LOST SOULS
BURNING SKY

written by **MEL ODOM**
created by **JORDAN WEISMAN**

RP|TEENS
PHILADELPHIA • LONDON

Dedicated to my son Nathan, a lost soul
who found himself and saved all of us!
—*Jordan Weisman*

For Chandler
Who, like his father, believes in heroes.
—*Mel Odom*

Library of Congress Control Number: 2009940140

ISBN 978-0-7624-3765-8

Cover and interior design by Ryan Hayes
Edited by Sharon Turner Mulvihill & Kelli Chipponeri
Typography: Caslon Antique & Mercury Text

Running Press Teens is an imprint of
Running Press Book Publishers
2300 Chestnut Street
Philadelphia, PA 19103-4371

Visit us on the web!
www.runningpress.com
www.lostsoulsbook.com and www.lostsoulsgame.com

Nathan hesitated on the next-to-last step and tried to push the sleep out of his head. *The sound was just your imagination. You've always imagined things. No big deal.*

For a moment he stood there, thinking about creeping back up to his bedroom before he woke anyone. His dad and Uncle William were okay with him staying up late as long as he kept to his room. Uncle William, though, only surrendered curfew under protest.

The cold outside clung to the big house despite the best efforts of the heater. It had been a cold winter in Chicago this year, and it was still cold in April. Nathan didn't mind. He loved winter as much as summer.

I should go back to bed. I've got school in the morning, and it's going to be painful. Seventh grade had been awful so far for Nathan, and he blamed his cousin Alyssa. She was two years ahead of him, a brainiac and cheerleader all rolled into one. The double whammy of popular and smart, and all the teachers loved her.

Nathan turned around and started back up the stairs. Then he heard the sound again.

Click-click. Click-click-click. The noise echoed through the house.

Nathan froze in place and looked around. This time he could tell where the sound was coming from; his head swiveled toward his dad's bedroom on the first floor.

Nathan checked the time on his phone and saw that it was only

11:56 PM. *I can't believe I went to bed so early. But in a contest between sleep and homework . . .* He realized that he'd only slept a couple of hours. *Weird.*

He stared down the hallway and didn't see any lights, but he felt certain his dad wasn't in bed. Professor Peter Richards put in a lot of late-night hours cleaning and cataloging Mesoamerican artifacts for the Field Museum, and William Richards blamed his older brother for tolerating—even encouraging—Nathan's night-owl habits.

Click. Click-click.

Nathan let out a breath he hadn't realized he was holding. He wasn't imagining the sound.

Curiosity killed the cat, he reminded himself, but crept down the steps anyway. Curiosity was his kryptonite. Nothing else hooked him as much as his own imagination.

At the bottom of the steps, he turned right, crossed the large living room, and headed for the hallway toward his dad's rooms. He caught movement from the corner of his eye and a glimpse of something about his height with dark, unkempt hair—then recognized his reflection in the surface of the big-screen television. His heart thudded like a jackhammer.

He glanced to the left and saw light through the cracks of his dad's workroom door. Nathan stared at the door for a moment, thinking, as always, that the only thing the door was missing was a sign that read CAUTION—PROFESSOR OF ARCHEOLOGY OBSESS-ING—ONLY OLD DEAD THINGS ADMITTED.

Click-click-click.

Nathan turned to focus on his dad's bedroom door. The sound had definitely come from there. Though he hesitated in the hall-way, Nathan knew what he was going to do.

Mysteries had to be solved. He didn't like them any other way.

He crossed to his dad's door, turned the knob, and found it unlocked. Ignoring the brief pang of guilt over invading his dad's privacy, Nathan opened the door and went inside.

An empty bed, a chest of drawers, and a large bookshelf. No television, no DVDs, and not even a radio. Nathan didn't understand how anyone could live like that. He was relieved to find that his dad didn't have a mummy's casket or a couple of skeletons in the bedroom. Those things often turned up in the workroom, and when they were there, strange things happened around the house that no one but Nathan seemed to notice.

Nathan let out a tense breath and stood in the doorway. *So where—?*

Click-click-click.

The sound came from the closet to Nathan's right. Involuntarily, he started forward. Weird light shifted in the edges of his vision, and he braced himself to dive away from it. He'd been killing nightmare creatures on his computer for the past few days. Apparently the gory graphics had inspired his subconscious more than he'd thought.

The weird illumination turned out to be a stray shaft of moonlight hitting a picture on the chest of drawers.

It's cool. Calm down. He stepped closer to the photo and immediately recognized Professor Felicima Diego Barrera Richards.

His mom.

She'd died giving birth to him, so he didn't really think of her as his mom.

In the picture, his parents stood in a small open-air café in the shade of some kind of trees Nathan couldn't identify. In the background, a man led a small brown burro pulling a cart of firewood.

If you knew what you were looking for, it was easy to see the physical influence of his mom's Hispanic and Mayan ancestors; she looked short standing next to his dad, and she had dark skin and black hair. Nathan couldn't believe how young she looked in comparison to his father.

His dad had been forty-one when he'd married his thirty-year-old colleague. In the picture, they held hands and were smiling, something Nathan hardly saw his dad do these days. Apparently she'd brought out a side of him that Nathan had never seen.

He'd always wondered what kind of a person she was. He figured she was different than his dad, more understanding and more giving. Then sometimes he wanted her to have been just like his dad so it didn't feel like he'd lost so much.

Click. Click-click-click.

Seeing the picture brought up a lot of stuff Nathan didn't like thinking about, so he was glad to turn his attention back to the closet.

Cautiously, Nathan opened the door and peered in. The closet held his dad's suits, shirts, and pants. Neglected fishing gear and golf clubs sat in one corner. Peter Richards mostly used the sports equipment when entertaining rich donors in pursuit of funding for the university.

Click-click. Click-click.

Nathan pinpointed the noise as coming from a scarred suitcase on the top shelf of the closet. Colorful stickers from other countries covered the scuffed surface.

Nathan grabbed the suitcase's handle and lifted it off the shelf. He laid it on the floor. Instead of a zipper, straps held the suitcase shut. The smell of old leather and dust curled into his nose and almost made him sneeze. His eyes watered from the effort of holding back his reaction.

Photographs, books, and other odds and ends filled the suitcase. Picking up one of the photographs, Nathan turned it toward the weak moonlight. The image showed Professor Felicima Diego Barrera Richards in a place that looked like a crypt. Her stomach was big, and Nathan realized with a start that he was actually in the photograph as well. He just hadn't been born yet.

Neat handwriting on the back said: *Palenque, Mexico. April 16.*

Nathan flipped the photograph back over and studied it. He had been born only eleven days later. In the image, Professor Felicima looked tired but happy.

Why were you there? I didn't have to be born there. And you didn't have to be gone.

The old anger swelled up inside Nathan, surprising him. When he was a kid, he often had wondered if having a mother around would have made his life any different. He flipped the photo back over and looked at her image again.

Mom. For a moment he thought maybe he'd said the word out loud. *How would we have gotten along, Professor Felicima? Would you have understood me any better than Dad? Or would you have kept your distance too? How did you love a guy who thinks more of dead and ancient things than he does of you?*

As he looked at her, he couldn't help wonder if her life with his dad had been as solitary as his. Maybe she'd gotten used to it, like he had. Or perhaps she had been just as solitary as his dad.

Not knowing bothered Nathan.

Forget it. It's not worth the time it takes to think about it. Nathan turned back to the suitcase. He lifted out the books and stacked them on the side, catching glimpses of titles that mentioned the Mayan people and Palenque. The only one that really interested him was a plain brown book that looked like a journal.

At the bottom of the suitcase, Nathan found a box carved from deep blue stone. The box was solid and heavy, and it felt smooth and polished.

Someone had chiseled three images on the surface of the box. On two of the sides, a fiery sun and a crescent moon lay diametrically opposed. In the center, a feathered serpent coiled in on itself.

Click-click.

Nathan had no doubt that the sound came from inside the stone box, as crazy as that sounded. He took the box out and searched for a way to open it. The box appeared seamless, but he knew there had to be a trick to it.

Unfortunately, this puzzle wasn't going to be easily solved. The box resisted pulling and prying, and Nathan started to get frustrated.

For all I know, it's just a really big coaster.

He tried twisting the top, but the secret to opening it—if there was one—eluded him. Then he heard his father moving around in the study. Nathan recognized those noises. His dad had finished whatever he was working on and was putting things away before coming to bed.

Nathan frantically stuffed everything but the stone box and the journal into the suitcase. He also kept Professor Felicima's photograph, unwilling to let it go after finding this picture of them together. Almost.

He slid the straps back into place and shoved the suitcase back onto the shelf. When he heard his father's footsteps out in the hall, Nathan knew he couldn't go out the way he came. Instead, he ran to the bedroom window and found it raised a couple of inches, like he knew he would.

Nathan slid the window open all the way and crawled over the ledge. Outside, he pulled the window down, sprinting away just as his father entered the room.

The backyard was big and deep with shadows from oak trees and a high fence that ran around the yard's perimeter. Nathan went around the corner of the house and stopped under his window. His room was still dark, which meant no one had noticed he was gone.

Stripping out of his T-shirt, feeling the chill of the night immediately bite into him, he tied the sleeves and tail together into a makeshift sling. He tucked the box, the journal, and the photo into the sling, pulled it over his shoulder and then grabbed hold of the gutter pipe and climbed the side of the house.

The pipe creaked a little and felt wobbly, but it held. He got back inside the house easily, because like his dad, he always left his bedroom window open. Once inside, he emptied his sling, pulled his shirt back on, and turned his attention to the curious stone box.

2

Twenty minutes later, on the verge of giving up, Nathan discovered the secret of the box. He had pulled and twisted and slid the thing dozens of ways, but with no results.

Something—in fact, *several* somethings—rattled and clicked delicately inside the box. The only difference from before was that now he was causing the clicking. Visions of something *alive* in the box fired his imagination. Not knowing what it contained was killing him.

He had been ready to open the window and sail the blue box deep into the backyard when, finally, he thought of pushing down on the sun and crescent moon. Even that needed a code, though. He discovered that pressing down on the symbols nine times in a staggered back-and-forth pattern that resulted in higher-and higher-pitched clicks opened the box.

When the final click sounded, the two halves of the stone box separated, leaving a slight gap. The box still wouldn't open, though, and Nathan had to play with it for a few more minutes before it gave up its final secret. He discovered that he had to twist the halves in opposite directions, and the top half had to turn in the direction of the snake's coils.

Inside the box, he found eleven tiny sculptures, five each carved from white stone and obsidian, plus one yellowish one. He recognized the symbol on one piece as a jaguar, but he didn't recognize the images on the rest of the pieces.

There was also a folded paper with a circular pattern on it. When he took out the paper and unfolded it, his first thought was that it was really old—maybe it was papyrus. Then he examined the design printed on it—concentric rings, each ring with a single repeated symbol.

The box also contained dice that looked like they had been carved from bone, gone yellow with age. *Maybe they were carved from human bone. Kind of gross, but pretty cool.*

Okay, obviously this was a game. That was a bonus, because he was good at games. With the way the board was laid out, he decided this was either a two-player game or a two-team game, but it was like nothing he'd never seen.

He laid the game board on a television tray by his bed. He set the pieces carefully on the board, dividing the black from the white and staying outside the circle. He noticed that the black and white sets had the same pieces, sort of like chess. Now he just had to figure out how to play the game—naturally, there was no ancient rulebook included. *Typical. The first thing you lose out of every game is the rules.* Most likely each player had to move through the circles somehow toward the center, but there had to be rules for movement.

He figured anything that had been around as long as this obviously had must have been researched and written about, so he logged on to the Internet to see what he could find—which turned out to be nothing. He was making the assumption that it was a Mayan artifact, given his mother's heritage and the subject matter of the books in her suitcase.

In general, he tried hard to not listen when his dad launched into his long-winded stories about the research methods he used when trying to figure out the history of an artifact. Now, Nathan appreciated the irony of needing those techniques. He couldn't see himself heading back downstairs tonight and sneaking into his father's workroom to grab reference material on Mayan board games.

Guess I'll have to go old-school and use the encyclopedia. Never figured the lamest birthday present ever would turn out to be useful. As he was blowing dust off the volume containing the Ms, he rediscovered a book on Mayan culture, a gift from a well-meaning aunt who wanted to make sure he had "the opportunity to explore his mother's culture," according to the inscription. He skimmed the encyclopedia entry and found it vaguely interesting, especially since there were several references to games. Armed with the names that historians had attached to the games, he turned to the book on Mayan culture. The book described one game that was similar to checkers and related to math.

Studying the carved game pieces for a moment, Nathan decided this particular game probably didn't have anything to do with math. He liked math at the same time that he hated math class. *Now there's a challenging puzzle; do they teach seventh-grade math teachers how to make such an interesting subject really boring, or does it come naturally?*

He found another game called Bul that was some kind of Mayan war game. According to what he read, Bul might have come from a dice game called Haxbil-Bul. But the game was played with corn, and with beans painted with a single dot on one side, most likely to represent dice.

Bul obviously wasn't the game Nathan had found, but it had an interesting history. It was a gambling game, and it appeared that Mayans could lose fortunes and even their freedom in the game.

Losers actually became slaves to the winners and had to serve them the rest of their lives.

That was pretty radical. Losing in Halo just meant respawning somewhere else and taking a lot of verbal abuse over Live. The idea of losing a match in Halo and having to do someone else's chores for the rest of his life was bizarre.

He put a bookmark in the page and kept reading. When it became clear that he'd found everything he was going to in the book, he snapped it shut in frustration and went to sit on the bed next to the game.

He tried moving the pieces around, setting them in different places to see if anything jumped out at him. Nothing. *I'm beginning to wish I'd never found this thing.* Then he admitted to himself that that wasn't really true: even though it was incredibly frustrating, this was an awesome puzzle.

As he moved all the pieces back outside the circle, he considered what he did know. There was a clear division in the number of pieces. Five pieces could compete with the other five pieces on the board, but what was the goal and the reason to get there?

Nathan lay back on his bed and stared at the game. He tried to make sense of the pieces through sheer willpower. That didn't work either.

He closed his eyes and visualized the game board in his mind. He moved the pieces around mentally, struggling to find a starting point. Somewhere in there, he fell asleep.

"Nathan."

Suddenly aware that his eyes were closed, Nathan

opened them. An emerald forest surrounded him. The stiff wind smelled like the breath of a predator.

Brilliantly colored birds stared down at him from the tall trees. He recognized them: scarlet macaws, turquoise-browed motmots, masked boobies, keel-billed toucans, and dozens of others. When he had been younger, he was fascinated by birds and had learned a lot about them. They cawed, clicked, and whistled, and the sound was horrendous.

Nathan stepped backward, clapping his palms over his ears. The riotous colors stood out against the greenery.

A lazy growl sounded overhead. Nathan slowly looked up. A beautiful but deadly-looking jaguar lounged on a thick tree branch. The big cat yawned lazily, and its pink tongue rolled out of its jaws. The tail curled and flicked.

When his eyes adjusted to the shadows of the forest, Nathan saw there were several big cats in the trees. Carefully, he started to edge away on the uneven ground.

This is just a dream. Don't freak out.

Except that this felt more real than any dream Nathan had ever experienced—and he had vivid dreams. He took another sideways step and tripped over an exposed tree root. He fell, but managed to catch himself on his hands and knees.

The jaguars came to life. They all turned their heads toward Nathan, and a few of them gracefully rose onto all fours.

"Easy." Nathan told himself not to look scared, but he didn't know if he was pulling it off. He'd always been told animals could sense fear in a human. "Everybody just chill." He moved slowly, rocking back into a squatting position.

He felt pretty sure that nothing would happen to him in his dream. After all, he had been brought down by zombie hordes, shot by aliens, and fallen off steep cliffs in dreams where he couldn't fly, and he had survived all that. But his survival was always a result of waking up.

This dream was much more interesting than usual. He didn't want to wake up until he dreamed a little more.

"Nathan, welcome."

The voice belonged to a man, but no one Nathan recognized. It was a pleasant baritone, a voice used to laughing. It was the kind of voice that inspired immediate confidence, like an athlete talking to a sports reporter after a big win.

"Who are you?" Nathan took another step back.

The jaguars stirred restlessly. A few more of them sat up on their tree branches.

"A friend. I thought it was time we met. We've got a lot in common."

That was weird. Even though his dreams were generally very detailed, usually the people in them only talked about things Nathan needed to know immediately. Like that the zombies were coming. Or where was the aliens' most vulnerable spot in their defensive infrastructure. Things like that. Necessary information.

Everyday conversation? Not so much.

"I really don't have jungle friends." Nathan looked around for an escape route. "Not even big on Tarzan." *And it looks like I definitely don't have any friends in the cat family.*

"This isn't the jungle. This is the forest."

"Whatever. This is my dream."

"Is it? Then what are you dreaming?"

"Stuff."

The man laughed. "It would be good if we could talk."

"About what?"

"'Stuff.'" The man chuckled at his own joke.

"Very funny."

"I would like to speak to you face to face."

Nathan had to admit that the guy sounded like someone he'd want to meet. Ordinary people wouldn't hang out in a forest filled with wild jaguars and who-knew-what-else lurking in the green shadows.

"You know where to find me." Nathan tried to pinpoint the direction of the voice. "You come here."

"Afraid the cats will get your tongue?"

Despite the threat of the jaguars pacing in front of him, Nathan had to smile.

"And maybe all the other pieces of me, yeah. Are these your pets?"

"No. I could tell them to back away if you're afraid. But I thought you could rise above the slight problem they present. Unless you like the idea of being a chew toy." The man laughed.

"Terrific." Although Nathan was afraid, he knew he was safe in the dream, and his competitive nature rose to meet the challenge. He turned toward the powerful voice, knowing that if this was a dream, he had one power the man couldn't foresee.

As he turned, the jaguars leapt. Their snarls and growls drowned out the sounds of the birds. Sunlight filtering through the leaves flashed ebony fire from the talons of the big cats.

3

Nathan kicked hard against the ground and hurled himself toward the sky. While awake, he wouldn't have gotten very far off the ground, but in his dream he could fly.

He soared up as the jaguars landed where he had been. Snarling in frustration, a few of them were quick enough to turn and jump for him. One of them caught his sneaker, but the claw pulled through.

The canopy of branches overhead slapped and tore at him, raising stinging welts on his face.

The startled birds took wing after him and spun into a twister of brightly colored feathers. When he burst through the trees into the bright blue sky, the birds peeled away from him and glided over the treetops like a rainbow-colored fog.

Grinning, loving the feeling of flying, Nathan wanted nothing more than to fly away and explore wherever it was his dream had brought him.

"For a minute there, Nathan, I didn't think you were going to make it."

"Are you kidding?" Nathan knew he had a goofy grin on his face. The guy sounded impressed. Now Nathan really wanted to meet him.

"Where are you?"

"Look straight ahead, and you'll find me."

At first, Nathan thought he was watching a slither of winged snakes take to the air. Then he realized they were birds. At least a dozen darters shot through the air at Nathan like arrows from a bow. They were on him with inhuman speed, but they didn't attack. They glided above, below, and around him without making a sound except for the fluttering of their wings against the wind.

"X marks the spot," said the voice.

Nathan flew downward to where the darters had come from. He protected his face with his arms when he flew back through the leafy canopy.

Monkeys scrambled across the upper branches, chattering angrily as they threw sticks and bark. Birds glided through the open areas.

A clearing occupied a large area under the canopy, and a stone building stood in the center of the clearing. It had three distinct stories, each smaller than the last. Narrow steps climbed the sides to the top. A man stood on top of the stone building.

He waved and smiled. "Welcome, Nathan. I've been waiting a long time for you."

The man looked pretty young. Nathan wasn't good at guessing the ages of adults, but he felt confident that the man was much younger than his father. He looked Hispanic, with dark smooth skin and jet black hair that hung down to his shoulders. His face was strong and clean shaven, and he was built like an Olympic athlete. He wore white tennis shoes, white cargo pants, and a deep-blue pullover sweater. He stood out against the weathered gray stone.

Nathan flew down to the top of the building. As he approached, he spotted the swamp behind the building. That explained where the darters had come from. To the left of the building, a high-walled rectangular courtyard sat vacant. Two hoops hung on walls at opposite ends, and a ball sat in the middle. It looked vaguely like the park-district basketball courts he passed every day on his way to school.

Effortlessly, Nathan dropped to the building. The darters flew past him and splashed into the swamp after fish. Other things, some of them big things, slithered in the shadows.

The man watched him. "You fly well."

"Thanks. I suppose you get a lot of flying people through here." Nathan couldn't help feeling annoyed that the man had taken the surprise of his flying ability so casually.

The man grinned and shook his head. "You're the first."

Nathan was proud of that but tried to keep it cool.

"Happy birthday."

An unfamiliar feeling twisted Nathan's insides. No one paid attention to the fact that it was his birthday. His dad seldom remembered it. In fact, Nathan had pretty much forgotten it himself until he'd seen his mother's photograph.

"I brought you here as part of your birthday celebration."

"You brought me here?" Nathan shook his head, but he secretly liked the idea that this man might have brought him to a dream world as a gift. That would have been totally cool.

Except for the part about the man being a figment of his dream and not capable of doing much at all.

"That would be awesome, but I'm just dreaming this."

"Really?" The man lifted an eyebrow and laid a large hand on Nathan's shoulder. "How many dreams have you had about a forest like this?"

Nathan hesitated. "Counting this one?"

"Sure."

"One."

The man smiled again. "There could be a reason for that."

Nathan shrugged. "With everything I dream about, I had to dream about a forest sooner or later. I dream about a lot of stuff. I dream about stuff people haven't even thought of yet."

"I know."

It was a novel experience, talking to an adult about such personal stuff—and having that adult acknowledge what he was saying with no questions. Nathan liked the way the man agreed with him, and it made him curious to know more about him. "How did you know it's my birthday?"

"I know many things."

"Then you might also know that I detest know-it-alls. Yoda in *Star Wars*? I thought he was an irritating little puppet. No way was he a scary Jedi warrior. So telling me that you 'know many things' isn't as impressive as you might hope."

"I'll keep that in mind."

"You also know that I love dreams where I can fly. Want to tell me why I'm standing here talking to you instead of flying around and enjoying this one?"

"I brought you here so that we could begin playing."

Nathan nodded to the ball court. "Basketball?" He laughed. "Unless you can fly too, you're gonna be at a real disadvantage."

"Not that game. And it's not called basketball. It's called Pok-A-Tok, or sometimes pitz. I'm going to teach you a different game."

"What game?"

"The game you found last night, in your mother's suitcase." A statement like that was weird even for a dream. The man definitely had Nathan's attention.

"What's the game called? Why did my mother have it?"

"It is just called the Game. And your mother had it because she was supposed to. Just as you're supposed to have it now."

"If you ask me, that name's not very creative."

"Maybe we can think of a better name for it."

"Speaking of names, who are you?" Nathan hated having to ask. In dreams, he usually knew everybody's name or assigned them names. Except for the zombies—those were always Larry, Moe, and Curly—and the hulking behemoths that he always named Arda Montoya, after his school nemesis.

"I'm Kukulkan."

"Tell me about the Game. And why my mom had it."

"Your mother learned to play the Game when she was young. She thought she would play it against me. She was mistaken. Instead, you and I are going to play the Game against each other."

"That doesn't seem fair. I don't even know how to play."

"You're intelligent, Nathan. You play a lot of games. I think you can figure this one out." The man gazed at Nathan with speculation. "As long as you don't doubt yourself."

"I won't doubt myself if I'm prepared."

"I'll make sure you learn. I promise."

Nathan hoped that this wasn't really a dream. He was enjoying Kukulkan's company and he knew that in his dreams, the characters rarely made a second appearance. Except for the zombies. They were pretty much a constant.

"You'll see me again, Nathan. Don't worry. Not everything is a dream." The man patted Nathan's shoulder. "And even dreams can be guided, once you learn their secret."

"If you say so."

"I do. Oh! Before I forget—you said you like to fly?"

"In my dreams, yeah."

"This isn't a dream, Nathan. It is one of the many frequencies. And my gift to you for your birthday is the ability to always be able to fly when you're in alternate frequencies."

Yeah, right. Nathan didn't let his doubt show. "Deal."

"Why don't you try?"

Nathan sailed easily into the air. The wind buffeted him and pulled him up as he glided and barrel-rolled over the building. He laughed in delight.

Below him, Kukulkan laughed as well.

Nathan braked and hovered ten feet over Kukulkan. The big man's smile was bright white against his dark face. "Not bad."

Nathan laughed again. "Only not bad? You think you can do better?"

Kukulkan lifted his arms and took flight immediately. He moved like he was born with wings.

"We need a finish line." Kukulkan pointed in the distance where a mountaintop stood up from the verdant forest. "There. Agreed?"

"Sure. Just say when."

"I'll leave that to you."

"All right . . . go!" Nathan willed himself forward and immediately rushed through the air. He kept his arms tight in front of his body, like a swimmer crashing through waves. The joy of flying washed through him as he spotted Kukulkan flying at roughly the same pace only a short distance away. The guy was big, and his size should have slowed him down, only it didn't. In fact, Nathan had the impression that Kukulkan was holding back.

Nathan willed himself to go faster, and the wind whistled past his ears. The sensation was like nothing he'd ever dreamed about before.

He was more than halfway to the finish line when the shadow

dropped suddenly out of the sky. He glanced up. Terror ripped through him when he saw the creature swooping toward him.

It was some kind of vulture, but it was bigger than any vulture Nathan had ever seen. At first glance he thought it was an American black vulture because it was covered in plumage so dark it glistened blue in the sun. But it was far bigger than it should have been. Normally an American black vulture had a wingspan of about five feet. This one's had to be nearly twenty feet across.

All buzzards and vultures had featherless heads and wrinkled skin. Nathan thought they all looked loathsome and evil. This one looked worse because its features were almost human. The vulture's face looked like an old woman with a flaring nose and sharp lips. The creature flexed tiny hands on the front edge of its wings.

No way! Stunned, Nathan watched as the vulture closed on him like an attacking fighter jet.

"Nathan, get away from it!" Kukulkan yelled.

Galvanized into moving, Nathan tried to take evasive action, but the vulture was too quick. It banked and changed directions with him, close enough now that Nathan could've sworn he smelled its revolting breath.

One claw flicked out and closed in Nathan's hair. With a yank, it brought him to a dead stop and his own anguished screams rocketed through Nathan's skull.

4

"Get off me! Get off me!" Nathan fought the vulture's unrelenting grip, kicking and flailing his arms. Then he realized he was battling twisted sheets and blankets. He was back in his bedroom—and he wasn't alone.

Alyssa stood halfway into his room, arms crossed and a disapproving look firmly in place. Her golden hair cascaded past her shoulders in waves that hair stylists promised but could never deliver, and of course it was all natural.

She was a full head taller than Nathan and slender. She wore a charcoal-colored pencil skirt, a kelly-green sweater, a black jacket, and calf-high leather boots. That was the cheerleader side of her.

She raised her eyebrows in mock astonishment. "Clearly, those video games have succeeded in rotting your malformed brain."

Nathan sat up and tried to straighten out his sheets. The dream had seemed really real.

Exhaustion weighed him down. He wrapped himself in his blankets and tried to get warm, but the chill wasn't just from his open window. He could still feel the vulture's talons tangled in his hair. Unable to stop himself, he ran a hand through his hair to check for blood. Nothing.

That dream was so real.

"When did you go to bed?" Alyssa looked at his room like she was afraid of catching a disease.

Comics, books, and video games stood in piles everywhere. Controllers littered the floor, along with half-finished models and dirty clothes.

"Before twelve. You know that. I heard you check on me."

"Did you get up last night?"

"No." Years of practice allowed Nathan to lie both convincingly and effortlessly.

"Sure you did. Look at you. You're barely awake. You look like death warmed-over. And you smell like it, too."

"Thanks for that. Now I know I should take a shower. I was a little unsure before."

"Admit it. You got up last night." Alyssa pointed at the computer. "All I have to do is check the history on your computer."

Shoot. He hadn't cleared the history last night when he'd finished with the computer. He'd been so distracted by finding the Game that he hadn't thought about it.

"If you had the pass code, you could probably do that." He smirked.

"Oh please. iwillrockyourworld, giveupnowandiwillshowmercy, iwilluseyourthighboneasabackscratcher. Sound familiar?"

Nathan frowned. Those were all recent pass codes. The last was his current one.

He drew his knees up to his chest and leaned his head back against the wall. "Fine. I got up. I couldn't sleep."

Alyssa shook her head. "You are so abnormal. You're driving my dad crazy, you know that, right?"

"Hey, I do my best to avoid your dad."

"I know. He knows. That's one of the things that's driving him crazy."

"Being around your dad drives me crazy."

Alyssa put her clenched fists on her hips. "I don't know why my dad bothers. But the problem is he does. And because he does, so do I. Which is what brings me here this morning."

"You really didn't have to come."

"You're right. I had a choice." Alyssa looked around. "I could've asked the CDC to come in, condemn your room, and bring you out at gunpoint."

The Center for Disease Control? Nathan had to hold back a smile at that one. She was good. Almost as good as him.

He glared at her to keep the smile from his face. "What's your point?"

"It's your birthday."

"Thanks. I didn't know you cared."

Alyssa rolled her eyes. He admired that eye-roll; it was one of her best dramatic skills. Her cell phone chirped for attention. She took it out of her pocket, glanced at it, texted with her usual blinding speed, and slipped it back in her pocket without missing a beat.

"I don't. Dad does. He cares enough to throw you a birthday party."

Nathan was immediately horrified. Visions of Alyssa's many perfect princess parties unfurled in his mind. He remembered the ones he'd gone to as consistently horrible experiences.

"He can't. You've got to stop him."

"Believe me, I tried. But he's sat by and watched your dad forget your birthday year after year. Now that he's living here, he's determined to not let that happen again."

Nathan thudded his head against the wall behind him. "Birthdays are supposed to be good things."

"This one will be."

"No, it won't. I like getting to do what I want on my birthday."

"Yes, it *will*. You're going to do everything in your power to make sure that you do your part to enjoy the party."

"*My* part?"

"The being-happy part. That's important to my dad. It's kind of what he lives for."

"Do you remember your fourteenth birthday party?"

"Duh. It was *my* party."

"Your dad made you wear one of those stupid birthday hats."

"Yes, that's what my dad does."

"And you had to put pictures of your birthday on FaceSpace?"

Alyssa grimaced. "Okay, that was a little uncomfortable."

"For Little Miss Perfect, it was a little uncomfortable. Do you know what will happen at school if any pictures like that get posted on *my* FaceSpace page? I'll be mincemeat. Arda and his fellow creeps will make it even more of a point to brutalize me."

"I know. I'm really sad for you. Here. On the inside. Where it really matters." Alyssa laid her hand over her heart. She didn't look sad.

"You have to stop him."

"This isn't about you." Alyssa looked keenly serious. "This is about my dad, whom I love very much."

Frantically, Nathan examined his options. Option one was—

"Don't you even think about ducking out on this party and not showing up." Alyssa looked at him. "I know that's what you're thinking. If you do that, I will make your life completely miserable."

"That's funny. I hadn't noticed that any misery coming from you was incomplete."

"There are a few areas I could work on."

Nathan believed her. In her own way, Alyssa was even scarier than the vulture in his dream. At least he could wake up from a dream and the vulture would be gone.

He laced his fingers behind his head, closed his eyes, and sighed deeply. "When is the party?"

"Dad wants to start early."

"Great."

Alyssa ignored him. "Shortly after school. Say around five. Don't get home before then. That'll give you a couple hours to do whatever it is you do before you come home. Dad figured you might want to go hang with your friends later. So when five o'clock gets here, be sure you act surprised. Dad likes it when you're surprised."

Terrific. Nathan felt a headache coming on. He looked out the window and wished he could just jump out and fly away.

Alyssa's phone chirped again. This time she answered the call. "Courtney, how are you?"

She sounded so sickly sweet that Nathan wanted to scream.

"I'm great." Courtney had an equally perky voice—and was loud enough to be heard by everyone else in the room. "Looking forward to today. We're going to kill in speech."

"Go us."

"I wanted to let you know that I picked up the information on those unsolved cases for journalism. I really like the one about the police officer who got killed and was suspected of being involved in the burglary ring. Being shot down in the tunnels like that is kind of creepy. We'll get double bonus for the creep factor."

"That's fantastic. We're ahead of schedule."

"With you in the group, we're always ahead of schedule. And I knew you had that thing with your cousin tonight."

Alyssa glanced meaningfully at Nathan. "I do have that thing."

"I wanted this to be one less thing you had to worry about."

"You are so considerate."

"I had a good teacher. Anyway, so after that *thing*, and now that the files are posted on your website for us to review, I thought maybe we could go to a movie."

"Sounds great. I'll see you at school. Ciao." Alyssa slid her phone back into her pocket. "To recap." She ticked off points on her fingers. "Party tonight at five. Be surprised. Be polite. Be appreciative. Any questions?"

Nathan shook his head.

"I shouldn't have to tell you, but I'm going to anyway. Screw this up and you're dead." Alyssa gave him a fingertip wave. "Oh, and happy birthday." Her cell phone chirped again before she was out the door.

Tired, and still groggy despite the early-morning wake-up threats, he glanced at the clock. It was 7:08. He could have slept another twenty-two minutes before he had to get up.

Nathan yawned and forced himself out of bed. Maybe he'd lost twenty minutes of sleep, but he'd gained twenty minutes of Internet time.

He glanced at the game board. Then he froze. The pieces had been set up around the edge of the board, and one of the white pieces was now in the outer circle.

Someone had made the first move.

5

The opponent's jaguar piece had been placed on the outer ring.

Nathan studied the game board. Was it a power move? Or just an opening gambit?

He reached for his jaguar piece, thinking to shadow the move, but something held back his hand. He couldn't have explained why he didn't pick up the piece, except that every time he decided to pick it up, he immediately decided not to.

For a moment Nathan just glared at the pieces. He felt compelled to do something just as strongly as he felt compelled not to pick up that first piece. He forced himself to not touch anything because he didn't want to make a play until he knew more about what was going on.

It's a two-player game. Since I didn't make the first move, the second move is obviously mine. Nathan took a deep breath and let it out. *Except that I don't know what I'm doing.*

He backed away from the Game, and the desire to move something faded a little. Distance definitely made a difference.

Showered and dressed, teeth brushed, and hair more or less combed, Nathan slid his netbook into his backpack, hoisted it over one shoulder, and walked downstairs. The whole time he'd been in the shower he'd been thinking about the dream, mostly the good parts. Like flying and meeting Kukulkan. He'd had such a great conversation with him, and he wanted more.

Uncle William heard him when he hit the bottom step.

"Nathan? Breakfast is ready. Come get it." His uncle waved tongs at him from in front of the stove.

A little overweight like his older brother, Professor William Richards had frizzy hair, a full red beard, wide blue eyes, and freckles across his nose and cheeks. As usual, he wore a sweater, bow tie, and black slacks. Although he was divorced from Alyssa's mother—against his wishes—he still wore his gold wedding ring.

The man has ears like a hawk. Nathan trudged into the large kitchen and dropped his backpack into one of the chairs at the breakfast table.

Alyssa was already halfway through her breakfast.

Nathan sighed. "I'm not really hungry."

"Nonsense." Uncle William took a fresh waffle from the waffle iron and placed it on a plate. "This is breakfast. And what do we say about breakfast, Alyssa?"

Alyssa smiled brightly at Nathan. "Most important meal of the day."

Nathan ignored her. He sat down, and his uncle put the waffle in front of him. Obediently, Nathan smeared butter on the waffle and added syrup, pausing only when his uncle scooped a couple of sausages onto his plate as well.

Alyssa gestured at Nathan to eat and narrowed her eyes in warning.

Nathan was tempted to ignore her prompt but just didn't have the energy for the fight this morning. "Thanks."

"My pleasure." Uncle William beamed.

Once Nathan started eating, he discovered he was actually ravenous. He devoured the first waffle and asked for a second, much to Uncle William's delight.

Uncle William filled the waffle iron again. "So, does anybody have a big day planned?"

Alyssa locked eyes with Nathan, then spoke first. "Just the usual, Dad."

"Tell me again about the special project in journalism."

"I think it's going to be fascinating. Ms. Champlain wants everyone in honors journalism to do field investigations into cold cases. You know, murder investigations that haven't been solved. She wants to know what we think about the crimes."

Uncle William turned to stare at her apprehensively. "Murder investigations?"

"Exactly." Reading displeasure into her father's question, Alyssa hurried on. "It's no big deal, really. Just reading a lot of newspapers and making a few phone calls to homicide detectives and the district attorney's office."

Now that's interesting. But Nathan made sure his curiosity didn't show on his face. If Alyssa saw that he was intrigued, she'd never let up—it would give her the perfect opportunity to rub into his face that he could do this kind of stuff too if he just applied himself and got better grades *blah blah blah*. He got enough of that already from Uncle William.

"Homicide detectives?" Uncle William was still on the trail.

"Dad, it's going to be okay. I mean, it's not like the police officers killed anybody."

"That doesn't sound exactly appropriate for freshmen." Uncle William wiped his hands worriedly.

"It's an honors class. It's not supposed to be appropriate for freshmen. It's supposed to be challenging for students who excel and want to learn more."

Uncle William looked at Alyssa with a doubtful expression. "You want to do this? Because you don't have to, you know."

"Dad, I *want* to do this. I think it's going to be really cool."

"Cold cases sound really cool?"

"They're really called Open, Unsolved cases. That was one of the first things Ms. Champlain told us. The police don't like calling them cold cases because it gives the public the idea that they're not working on them."

"But they are working on them?"

"Of course."

Uncle William still wasn't convinced. "And exactly what is it your teacher expects you to learn from this?"

Alyssa ticked off points on her fingers, like she always did when she got really serious. "How the police work. How investigations are run. How emerging forensics and technology change the way those investigations are handled. In fact, there have even been a few cases where investigations by high school and college students have helped get someone off death row."

For just a moment, Nathan played with the idea of getting certified as an AP honors student. Going to a school associated with the university where both his dad and his uncle taught had some advantages; because the junior high and high school classes shared the same campus, it was easy to get access to cool AP classes. The big downside was that he was going to follow in Alyssa's footsteps all the way through.

Getting a chance to do something like researching cold cases in class would be really fun and challenging. But, when it came down to it, it sounded like too much work.

"Something like that could be really bad." Uncle William knotted the kitchen towel he held, and Nathan knew he was holding himself in check. "If you get involved with the wrong thing. Don't those cases involve murders?"

"Usually. Sometimes missing people."

"Don't you think this might be a little scary?"

Alyssa raised innocent eyebrows. Nobody could pull off innocent eyebrows like his cousin. "More scary than television news stories? Because that's what these case files essentially are. Documentation on information that's already been released in the media. An Open, Unsolved investigation only has that information to go on. It's not like we go creeping around looking for clues. It's just developing a new line of thinking about an old crime."

Uncle William still clearly wasn't happy. "I suppose you told your mother."

"Mom's totally on board with this. After all, we'll have to talk to the district attorney's office as well. She's agreed to be a liaison for us."

Jennifer Richards was an assistant district attorney for the city of Chicago. She was often in the newspaper in stories about criminal proceedings.

"Oh." Uncle William suddenly looked grim. "Well, I guess your mom would like to spend a little more time with you. I know she works a lot of hours."

"I think she's looking forward to it."

"She'll get to see you and not have to leave her office. She'll count that as a win-win situation."

Alyssa winced.

For just a moment, Nathan felt sorry for her. She was torn

between her parents. Both of them loved her unconditionally and doted on her.

He had no idea what that must be like.

Uncle William grimaced. "Sorry about that, honey. I didn't mean that."

"I know, Dad." Alyssa put on another smile, but Nathan saw this one took effort. She stood up from the table, cleared her dishes, and put them in the dishwasher.

Nathan glanced at the pile of papers in the thick folder Alyssa had in her notebook. OPEN, UNSOLVED was written in big, black letters in her handwriting. He itched to open the file.

Movement stirred on the surface of the glass of orange juice beside Nathan's hand. As he watched, a man's face appeared on his juice glass. The man's head was blocky, muscular looking. He wore his hair short, like someone in the military, and had a pencil-thin moustache that traced his lip. Though his image on the glass was grayed out, he looked Latino.

Nathan. The voice was hoarse and whisper-thin, like it had almost been entirely used up. *Listen . . . listen to me. I need your help.*

Feeling totally creeped out, Nathan dropped his fork onto his plate and closed his eyes. When he opened them again, the image on the side of his glass was gone.

I did not imagine that. Who was that guy?

Nathan.

This time the voice sounded like it was coming from Alyssa's special project folder. That was definitely creepy. Nathan couldn't stop staring at the folder and was afraid to look at his juice glass.

I hope I'm imagining this. Not enough sleep. And that dream . . . His birthdays were always a little odd, but this one was particularly weird.

Nathan . . .

Alyssa scooped up the folder and put it in her messenger bag. Nathan felt instant relief when the folder disappeared.

At that moment, Nathan's dad carried a skull into the room and deposited it on the breakfast table. He never even looked at Nathan. But Nathan didn't take it personally because his dad didn't look at anyone when he was preoccupied.

Professor Peter Richards was in his sixties, going gray now. Nathan knew that he got his above-average height and his hazel eyes from his dad's side, and his dark hair and permanent tan from his mom's side. He was good with all that, but he was hoping for a better fashion sense than his dad, who looked permanently rumpled. Today he wore suit pants with suspenders, a faded University of Chicago T-shirt, and fuzzy slippers.

The skull was more or less intact and rocked gently on the table. A hole about the diameter of Nathan's little finger had been punched into the back. Jagged bone edges surrounded the hole.

lyssa turned around, saw the skull sitting on the breakfast table, let out a little "eep" of surprise, and took a step back. Nathan smiled. It wasn't often his perfect cousin was caught off guard.

Nathan's dad cruised on autopilot through the kitchen, picking up a waffle, some scrambled eggs, and sausages. He looked around for a moment, spotted the syrup, and helped himself. Without a word, he sat down at the table and stared at the skull.

"Peter." Uncle William hurried over with a kitchen towel and reached for the skull. "Did you have to bring that in here?"

Nathan's dad clapped a hand on the skull and pinned it to the table. He blinked owlishly behind his glasses and looked around as if he'd just then noticed there were other people in the kitchen.

"Don't touch the skull, William."

"But at the breakfast table?"

"Don't. Touch. The. Skull."

His face pinched with disapproval, Uncle William turned back to the frying pan and scrambled eggs.

Nathan's dad waved at the skull. "Don't worry about this. This is nothing." He shrugged. "I mean, it's not nothing. I hope it's something. And in fact, I think it is something." He frowned and tapped the skull with his fork. "I just don't know what it is. Yet. But I will."

He stabbed a chunk of sausage and brought it to his mouth.

"Uncle Peter." Alyssa's voice tightened with astonishment. "You did not just touch that skull with your fork and eat off it."

"It's a perfectly clean skull. A lot cleaner than these dishes, even from the dishwasher. I know because I cleaned that skull myself." Nathan's dad licked syrup from the fork tines and dug in again. "You could eat off that skull."

Alyssa shook her head. "No. I couldn't."

Nathan grinned. "Personally, I think it would make a great queso dip bowl at Halloween. We'd have to plug up the eye sockets and ear holes. Maybe leave the nose holes open so it would look like drainage."

Uncle William grumbled, "Clean or not, you don't bring a human skull to the breakfast table."

Nathan's dad shook his head and tapped the skull with his fork again. "If you'd gotten a real degree instead of one in the soft sciences, you'd know this isn't a human skull."

"It's not?" Alyssa picked up the small artifact. She balanced it on her fingers and looked it in the face. "It's not. This is from a monkey."

"Evidence, if you please."

Alyssa turned the skull over in her hands, poking and prodding at it. The jaw moved easily, and the metallic gleam in the tiny mouth revealed that screws had been bored into the hinges, keeping the lower jaw from falling off.

"First of all, the size, and the fact that it's near-humanoid. The heavy, outthrust jaw also suggests a monkey."

"Good. What kind of monkey?" Nathan's dad ate while he listened.

Holding the skull so that it faced her, Alyssa stared into the empty eye sockets. She seemed stumped at first, then her lips curled into a smile. "A spider monkey."

"You're guessing." Her uncle leaned back in his chair and observed his niece with interest.

"Nope."

"Then how do you know?"

"Because of the nostrils." Alyssa swiveled the skull around so everyone could see.

Despite the fact that he didn't want to show any interest, Nathan stared at the monkey skull and tried to figure out what she had seen. The nostrils were just holes like the eye sockets. No big deal.

"What about the nostrils?" Nathan's dad ran a thumb under his suspenders.

"They're set really wide apart. That's a distinguishing feature on a spider monkey." Alyssa's blue eyes gleamed in triumph. "I did a report on monkeys for my earth science class in seventh grade. I remember reading that."

"Precisely. Good job, my dear." Nathan's dad clinked his fork against his orange juice glass to toast her.

Willing himself to show no reaction, Nathan got up from the table and walked to the sink.

Nathan's dad forked up another piece of waffle. "You know, William, if you make sure this young lady gets a proper education, in a serious field of study, she will be an excellent student with a wonderful academic future."

Nathan blew out his breath in disgust. *If all I wanted to do was look at nose holes, I could probably be an excellent student too.*

He rinsed the dishes and put them in the dishwasher. It bothered him that Alyssa got his father's attention without even trying.

It bothered him even more that he let himself be bothered by that.

"Thanks, Uncle Peter." Alyssa gushed enthusiasm.

"You're very welcome. Do you want to know what's so interesting about this particular skull?"

"Sure."

"Turn it over."

"What? Does it tell fortunes like a Magic 8 Ball?" Alyssa flipped the skull upside down and peered into the skull cavity.

"Maybe."

Nathan.

Nathan heard the voice again and suddenly realized he was standing next to Alyssa's messenger bag. He took a couple of steps away. He wanted to be out the door and gone, but now he was curious about the monkey skull.

Interest flashed in Alyssa's eyes. "Hey. There's writing inside the skull."

"Actually, that's engraved, not written."

"Someone carved up the monkey's skull?"

"I'm sure he was well past caring at the time," Nathan's dad commented, quite seriously.

"Why would they do that?"

"I don't know. That's one of the things I'm trying to find out. No one has recognized those glyphs yet. So it's either an unknown language, or it's gibberish."

"It's better if it's an unknown language, right?" Alyssa guessed.

Nathan couldn't resist the joke. "I guess that monkey had a lot on his mind when he died. Maybe he'd been taking some mental notes." He grinned, waiting for someone to join in.

Everyone stared at him for a moment then went back to what they were doing.

Okay, I thought that was pretty funny. He shrugged, dried his hands, and headed for the door.

"Hey." Uncle William cleared his throat and waved at Nathan with the dish towel. "Just a second."

Startled, Nathan turned around.

His uncle pointed to his backpack. "Forgetting something?"

"Yeah. Thanks." Nathan grabbed the backpack and hooked it over his shoulder.

"Peter." Uncle William walked over to the table.

"Hmmmm?" His dad was lost in the skull and breakfast.

"Isn't there something you're supposed to say to your son this morning?"

Nathan's dad frowned over the top of the monkey skull. "What?"

Uncle William indicated Nathan.

His dad thought for a moment then noticed the backpack over Nathan's shoulder. "Right. Have a nice day." He turned his attention back to the skull.

Unwilling to make it obvious that he wanted Nathan's dad to wish Nathan happy birthday, Uncle William nodded morosely and said good-bye as well.

O utside, Nathan crossed the immaculately kept yard. He missed the old, overgrown look, but that had vanished when Uncle William had come to live with them after the divorce a few months ago. The trees were beginning to bud, and soon there'd be a green canopy overhead. He was looking forward to that. Once it got a little messy, the yard would feel lived in again.

A sleek red Mustang GT slid to a stop at the curb near the towering oak tree. A girl in a letter jacket sat behind the wheel. She adjusted the rearview mirror so that she could see to apply lip gloss with her finger. Loud rock music blasted the neighborhood from the sound system.

"Want a ride?" Alyssa walked past Nathan. Carrying her black messenger bag over one shoulder, she looked like a business executive.

"I'll walk."

Alyssa stopped and turned to face him. "Look, this morning kind of sucked. Your dad . . . well, he should've wished you happy birthday."

Nathan grimaced. "If my dad had wished me happy birthday this morning, we'd have had to worry about an invasion of body snatchers."

Alyssa smiled, but looked a little sad. "In all seriousness though, Genevieve won't mind giving you a ride."

Nathan looked past his cousin at the beautiful brunette playing with her hair. He shook his head.

"Really don't think I'm a ride-with-girls-named-Genevieve kind of guy."

"Have you ever ridden with any girls named Genevieve?"

"Let me think." Nathan paused for just a second. "No."

"Then this could be a first."

"Nope. I've got a reputation to maintain. I suppose Genevieve got held back? Not as smart as your usual friends. That's how she got her license in ninth grade?"

"Genevieve had a serious illness in first grade. It put her back a year." Alyssa brushed a stray lock of blonde hair from her face. Her eyes turned arctic. "You know, you can be a real jerk sometimes."

Nathan smiled and winked. "Now *there's* that reputation I was talking about."

"Come on, Alyssa." Genevieve waved. "I'm starving. Some of us don't have fathers who make breakfast for us every morning."

"Don't forget about the party, Nathan." Alyssa turned and walked toward the waiting car.

Nathan put his face into the cold wind and followed it toward school.

T hree blocks from school, Nathan heard the final bell ring. He thought about running and decided against it. Running wasn't going to help. He was still going to be late. Running would only mean he'd be slightly less late, and he'd stink like a gym locker. He could live without that.

When he reached school, there were a few other stragglers. None of them was running either.

Fashionably late. Nathan thought maybe he could put in some time at the principal's office getting a note and maybe get a few laughs. Kids who were in trouble loved it when he was in there with them.

When he put his hand on the door to push it open, he saw the reflection of a Chicago uniformed cop standing just behind him in the glass. Nathan recognized the guy from his orange juice glass at breakfast.

Nathan felt a sudden spike of fear. He hadn't heard the guy come up, and he was big. Football-player big. Somebody that size should have made some noise. His badge gleamed on his broad chest.

Nathan. The cop spoke in a hoarse voice that sounded about a million miles away. *You and me. We gotta talk, kid. You're in a lot of trouble. I can help. But you gotta help me too.*

7

athan stared at the officer's reflection in the glass. One more step and he would've been inside. Would the man—or whatever he was—be able to follow? Was he even there? When Nathan turned around, the police officer was gone.

Chas Burris stood there instead. He was on the football team, and he was one of the guys who hung with Arda and who Nathan tried to avoid on a daily basis. Chas was big and heavy. His fair skin had burned red from the cold, and his nose was running. He wore a letter jacket that was big enough to qualify as a tent.

Chas was pretty universally disliked, but he was too big for anyone to be willing to tell him that to his face. His dad owned a car dealership and was a generous supporter of the school football program. Rumor had it that sponsorship was the only reason Chas managed to stay on the team.

Nathan often repeated the story that Chas used to have two younger brothers, but he got up hungry one morning and ate them both. The real story was that they were Chas's stepbrothers and they moved away after his dad got divorced. But the other kids liked the way he told the story, so Nathan kept it up.

Of course, if Chas and Arda hadn't ambushed Nathan on his way home one day in fifth grade, yanked his pants down around his ankles, and pushed him into a flock of eighth-grade girls, Nathan probably wouldn't have come up with that story or told it so many times.

"What are you looking at, freakazoid?" Chas huffed gray clouds in the cold air.

"There was a police officer here just a second ago." Nathan's amazement at how fast the man had disappeared dulled his sense of self-preservation. He tried to step around Chas to look behind him.

No police officer in sight.

"Did you see him? He was standing right here."

"The only person standing here is you, taking up space as usual." Chas laughed at his own joke.

"There was a police officer."

"You're making me later, lame-o. Stop blocking progress." Chas grabbed hold of Nathan's hoodie and tried to shove him aside.

Normally, Nathan would have moved and let Chas win the shoving match. Because he was still trying to figure out what he was seeing—or not seeing—he stayed where he was. Chas actually wasn't all that strong, so he was easy to resist.

What Chas lacked in strength, though, he more than made up for in bulk. He twisted suddenly and put a massive hip into Nathan's stomach. Hammered by the weight, Nathan fell backward over the low wall. He landed in the middle of a row of scratchy bushes along the school building.

There's never a cop around when you need one.

Chas leaned over the low wall and hooted like a gorilla, clasping his hands overhead like a champion.

"That'll teach you to stay out of my way, jerk."

Carefully, Nathan pushed himself up and untangled himself from the bushes. One of the branches caught him over his right eye and hurt bad enough to make his eye water. He covered his eye with his hand and tried to back out of the bushes.

Nathan.

Recognizing the police officer's deep voice coming from in front of him this time, Nathan kept his hand protectively over one eye and stared through the school's basement windows into the dark room beyond.

The police officer was inside the basement.

"What do you want? How did you get down there so fast?"

The police officer stared at him earnestly. *Talk to me, Nathan. I need you to talk to me. I can help you. You can help me. I need to find a way to help my family, and you're the key.*

Not quite believing what he was seeing, Nathan didn't move. *No way he can reach through the glass.*

Then the man's hand reached through the window like the glass wasn't there.

Frantically, Nathan jerked himself out of the bushes. *This isn't real! You're just imagining this! The way you used to imagine things when you were a kid! Just breathe!*

I need your help.

"Help doing what?" Against his will, against his better judgment, Nathan was becoming curious. He had a faint feeling of déjà vu, like this was a conversation he'd had back when he was a kid.

Nathan. There was another voice, behind the police officer.

A handful of other voices turned his name into a weird, unbalanced chant. Nathan's stomach churned.

Other, grayed-out people moved in the basement, trying to get to the windows. The voices grew louder.

"Not happening!" Nathan told himself desperately. "This is so not happening! You didn't get enough sleep last night! That's why you're seeing this!"

Nathan jumped but stayed on the ground. Unless this was one

of those dreams where he couldn't fly, he wasn't dreaming.

You can't hide from them. The police officer stared at him. *For your sake, you gotta get it together, kid. If you don't get control of your powers, they're going to be all over you like ants at a picnic.*

Suddenly, a light came on in the room. The police officer and all the other people turned translucent and disappeared. His heart thudding in his ears, trying not to hyperventilate, Nathan watched Mr. Lewiston, one of the school janitors, take a mop and bucket from the wall and head back to the door.

Before Mr. Lewiston could reach for the light switch, Nathan turned and fled up the steps. He didn't want to know if those people came back when the window went dark again.

□—□—□

As Nathan ran, his vision was flooded with the game board. Before his eyes, a black piece with an animal head on it moved swiftly onto the first colored ring and the sun piece, the yellow piece, moved one square in the outermost ring. The die rolled, and the white jaguar piece moved two squares. It was Nathan's turn once again.

What does the sun mean? Is it marking time? Does the Game have a deadline?

Panic flooded Nathan as he surveyed the game board. *How am I supposed to learn a game when there's a ticking clock? It's not fair!*

More than that, it was his turn to move again. But what was he supposed to move?

□—□—□

"You're late, Mr. Richards." Mr. Lloyd reminded Nathan of the Scarecrow from *The Wizard of Oz*. His hair was frizzy and he had a hooked nose. "Again."

"I know." Nathan waved the slip of paper in his hand cheerily. "That's why I brought the late slip and everything. They told me you can't bring one early."

A few of his fellow math-class students cracked up. With effort, Nathan kept his face straight and somewhat innocent. Maybe he didn't have a lot of friends, but he had a lot of fans when he was on a roll.

"Don't get cute with me, mister."

"I wouldn't dream of it."

Mr. Lloyd pursed his lips and frowned. "You know, you could learn a thing or two about responsibility from your cousin."

Despite already being late, Nathan couldn't resist the comeback.

"I know I could, but I got pre-Algebra class with you. They couldn't get me into hers."

A few more of the students cracked up.

The tips of Mr. Lloyd's ears turned bright red. "Take your seat, Mr. Richards. But if you get another tardy in my class, you're going to get detention."

"Yes, sir." Nathan went to his seat. He was happy that the seating chart allowed him to sit in the back of the room.

He dropped into his seat, opened his backpack, and took out his math book and then closed the backpack and shoved it under his desk. A quick glance at the open book of the guy next to him told him what page they were on.

Nathan sat back and studied the page. It was simple. He'd gotten bored with it weeks ago. He'd had to learn more complicated math than this in order to program his computer. He groaned and stretched out his legs.

Mr. Lloyd wasn't much of a speaker. Fortunately, math didn't need much of an introduction. Unfortunately, his teaching method was to "talk" math into the students' heads, and he made no allowances if that wasn't how you learned.

Nathan zoned out, aware of the teacher's voice, but not hearing a word. He wanted to relive flying in his dream, but his mind kept going to the police officer who had been haunting him since breakfast—and now there was that strange flash of the game board changing. He stared at the touch-screen board Mr. Lloyd was using to teach the lesson, but didn't see a thing.

The forest from his dream called out to him.

He took a deep breath and closed his eyes. When he let his breath out, he was no longer in the classroom.

□—□—□

Nathan stood on a riverbank in the deep emerald shade of trees that towered overhead. Muddy logs lay nearby on the ground. The water moved rapidly over rocks that had worn smooth over centuries. The constant gurgling noise of the river filled his ears.

Watching carefully, Nathan took in his surroundings as he turned a slow circle. Colorful birds twisted through the branches and skated just under the leafy canopy. A few spider monkeys threw themselves across incredible distances, twenty and thirty feet with each leap. They looked like darting shadows and screeched like banshees.

None of the animals seemed to have noticed him this time. He stood at the river's edge and looked around for any sign of the tall building. The trees looked different this time, and in the distance he saw the crumbled remains of a village. This wasn't the same forest Kukulkan had drawn him to.

Straining to see through the trees, Nathan didn't see what touched him on the leg. When he looked down, he saw that the nearest logs had sprouted eyes and weren't really logs after all.

Five giant crocodiles jerked into sudden motion on strong little legs. Their gray-green scales rippled over powerful muscles. They remained low to the ground and moved with the rapid, sinuous motion of a snake. Each of them had to be at least nine feet long. Fangs stuck out from their long snouts and curved around both upper and lower lips, looking like thick stitches that had been pulled into the scaly flesh.

Nathan yelped, and the closest crocodile opened its mouth and exposed a pink gullet surrounded by sharp teeth.

Nathan started to run and then recovered his wits and threw himself into the air, hoping that this was a dream because there were a lot more crocodiles ahead of him.

He hovered in the air a few feet above the crocs, suddenly feeling safe and pretty confident of himself. Below, the crocodiles snuffled and coughed their displeasure. A few of them headed into the water and thrashed around.

"Yeah, the flying boy would taste really good, but he's not on the menu, is he? *Nooooooooo.*"

Grinning, Nathan looked up and down the river and wondered if Kukulkan was anywhere nearby. He also wondered why it was he dreamed himself into something nasty every time he closed his eyes.

"Because the Game is filled with danger."

Nathan spun in the air, looking for the source of the tiny, squeaky voice. Then he looked suspiciously back down at the crocodiles.

"Crocodiles don't talk. Are you some kind of idiot?"

This time Nathan tracked the voice to a spider monkey sitting on a limb only a few feet away. *Awesome. Now I'm dreaming about stuff I find out from Alyssa at the breakfast table.* The spider monkey was a little over a foot tall, had an old man's face framed in gray and black fur that matched its coat, and was eating a banana.

"You're a monkey." Nathan knew he shouldn't be amazed. He was in a dream, and he knew anything could happen in his dreams. For example, he was flying.

The monkey took a bite of banana, chewed, and swallowed. Then he picked an insect from his left ear and ate it. The bug crunched. "I am. And I'm smarter than you."

"Monkeys can't talk. And I would never eat a bug I picked out of my ear."

8

The monkey took another bite of banana and chewed thoughtfully.

"Well?" Nathan stared at the creature and wondered if the skull at the breakfast table had inspired him to imagine it.

Lifting his thick brow ridge, the monkey remained silent and chewed carefully.

"Aren't you going to say anything?"

The monkey rolled his eyes at near Alyssa-strength. "What do you want me to say?"

"That you can talk."

The monkey scowled and bared his teeth. "You are the epitome of idiocy." He stood and flung the empty banana peel at Nathan.

Although Nathan tried to avoid the peel, it somehow plopped onto his head, spreading out like a yellow octopus.

"There." The monkey preened in satisfaction. "I crown you king of the idiots."

"Why are you talking to me?" Disgusted, Nathan pulled the peel off his head and dropped it into the river. A half-dozen crocodiles immediately swam for it and started fighting over the refuse.

"You've probably noticed that the crocodiles aren't scintillating conversationalists." The monkey shot the creatures a disparaging look. "Besides that, they would eat me if they got the chance. Not exactly a good conversation starter." He looked back up at Nathan.

"You know, I could choose to disbelieve in flying boys."

"Like that would do a lot of good." Nathan waved his arms at his sides. "Look at me. I'm flying."

"And I'm talking." The monkey crossed his arms over his thin little chest and deliberately looked away.

Nathan sighed. His dreams were becoming more and more unmanageable. "Truce?"

The monkey turned his head enough to catch Nathan from the corner of his eye. "What?"

"If I believe in you, then you need to believe in me."

"Do you realize how juvenile that is?"

Nathan shrugged. "Works for me."

The monkey sighed. "Idiot. How do we do this? Do we need to go through some silly ritual that binds both of us to your agreement?"

"Never mind. How did you know I was going to be here?"

"Kukulkan told me."

Anticipation buzzed through Nathan's veins. He'd been looking forward to seeing Kukulkan, and he was excited about him being in his dream again.

You were able to fly like he promised you.

"Where is he?"

"Busy with other things. He can't spend all his time getting you up to speed on the Game. You're going to have to do some of this yourself. You're not going to be spoon-fed."

Nathan felt disappointed. If this was his dream, why couldn't he have what he wanted?

"Because this isn't a dream." The monkey picked another bug out of his ear and ate it with a loud pop.

"Would you stop doing that? It really creeps me out."

"Doing what?"

"Reading my mind. Eating bugs. All of the above."

The monkey rolled his eyes and picked up a small bunch of bananas with his foot. Deftly, he pulled one off and started peeling it.

"Insects are a good source of protein. And it's not like you're thinking really deep thoughts. I'm certainly not intruding on anything interesting. 'I don't believe in talking monkeys.' 'Where is Kukulkan?' 'I can't believe the monkey just read my mind.' You should be concerning yourself with thinking what your next move is going to be."

Nathan couldn't stop himself from thinking how irritating the monkey was. And a few other things.

"Okay." The monkey stopped in mid-bite. "Thinking those things wasn't necessary. Or polite."

"Why are you here?"

"To give you more information about the Game."

Nathan focused on that. "What is the Game?"

The monkey raised his thin shoulders and dropped them. "It is what it is. It can be everything."

"Everything."

"Repeating what I say isn't going to get us very far. We have limited time. Do you think Mr. Lloyd is going to let you sleep forever?"

The way this dream world mixed with the real world was freaking him out. None of his other dreams had done that in quite the same way. And there wasn't a zombie in sight.

"What am I supposed to do in the Game?"

"Learn more about the world."

"My world? Or this world?"

The monkey shook his head. "As far as worlds go, there is only one. The others are merely set at different frequencies."

"Frequencies," Nathan repeated.

"You're repeating again. You're not going to learn anything that way." The monkey threw the empty banana peel at Nathan.

Dodging away, Nathan thought for sure he'd escaped the peel this time. Then, incredibly, the banana peel twisted in the air like a live thing and landed unerringly on Nathan's head.

Stupid monkey must be some kind of banana peel ninja. Nathan reached up to pull the peel away and then got hit with another one that wrapped around his lower face.

"Quit that." Nathan pulled both peels away and dropped them to the river. "What am I supposed to learn about the world?"

The monkey shook his head. "The most important thing, of course: your place in it."

"I know my place."

"Please. You don't interact with the world. You don't look around you and make changes when the opportunities are given to you. To become a Player, to play the Game properly, you have to seize those opportunities and make the most of them." The monkey held up a long-fingered hand just before Nathan could respond. "Don't object. Mr. Lloyd has already noticed that you're asleep."

Nathan immediately tried to wake up.

"We're not done here. We have a little time."

"If Mr. Lloyd catches me sleeping in class, I'm going to get detention. If I get detention, Uncle William will probably decide I need counseling."

"You're getting counseling. From me. Listen. You've been hanging onto the world with your fingertips. Barely even making a ripple in the things that go on. Your days of being a wallflower are over."

"What does my participation in the world have to do with the Game?"

"Everything. Your participation in the world, your interaction with others, is the heart and soul of the Game. You've kept yourself from caring about anyone and anything for far too long. That has to change. Now."

"What if I choose not to interact?"

"Then you'll lose the Game." The monkey looked at him sadly. "That would be bad. The Game will take something from you that you value. Perhaps something you didn't even know you would miss. But the Game knows. There are always stakes in a game, and your stakes will rise with every Game. You have to learn to play brilliantly."

"Great. No pressure there. And if I don't play brilliantly?"

"Epic failure. You can't even imagine the badness that will follow." The monkey gave him a tiny smile and leaped up to the next branch. "Good luck. Personally, I think you're going to need it. You're not going to be safe while you're learning."

"Wait."

The monkey paused. "I didn't go too fast for you, did I? I used small words."

"What do you mean I'm not safe?"

The monkey's small face wrinkled in puzzlement. "What can possibly be unclear about that?"

"What am I not safe from?"

"Many things. You had a narrow escape from the soul vulture earlier."

"Soul vulture?"

"Dan-ger-ous." The monkey spoke slowly and deliberately. "Bad. Eee-vil."

"Got that. Why do you call it a soul vulture?"

"Because it traps souls in its feathers. If you get a chance to see one up close, though I would hardly recommend it, you can see the imprisoned souls screaming in each of its feathers."

The thought chilled Nathan. He'd never heard of anything like that. Well, he'd heard of things that trapped souls, possessed souls, and killed souls, but he'd never heard of a vulture that did that.

Nathan needed more information. He needed to speak to Kukulkan. A mistake had been made, and if it could get him killed—or worse—it needed to be corrected. Now.

Someone shook his shoulder—

—and he woke up in math class with Mr. Lloyd staring down at him. The rest of the class waited in anticipation to see what would happen.

Detention loomed.

9

"**M**r. Richards, were you *sleeping*? In *my* class?"

Nathan was momentarily stunned. His life was in danger from some dumb game he wasn't even playing, and Mr. Lloyd was going out of his way to give him grief?

Worst birthday. Ever.

"No one sleeps in my class." Mr. Lloyd spoke in the voice he used when students went to the boards and continually did the work wrong.

A few of Nathan's classmates cracked up, expecting him to be shredded. Mr. Lloyd was a take-no-prisoners kind of teacher. But others waited for Nathan to strike back. He was known for his scathing wit, which most of the students were afraid of having turned in their direction.

Nathan thought quickly. Detention didn't scare him. He could do detention standing on his head. He had once, which had earned him further detention, so that proved counterproductive to the whole process.

Thinking about the "surprise" birthday that was waiting for him after school put pressure on him, though. If he wasn't there, the possibility existed that Alyssa would kill him. He didn't mind having her mad at him. That was another thing, like detention, that he could live with.

Having Alyssa gunning for him was another matter. She could

make his life insufferable. There was no sense in risking that.

Nathan cleared his throat and tried to look extremely attentive. "No."

"You're telling me you weren't sleeping?" Mr. Lloyd's face got redder.

For a second, Nathan wondered whether it was possible to make the math teacher so angry he passed out. *That could happen, couldn't it?*

"That's right. I wasn't sleeping."

"You were sleeping." Mr. Lloyd pointed his finger at Nathan, and it jerked back and forth like machine gun fire. "In my class."

"I wasn't." Nathan maintained eye contact.

"Whiner." Chas's assigned seat was in the corner of the room. "Shut up and take your medicine, dweeb."

"That'll be enough from you, Mr. Burris. You've earned yourself a detention." Mr. Lloyd spoke without turning to Chas.

That actually made Nathan happy. Getting Chas in detention was worth whatever he had to suffer. Mr. Lloyd was one of the few teachers who wasn't afraid to give Chas detention.

Choosing his course of action, Nathan sat up straighter. "I was having a . . . psychic vision."

Silence filled the classroom.

Then it erupted in laughter. "Did you see a cat in a tree, Nathan?" "What's the winning lottery number, nerd?" "Tell me who's going to win the Cubs game this weekend." "Even I could tell you who's going to win."

"Quiet!" Mr. Lloyd's voice cut through the din and ended the chatter instantly. "This class will not follow Mr. Richards's inexcusable inattentiveness."

The room quieted. Everyone looked expectantly at Nathan, as if he were going to spontaneously combust. Nathan figured that might be a good plan. Maybe even less painful than the plan he was working on.

"All right, Mr. Richards." Mr. Lloyd glared at him. "Let's hear about your vision. But I warn you now, if you use this moment to make things worse for yourself, I'll make sure they are indeed worse."

Nathan tried to stay cool, but it was hard. He enjoyed being the center of attention when he was calling the shots, but this was risky. He'd stumbled onto a math trick a few weeks ago while cruising the Internet and had decided to save it for a time when he needed to blow Mr. Lloyd's mind.

Of course, he was hoping Mr. Lloyd wasn't already familiar with the trick.

"In my vision, I saw you write a problem on the board." Nathan looked as innocent as he could.

"No big deal there. Mr. Lloyd's always writing problems on the board," someone piped up.

Mr. Lloyd clearly wasn't impressed. He folded his arms. "I suppose you're going to tell me what the problem was."

"Nope. That would screw up the whole space-time continuum."

Someone hooted in the corner. "Warning: Nerd alert."

Nathan ignored the comment.

"So you're *not* going to tell me?" Mr. Lloyd clearly wasn't happy.

"If I tell you, you'd just change the numbers."

Mr. Lloyd's face got even redder, and he pursed his lips, a sure sign that he was fast approaching the breaking point. "If you can't tell me the numbers, how are you going to prove your . . . psychic *vision*? Or do you intend to tell me that we're at an impasse?"

"You're going to write down the first number of five and then

I'm going to tell you what the sum of all five numbers will be—before you write down the other numbers. You'll write down four more after I give you that total. I'm going to give you two of them, and you can get two more from anyone in the room." Nathan had decided it would be better if everyone in the class got blown away at once.

"Really." Mr. Lloyd's tone was decidedly sarcastic.

"Yeah."

Mr. Lloyd stood there, and for a moment Nathan was afraid the teacher wasn't going to go for the bait. But in the end, Nathan was certain Mr. Lloyd would. The man lived for putting jocks and slackers in their places. And he seemed to have a special need to get Nathan. Especially if he could accomplish his goal using math.

"We're talking about extra detention if you're wrong." Mr. Lloyd rubbed his hands enthusiastically.

"I won't be wrong."

"I might remind you that your work in here has been less than stellar so far this semester, Mr. Richards."

Thanks for that. Nathan knew it wasn't his inability to grasp the concepts Mr. Lloyd taught. Nathan's present C grade just reflected his dislike of homework.

"How many digits?" Mr. Lloyd picked up his light pen and prepared to write. "I warn you, two or even three digits won't be acceptable. I could add a column of three-place digits in my head as I wrote them."

"Seven places." The material Nathan had read had only shown a three-place value, but the article said that the method would work for any number.

Without hesitation, Mr. Lloyd wrote down 7,431,658. He looked up at Nathan when he'd finished. "You said we're going to write down four other numbers."

"Right. But first, I'm going to tell you what all five of these numbers are going to add up to when we're finished."

The students cracked up, Chas leading the pack with his braying laughter.

"How do you propose to tell me the sum of numbers we haven't even chosen yet?" Mr. Lloyd smiled, clearly believing Nathan was about to fall flat on his face.

"Because I saw the total in my vision."

"Very well. What is your proposed total?"

Nathan answered immediately. "Twenty-seven million four hundred thirty-one thousand six hundred fifty-six. I clearly saw that in the vision."

Mr. Lloyd wrote the number down and smiled. "Okay, what is the next number?"

"Have someone else pick it." Nathan figured getting the other kids involved would be ideal. That way everyone would have something at stake. He knew a lot of his peers would be happy to see him blow up on this. And that was fine. They could all eat dirt.

Chas held up his hand, probably the first time all semester. "I have one."

"You can't even count that high." That came from the geek corner of the room.

"Who said that?" Chas twisted around in his chair and glared.

"Give me the number, Mr. Burris." Mr. Lloyd remained calm.

Nathan knew the math teacher really wanted to put him in his place if he was going to let the girl's comment go without assigning a detention. Mr. Lloyd didn't allow much in the way of negative comments in his class. Nathan laced his fingers behind his head and closed his eyes, acting like he had all the time in the world.

It took Chas a minute to remember all the place values. "Two million six hundred fifty-nine thousand one hundred and twelve."

Nathan pictured Chas's number in his head and answered before Mr. Lloyd could write the number on the board. "The next number is seven million three hundred forty thousand eight hundred eighty-seven."

Mr. Lloyd wrote both numbers on the board. "You give us this one and one more, correct?"

"Yes. So you need to come up with one more number." Nathan kept his eyes closed and looked relaxed. It was all about the show now. He was sweating it, but no one would know. He had to be free to go to that stupid *surprise* birthday party.

"Me." A girl he knew was on the soccer team called out. "Please, Mr. Lloyd, I have a number."

"All right, Miss Marcussen."

"Four million two hundred sixty-nine thousand four hundred sixty-one."

"Mr.—"

Nathan cut the teacher off but still didn't open his eyes. Giving the number was almost as scary as hovering over a river of crocodiles. "Five million seven hundred thirty thousand five hundred thirty-eight." He opened his eyes.

Without speaking, Mr. Lloyd wrote the numbers down in order above the proposed total.

$$7,431,658$$
$$2,659,112$$
$$7,340,887$$
$$4,269,461$$
$$5,730,538$$
$$27,431,656$$

Everyone in class held their breath as Mr. Lloyd started working the problem below Nathan's "vision." When the six showed up under his "guessed" number, the students started talking. When the five showed up in quick succession, followed by the second six and then the one, you could have heard a pin drop.

Nathan smiled. As long as those numbers had shown up, he knew that every other number had to fall into line. Now the real test was whether Mr. Lloyd would see the trick.

When Mr. Lloyd finished adding, he just stared at the smart board in confusion. "That's not possible. You couldn't have added those numbers that quickly. I couldn't add them that quickly." He turned to face Nathan. "How did you do that?"

"Vision." Nathan tapped his forehead. "I think my mutant power must be kicking in or something."

The weird thing was the explanation sounded even more real than what was actually happening to him. He could only imagine the conversation if he'd told Mr. Lloyd about his witty banter with the talking monkey.

Mr. Lloyd turned back to the smart board and went over the numbers again. He shook his head in dismay. "You can't have known these numbers would add up. You didn't know what numbers your classmates would pick."

The bell rang.

Nathan shoved his book into his backpack and got up, moving into the shuffle of other students. He noticed that most of them tried to stay away from him.

"Freak." "You don't have any mutant ability." "Geek."

Nathan ignored all the comments. He'd knew he'd stumped them all. It felt pretty good.

"Mr. Richards." Mr. Lloyd looked at him sternly. "I want you to show me how you did this."

"It was a vision," Nathan insisted, never breaking stride. "I didn't do anything."

"Mr. Richards, I insist."

"I'm here to learn, not teach." Then Nathan was out the door. He knew he was going to pay for that at some point, but he wasn't going to pay for it now.

He trotted to his locker and ignored the few people that wanted to know how he'd worked the math problem. He opened his locker and rummaged through the books to find his earth science book. It was another boring class, but at least Mrs. Sommers usually just read from the book or showed a film. He hoped there was a film today because he could use a nap. That would tide him over till lunch.

Movement flickered at the edge of his vision. When he looked, he saw the mirror he'd stuck on his locker door.

Only he didn't see his reflection there.

He saw Professor Felicima Diego Barrera Richards—his mother. And she didn't look happy.

10

Professor Felicima looked intense, but mostly she looked like she really wanted to talk to Nathan. And it wasn't going to be a pep talk.

She gestured impatiently and waved him closer.

Nathan was mesmerized by her appearance and leaned nearer. The noise of the crowd passing through the hallway behind him swelled and receded.

Nathan.

He read his name on her lips. He wondered how she had known his name. His father had never mentioned if it was one they had picked out together, or one that he had simply come up with himself.

Nathan.

"What?" In his dreams, he'd imagined getting to meet his mother, imagined what his life would have been like if she'd lived. He'd never imagined what that first conversation would be like, but asking "What?" didn't seem like a great start.

We need to talk. Professor Felicima stretched out a hand toward Nathan but stopped at the mirror's surface. Involuntarily, he touched the mirror. Suddenly, everything went dark around him.

Nathan felt weightless, and the accompanying vertigo was bad enough to make him light-headed. Then he blinked his eyes open and found himself in a small cave.

Small, closed places panicked Nathan. He blew his breath out and tried to remain calm. Flickering light danced across the stone walls, and he tracked it back to a pitch torch hanging on the wall behind him. Black soot stained the stone overhead.

"Are you all right?"

Nathan spun around and saw Professor Felicima standing there. She wore the same khaki outfit she'd been wearing in the picture of her he'd found.

"I get kind of claustrophobic. Don't know why." Nathan barely managed to stay standing. He looked around. "I haven't really been in a cave before. I never had any desire to explore one."

"I'm sorry." She looked around. "This was the only place I could meet with you."

"Really?" Nathan shook his head, and the disorientation swirled within him again. "Because I can think of hundreds of other places we could have met." He looked at her. "But then again, I didn't know we could meet. If I'd known that, maybe we could have done this before." He couldn't keep at bay the sudden surge of pain and anger he felt. Unleashing the anger was easier than dealing with the pain.

She pursed her lips and nodded. "I've done the best I can, Nathan. I haven't been able to talk to you before today."

"How did you know my name?"

"Peter and I picked it out. Actually, I'm surprised that he named you Nathan. It was the only name we agreed on, but it wasn't the name he really wanted. I think you get a lot of your stubbornness from him."

The stone wall felt rough under Nathan's hand. "How far underground are we?"

"Thirty feet or so. We should be safe here."

He looked at her. "Safe from what?"

"The soul vultures, for one. There are a lot of other creatures out in the frequencies that will prove dangerous to you."

"That's what the monkey said." Nathan held onto his anger. "I'm getting really tired of people—and monkeys—talking to me but not really answering questions."

"Kukulkan will give you the answers you seek, Nathan. The rest of us are here to help you learn to travel the frequencies and manage your gift."

Nathan looked at her, wishing he felt like running over to her and hugging her. He thought that's what he should be feeling. But he didn't. She was a stranger.

"Are you really my mom?"

Tears glittered in her eyes, and it surprised him to feel bad that he'd caused her pain.

"Yes." She nodded. "I am."

"Why—?" Nathan's voice broke unexpectedly.

"Why wait all these years before I saw you?"

"Yes."

She smiled at him. "I've seen you a lot, Nathan. From the time you were a baby until now. I've always been with you. But you haven't been able to see me."

"Why?"

"Because . . . death is on a different frequency. Or at least I am no longer able to access your frequency."

"The monkey talked about frequencies."

"Yes." His mother wrapped her arms around herself. "You have to think of the frequencies as worlds, Nathan. There is your home frequency, the world where you live, and the rest of the worlds—the frequencies—are just a bit different, like recordings with some of the details left out, a little less than the original world. Or sometimes totally different. I don't know. I've only heard stories from Kukulkan and others."

The idea fascinated Nathan. Some of the video games he played and graphic novels he read talked about things like that. Science had a string theory of different worlds. And the last *Star Trek* movie had created a whole new time line for the reboot.

"I can't come to your frequency." Professor Felicima sounded frustrated about that. "I'm blocked."

"Because—" Nathan stopped himself.

"Because I'm dead, yes."

"How did you die?" Nathan had never gotten a good answer to that question.

Professor Felicima shook her head. "There's no time for that. We can talk about the past later. Right now, we need to talk about what you're doing in the present."

"What I'm doing?" Nathan laughed shortly. "I'm kind of hoping I'm not going to end up in a mental institution."

Professor Felicima smiled. "Your fate is one thing I know, Nathan. You're destined for great things. Important things. You can't even imagine the things you're going to see and do. You've got great power." His mom stared at him. "I don't want to see it squandered." She paused. "I have to admit, Nathan, your behavior at school and in your life is surprising to me. You're an intelligent young man, but you don't bother to even try."

Oddly, Nathan felt embarrassed. "School is boring."

"Because you're smart. You need to seek out challenges in your education, or have your teachers push you."

Yeah, like I'm gonna ask for extra work.

"Or get your father and your Uncle William to supplement your studies."

I'd rather have a third eyeball.

His mother grimaced, and he had the distinct, uncomfortable feeling she knew what he'd just thought. "You could even talk to your cousin, Alyssa."

A diseased third eyeball. Nathan folded his arms. "If you haven't been able to contact me before, why can you do it now?"

"Because your power has started to blossom. It has created a gateway. A potential for several gateways, actually. That's why the dead are starting to seek you out. You're a magnet for them."

Now there's a truly creepy thought. Nathan shuddered as he remembered the gray shapes standing in the basement.

"Many of them simply want understanding." His mother looked at him. "They want to know someone can still hear them. Others need more substantial things. Like the police officer who's been talking to you. His name is John. I think you should try to help him. He seems like a good man."

"Let's say that I agreed to help him, which I'm not agreeing to, by the way, but if I did: how can I help him?" *Better yet, how can I get him to go away?*

His mom shook her head. "I don't know how you can help him specifically. That's for you to figure out. And you can't simply make him go away." She frowned a little. "For one, that would be very impolite, and for another you don't have the power to prevent him from contacting you. Not yet, anyway."

Great. Everybody reads my mind.

"That's not as hard as you think."

"So I'm going to be haunted for the rest of my life? That stinks."

"Watch your tone. And I haven't been haunting you. I've been looking out for you."

Nathan didn't have the heart to tell his mother he didn't believe her.

"You've been given a great gift. You need to learn how to use it."

To Nathan, the speech sounded way too familiar, a lot like what he'd been hearing at home since Uncle William moved in. "You know, this is my life. I think I should be able to choose what I do with it. And if I'm happy, people should just leave me alone and let me be happy."

His mother looked at him. "Are you really happy, Nathan?"

"Yes."

His mother drew herself up, and he felt the distance between them all of a sudden. She didn't like that answer. "You're playing the Game now. Keeping to yourself is no longer an option." She paused. "You need to return to your frequency before anyone notices you missing."

"You disappeared me in the middle of the hall. Don't you think someone will have noticed?"

"Time can move differently in the frequencies, Nathan." His mother smiled and started to fade. "Sometimes that's a blessing."

"Hey." Nathan stepped toward her, suddenly realizing she was going and there was nothing he could do to stop her. He really didn't need her popping into his life and acting like a mom after thirteen years, but he really did want to know more about her.

Then the cave melted around him and he was—

—staring into his locker. The noise of people shuffling through the hallway was still all around him. He stood there and wondered what he was supposed to do.

He felt nauseous and closed his eyes. Rather than seeing the calming darkness, he saw the game board before him once again. This time, there were two white pieces on the board, a new unidentifiable one in the outermost ring and the animal head piece in the second ring. Kukulkan had taken his turn. Nathan observed that the black piece he saw move last time, his piece, was in its same place, but as he watched, it moved boldly toward the white piece. As his piece moved, the yellow sun piece moved one space forward in its orbital path.

Then someone roughly shoved him into his locker. His chin struck the edge, followed closely by his ear, and his forehead banged against the door.

When Nathan reeled back, the mirror was just a mirror again. His moth—Professor Felicima had vanished, replaced by the reflections of the guys who had shoved him into his locker.

Arda. Great. Just what I needed today.

11

Arda Montoya had one huge hand wrapped around the back of Nathan's neck, and he was squeezing hard enough to hurt. Nathan fought to turn around, but Chas and Barkley, another boy from the football team, caught Nathan's arms. Together, the three of them banged Nathan's head into the locker again.

"Hello, shrimp." Arda grinned hugely, exposing his big teeth. "I guess you forgot my out-of-school suspension ended today."

Nathan had forgotten. *This birthday just keeps on giving.*

A week ago, in retaliation for Arda slipping a dead rat into his locker, Nathan had goaded Arda into taking a swing at him in front of Mrs. Myers, the vice principal. Nathan had rolled with the punch, but he'd gone to the floor like he'd been body-checked by Shaq.

Mrs. Myers had given Arda three days of detention and let Nathan hang out in the school infirmary for a couple of hours. At the time, Nathan felt like the bruising had been totally worth it. Over the past two years, Nathan and Arda had been at each other's throats on a weekly basis, but it was hard to say who was winning their feud.

Arda had painted Nathan's favorite skateboard pink last year, filled his backpack with garbage, popped Alyssa's game-winning soccer ball when she'd given it to Nathan to hold after the game, and inflicted body slams and punches on Nathan in every school hallway at amazingly regular intervals.

Nathan had fought back physically and was a little surprised when he'd held his own. But Nathan was particularly proud of one-upping Arda in the dirty tricks department. In earth science, Nathan had tainted a chemical experiment Arda was working on so that it blew up, giving Arda's skin a blue tint that had taken days to wear off. Unfortunately, two of Arda's lab partners had gotten the treatment as well. There had been a few unhappy parents after that incident.

And then there was the FaceSpace hack Nathan used to distribute pictures of Arda getting kisses from his pet Chihuahua, Muffy. It had taken Nathan nearly a month to get those pictures, and he still laughed every time he thought about Arda walking through the halls while all the boys made kissing sounds and all the girls talked about how cute his dog was.

"You look surprised to see me, dork." Arda spoke into Nathan's aching ear. Arda was big and really athletic. He was a running back on the football team, and everybody at school thought he was a big deal. He wore his bronze-colored hair cut short and looked older than thirteen. "I can't believe you'd forget about me. I sure didn't forget about you. Thought about you every day. And what I was going to do to you when I got back."

Nathan struggled to get free, but Chas and Barkley kept him squashed up against the lockers. *I could really use my flying power right now.*

But this was the real world. He couldn't fly.

Arda banged him against the locker. "Do you know where I spent the last three days? Helping my mom clean other people's houses. She thought getting me to help her at work could be part of my punishment for getting tossed out of school. Kind of make me appreciate the opportunity for education, you know?"

Nathan couldn't resist. "Got a bad case of dishpan hands, did ya? They have lotion for that. Probably make you smell better too."

Chas laughed and then started fake-coughing when Arda glared at him. "Something in my throat." Chas coughed again. "There. I think that got it."

"*It* better have." Arda glared at him.

Nathan looked desperately for a teacher. None was in sight. It was almost like a conspiracy—some kind of Get Nathan Day.

Arda banged Nathan against the locker again. He felt like he was in the gorilla cage at the zoo. "I didn't get dishpan hands, but I cleaned a lot of toilets."

"Wow." Nathan put as much fake enthusiasm into his words as he could. "A job skill. Who knew? Your mom must be so proud. And they said you were untrainable."

"Keep yucking it up, shrimp. You got some payback coming. I've been thinking about this. I got really good at cleaning toilets. Thought I'd demonstrate." Arda jerked his head to the other guys.

Chas and Barkley grabbed Nathan under the arms and lifted him off his feet. Nathan tried to kick them and managed to get Chas in the stomach. Chas used a few choice words and then shifted to grab Nathan's ankles and pin them together. Nathan jerked and tried to get free, but it was impossible.

Several of the students stared at him as Arda and his crew carried him through the hall. None of them wanted to go up against Arda.

"A little help?" Nathan squirmed again. "Maybe a principal? I'd settle for a teacher. Or the lunch lady. Can somebody maybe find Mrs. Squigbottom? Just follow the stench of mystery meat. She'll be the one with the rusty spatula."

Some of the students burst out laughing at Nathan's plea for help.

"Somebody shut him up." Arda tried to clap a big hand over Nathan's mouth. Nathan tried to bite him.

"Hold on." Chas stopped, kicked off one of his shoes, and pulled off his sock.

"Don't." Immediately grossed out, Nathan fought harder, but still couldn't break free.

Then Barkley held Nathan's nose. When Nathan couldn't hold his breath any longer, Chas shoved the sock into Nathan's mouth. Nathan choked on the rancid taste. He was sure he was going to die. If foot rot didn't get him, he would asphyxiate from the horrible stench. He retched and then wished he would have thrown up because then someone might have called the janitor.

No one did anything except watch and laugh. Nathan couldn't really blame them. If the situation had been reversed, he probably would have done the same. After all, he wasn't in any real physical danger. Was he?

Arda pushed the bathroom door open. "Take him to the stall."

No! Nathan tried to shout, but the sound he made didn't even sound human. *"Nnnnrrrrppphhhh!"*

"Gimme his head." Arda shifted his grip and reached for Nathan's head.

Nathan wriggled like a worm on a fishing hook, and just like a worm on a fishing hook, he didn't manage to do much more than squirm.

Arda seized the front of Nathan's hoodie and his belt. Then he tilted Nathan and shoved him headfirst into the toilet bowl. Cold water went all the way up to Nathan's neck. He closed his eyes and was grateful the toilet was clean.

At least, it had looked clean.

Can you die from exposure to toilet water? In just a few seconds, Nathan stopped worrying about that and became afraid that Arda was really going to drown him in the toilet bowl. Arda, or someone, flushed the toilet, and the water swirled around Nathan's head.

Just when Nathan thought he couldn't hold his breath any longer, they brought him up out of the water. He gasped and blinked. Arda thrust his face into Nathan's.

"Not so tough now, are you, dweeb?"

"I never said I was tough." Nathan kept talking. As long as Arda was yelling at him, he wouldn't be drowning him. It wasn't exactly a win-win situation, but Nathan was working through the main problem.

"You think you're clever."

Nathan couldn't bring himself to disagree with that one. He did think he was clever. Except for the whole Let's-Give-Nathan-A-Swirly thing. That was something he hadn't seen coming. "Smarter than you, moron."

"Well, you're not so smart now, are you?" Arda shoved Nathan's head back into the toilet bowl and flushed again.

Water hammered Nathan's face. This time it filled his nose. It might have filled his nose last time, but he'd been too concerned about drowning to notice.

"What do you think you're doing?"

Even under water, Nathan recognized Alyssa's voice. Arda and the others yanked him out of the toilet and dropped him onto the sopping tiled floor. He landed with a bone-jarring thump.

"Hey, you're not supposed to be in here." Arda put his big hands on his hips and gave Alyssa a defiant glare.

Alyssa stood with her books folded into one arm and glared at Arda. "Do not tell me what I'm supposed to do, you Neanderthal."

"Hey." Chas took a step back as if fearing attack. "That's the dork's cousin."

"So?" Arda didn't look away from Alyssa.

"She's one of Principal Masterson's favorite students is so."

Silently thanking Alyssa for her timely arrival, Nathan reached under the stall, grabbed the dividing wall, and propelled himself under and into the next stall.

Barkley looked under the stall. "Hey, the doofus is getting away."

They rushed the stall door, but Nathan locked it and stepped up onto the toilet to get out of reach. They'd either have to climb under, which he didn't think they'd be willing to do with water covering the floor, or they'd have to climb over the stall. If they tried that, he thought he had a good chance at defending himself. He made a fist.

"Leave him alone." Alyssa's voice sounded loud in the bathroom.

"Oh yeah?" Arda smirked at her. "What are you going to do if we don't?"

Nathan peered over the top of the stall. Alyssa thrust her phone at Arda like she was using a crucifix on a vampire.

A picture filled the screen. The woman was instantly recognizable to everyone in the bathroom. Principal Mary Margaret Masterson ruled the halls and classrooms with military precision.

"Principal Masterson." Alyssa cocked a lethal eyebrow. "On speed dial." She looked like a villainess out of a James Bond movie. "What do you have?"

Arda hesitated only a moment then he walked toward the door. He turned and walked backward for a few steps, staring at Nathan as he went. "This ain't over, dork."

"No, it's not." Nathan smiled despite the water dripping onto his shoulders. "I'm going to make sure you get more on-the-job training with your mom, baboon boy."

When the door swung shut, Nathan sighed in relief. He opened the stall door and looked at Alyssa. "Thanks for the save."

Alyssa glared at him. "Oh, I didn't come in here to save you."

Nathan stood on the toilet and felt confused. "Then why did you come in here?"

"Because I just heard what you did to Mr. Lloyd. How could you? You know math is his life. You can't just stump him with a math puzzle and walk away."

12

"What?" Nathan couldn't believe what he was hearing. "I don't even see how this is a problem."

"You were sleeping in his class." Alyssa shook her head. "You should know by now that he hates that."

How does she know all this stuff? She must have spies everywhere.

"I didn't have a choice."

"About sleeping?" Alyssa frowned. "Maybe you should try sleeping when normal people do."

"I didn't have a choice about stumping Mr. Lloyd with the math problem. If he'd caught me sleeping in class—"

"He did. You were."

Nathan shrugged. "I was going to get detention. Detention would have meant missing the—" he hung air quotes and dripped as much sarcasm into his words as he could "—*surprise* birthday party."

"That's not Mr. Lloyd's problem. You were disrupting his class, and he was doing the best thing for you."

"By giving me detention? Are you wack?"

"He didn't deserve what you did."

"I didn't do anything to him."

Alyssa just stared at him.

"He's the one who always says math is the solution to any problem." Nathan brushed futilely at the water soaking into his hoodie.

"He's a good teacher and a great mathematician. Given time I'm sure he'll figure out your little trick."

"It's not my trick. I just borrowed it." Somehow it was easier to justify his actions when he could say that the trap he'd set wasn't his own. Nathan could see how being proven wrong might make Mr. Lloyd upset. He liked to be right. Being wrong must have felt like Nathan would feel if he got a Nanovor evolution or Transformer question wrong.

"You're going to apologize to him."

"For what? Being smarter than him?" Nathan started to get angry. It was easy to do while standing there dripping water all over himself.

"Says the boy who just had his head used as a toilet brush."

Nathan took a deep breath and instantly regretted it. He smelled like a pine-scented urinal cake.

"You know, this is probably not the most appropriate place to have this conversation."

"When did you become an expert on *anything* appropriate?"

"In order to know inappropriate, you first have to know appropriate. Something can't be inappropriate without a foundation to disrupt. You answered your own question. I know appropriate. And this ain't it." Wordplay was the one area where Nathan knew he could hold his own with Alyssa, and he took the opportunity every chance he got.

The door opened and a boy walked in, another seventh grader, but Nathan didn't know him. When he saw Alyssa standing there, the guy stopped and looked back at the identification plate on the open door.

"Out." Alyssa didn't even bother to turn around.

"But I'm in the right place." The boy pointed at the identification plate. "You're—"

"Do you want what he just got?" Alyssa pointed at Nathan.

After a quick look at Nathan, the boy shook his head. "Not me."

"Hey." Nathan waved his hands in protest. The last thing he needed was everyone at school thinking Alyssa had given him the swirly. "She didn't do this. Seriously. A girl couldn't give me a swirly."

Not bothering to wait around for further explanation, the boy backed out.

Someone knocked on the door. "This is Principal Masterson. I'm coming in."

Nathan sighed in defeat. *I'm gonna be here so long, maybe I should have packed a lunch.* He inhaled a fresh whiff of toilet water and pine cleaner and then stepped through the stall door to face his executioner.

Principal Masterson opened the door and walked into the bathroom without hesitation. She was a tall, narrow-faced woman with shoulder-length red hair. She always wore a suit and looked like a corporate executive. Crossing her arms, she looked around the room like a king's headsman looking for a victim.

"Mr. Richards. Why am I not surprised?" The principal's voice dripped disappointment.

"Probably because I'm surprised enough for the both of us."

"Was that an attempt at humor?"

Nathan weighed his options. Actually, under the right circumstances—for someone *not* wearing a wet hoodie and smelling like pine—the situation could be funny. "Maybe."

"Because I'm not in a humorous mood."

"Me neither. That was definitely not humor."

Principal Masterson looked at Alyssa, and her voice softened.

"What brings you here, Alyssa?"

"I wanted to talk to Nathan."

The principal sighed. "One of us really needs to be able to get through to him."

"I'm trying, but evidently I don't speak village idiot."

Principal Masterson patted Alyssa on the shoulder. "I appreciate what you're doing, but it's not your responsibility. You have enough to handle with everything that you do around the school, and everyone appreciates how hard you work. The last thing you need is Mr. Richards making everything more difficult for you."

Alyssa feigned embarrassment. Nathan knew she was faking. Alyssa loved getting praised. She lived for it.

"Thank you for understanding."

Behind the principal's back, Nathan mimed gagging, which drew an immediate glare from Alyssa.

"More difficult for her?" Nathan held his hands out in martyred disbelief. "She didn't just get attacked and have her head rammed into a toilet and flushed!"

Principal Masterson glared at him as though he'd just interrupted a very important meeting. "You're claiming someone did this to you?"

Nathan gestured at his wet head. "Not exactly something I would do to myself."

"A simple yes would suffice, Mr. Richards. The last thing we need here is your sarcasm. Trust me when I say that that is one particular talent of yours that has been seen and heard far too much."

"Yes." Nathan throttled a snappy comeback about the principal needing a sight and hearing checkup. "Someone did this to me."

"Who?"

"Arda."

"Mr. Montoya?"

"Yes."

"Do you have witnesses?"

"Alyssa saw Arda in here with me."

Principal Masterson looked at Alyssa. "Is that true?"

"There was a group of guys in here." Alyssa shrugged. "But I didn't know any of them."

"Arda plays football. You're a cheerleader. How can you not know a football player?"

"I rarely see them out of their pads and helmets." Alyssa put on one of her most innocent looks. "Plus, when I'm on the field, I have a job to do. I don't get to just sit back and watch the game."

"You shake pom-poms. That's not a job."

Alyssa arched an incendiary eyebrow at him. "How would you know? You never go to the games."

Principal Masterson cut off Nathan's blistering retort and addressed Alyssa. "Did you see anyone put Mr. Richards's head into the toilet?"

"There was a group of boys standing around the stall when I came in here to speak to Nathan. I couldn't see through them. I didn't see what they were doing."

"You can't have missed that." Nathan pointed at the stall. "Even a blind person would have seen them shoving my head into the toilet. *Twice.*"

Alyssa shrugged. "I didn't. And I wouldn't have minded seeing that."

Upon reflection, Nathan had to admit that maybe his cousin hadn't seen anything. The stall had been pretty tightly packed with bodies. But it didn't take a rocket scientist to figure out what had happened.

Principal Masterson tapped her finger on her chin as she considered. "So, for now, I only have your word that Mr. Montoya—"

"And henchfriends."

"—and possibly associates assaulted you."

"They did."

"And what do you think they will say when I ask them about your accusations?"

"They'll deny it."

"Yes. They'll probably say you slipped and fell in all on your own."

Nathan knew that was true. That's the story he would have told.

"You see my problem." Principal Masterson wasn't exactly sounding sympathetic.

Nathan pulled at his wet hoodie. "I didn't do this to myself."

"Mr. Richards, let me remind you of an incident that happened a little over a week ago. Mr. Montoya assaulted you then as well, correct?"

"Yes."

"And you told your story to the vice principal?"

"I did." Nathan sighed, knowing what was coming. He had nothing but bad luck when it came to Arda. But the war wasn't over yet.

"You neglected to mention that you set up Mr. Montoya for the whole encounter. In effect, you got yourself smacked around that day. I didn't find out about your little subterfuge until Mr. Montoya had already been punished. Am I now to assume that you're *not* faking this time?"

Nathan had nothing to say to that without going into the long history of dislike that stretched between Arda and him. And since he didn't understand it, he didn't think anyone else would either.

"You're the boy who cried wolf, I'm afraid, Mr. Richards." Principal Masterson eyed him levelly. "Obviously there is bad blood between you and Mr. Montoya. I suggest that the two of you seriously work at finding a way to patch that up. Or at least keep it out of this school. I will not tolerate any more of this destructive or abusive behavior. Especially when it's going to endanger others and result in damage to school property."

"But I didn't—"

The principal held up her hand. "I don't want to hear any more."

Reluctantly, Nathan closed his mouth. The wet clothing made him shiver. He sneezed, then couldn't help wonder if toilet water had seeped into his brain while he was submerged.

Principal Masterson glared at Nathan. "You know you're going to get detention, don't you?"

"Yes." Nathan had already resigned himself to that. He actually expected to be suspended at this point. He groaned inside. He hadn't been suspended since Uncle William had moved in. He could imagine what it would be like to have his uncle around all day fretting over how Nathan's attitude had to be corrected and how he needed to look at "the big picture."

"Would you consider allowing Nathan to start detention next week?" Alyssa asked.

Nathan couldn't believe what he'd just heard. His cousin was going to bat for him?

"Why? What do you have in mind?" Principal Masterson asked.

"My father is planning a birthday party for him today after school."

Principal Masterson glared at Nathan. "What you're asking for is a serious infraction of the rules, Alyssa."

"I'd consider it a favor."

The principal sighed, smiled at Alyssa and then frowned at Nathan. "You know, Mr. Richards, I get the feeling you don't know how truly lucky you are to have Alyssa as your cousin."

Nathan bit his tongue. No one else knew what a pain Alyssa could be.

As if reading his mind, Alyssa raised her eyebrow and smirked. Her face smoothed out an instant before Principal Masterson looked back at her.

"I'll do this for you, Alyssa." The principal shifted her attention to Nathan. "As for you, Mr. Richards, you'll help Mr. Lewiston clean up this mess. Then report to me, and we'll get you into your next class."

Great. Nathan couldn't believe it. *Alyssa is so well-liked that even the principal will set aside a perfect opportunity to make me sit around in toilet water for an extra couple of hours.*

Principal Masterson left the bathroom, already talking on her radio to summon the janitor.

Alyssa started for the door and then paused. "Don't get into any more trouble the rest of the day. I'm not going to be able to get you out of everything."

"I'm still getting detention."

"I didn't *try* to get you out of detention. You *deserve* detention."

"I didn't shove my head in the toilet."

"Not for that. For embarrassing Mr. Lloyd in class."

"He didn't give me detention."

"He should have."

"You know, if this is your idea of helping me, I really don't need it." Nathan shifted his weight to step off the toilet, but his foot slipped on the wet surface and he barely avoided smashing his face into the tiles.

"Alyssa? What are you doing in the boy's bathroom?"

"Oh my goodness! Is that your cousin?"

"He looks like a drowned rat."

"Is he all right?"

"He is so weird!"

"I can't believe you're related."

When Nathan looked up, he saw a group of girls gathered around Alyssa in the doorway. Some of them already had their cell phones out and were taking pictures of him. He was certain they'd be texting and tweeting in seconds. This episode was going to be all over the school.

Groaning, Nathan buried his face in his hands and wished he were somewhere else.

13

Nathan pushed himself to his feet. He hated the feel of the wet clothing sticking to him.

Mr. Lewiston rolled a creaking mop bucket up to the doorway. He stopped and looked at Alyssa and the girls.

"You ladies mind?"

They moved out of his way, and the janitor pushed the bucket into the bathroom. He surveyed the damage and then looked over at Nathan.

"You do this?"

"I've got enemies."

"Well, now you got a mop." Mr. Lewiston handed Nathan one of the mops attached to the bucket. "Just swish it around on the floor to pick up the water and then squeeze it out in the bucket." He demonstrated how to use the wringer.

"You're not going to be late after school, are you?" Alyssa checked the time on her phone.

Nathan gripped the rough wooden handle and wiped the mop across the floor. "No, I won't be late."

Alyssa left, taking her entourage with her.

"Girlfriend?" Mr. Lewiston squeezed his mop out in the bucket.

Nathan looked at the man in disbelief. "I just had my head shoved in a toilet. Do I really look like the kind of guy who would be dating someone like her?"

"Nope. I didn't think so. That's why I had to ask."

Nathan sighed. "Thanks for the vote of confidence." He wrung out the mop. "She's my cousin."

"So what is it you're not supposed to be late for?"

"My birthday party."

The janitor looked at him and smiled. "Today's your birthday? No kidding?"

"Nope."

"Happy birthday, kid."

"Yeah. Thanks." Nathan plopped the wet mop back onto the floor. "Ain't this the life?"

⊏─⊏─⊐

At lunch, Nathan grabbed a burger and fries off the cafeteria serving line, wrapped them in a napkin, took a bottle of water, and hustled back out into the hallway. He kept careful watch and made it past the open classrooms to the computer lab. Usually no one was there during lunch time.

He couldn't believe luck was with him and the lab was deserted. With the way the day had been going, he'd figured Arda and his group would have been lying in wait ninja-style.

Seating himself at one of the computers, he quickly brought up Alyssa's FaceSpace account. A barrage of photos and friends displayed to the thumping backbeat of a hip-hop song that Nathan immediately detested because his cousin liked it well enough to put on her account.

He clicked through her pages but didn't find her homework page. He knew she had one on there because she and her friends who did projects together used it. He'd heard her talking about it.

"Okay, so you've got it hidden." Nathan took a bite of his burger, cracked his knuckles, and started hitting keys. "You can hide it, but I can find it. I am Captain Sly, and I am a master of Google-Fu."

First he typed in all the obvious page names that he could think of. To hide a page, all a person had to do was create the page on the site but not provide a link to it from the homepage. Unless someone knew the page was there and knew the name of it, access was practically impossible from the homepage.

Nathan found the page pass code attached to a hyperlink of Alyssa's favorite movie, *The Princess Bride*.

"Wicked." Nathan took another bite of his burger and ate a few cold fries. He sipped his water as a chaser and returned to work. "When it comes to computers, you're the hound, and I'll always be the fox."

Several folders showed up on the hidden page. Nathan clicked on the one that read OPEN, UNSOLVED SPECIAL PROJECTS. That page opened and showed more folders. He looked for the name John. There was only one.

Chicago Patrolman John A. Montoya.

For a moment, Nathan thought the name sounded familiar, but he brushed off the feeling almost at once. He'd been hearing about John all morning. And seeing the guy. Of course the name sounded familiar.

When he opened the file, the first thing that showed up was a newspaper picture of John A. Montoya with a headline that read: DECORATED POLICE OFFICER'S DEATH SUSPECTED TO BE A RESULT OF INVOLVEMENT IN BURGLARY RING.

Nathan leaned away from the computer screen in confusion. *The guy was a crook? Why would I help a bad cop?*

He rested his head on one hand as he read the news article.

No one seemed to know what John Montoya had been doing

when he'd been shot in the back while inside a maintenance tunnel that was under repair. After he failed to respond to a call from dispatch, other officers had been sent to check on him.

Finding Montoya took some time. He'd left his car at the curb in front of Manny's Café and Delicatessen on South Jefferson Street. Montoya's body was found a couple of hundred feet inside the maintenance tunnel. The only person anywhere near the scene was a maintenance worker installing fiber lines. The police interviewed him and determined that he had no involvement in the case. There were no witnesses.

According to the news article, Montoya was a highly decorated and award-winning police officer. He was survived by his wife and son. The article concluded by stating that the murder was under investigation.

That had been two years ago.

Nathan finished the last of his burger and thought about the murder. Students were starting to trickle back into the hall. He checked the time on the computer and discovered that lunch period was nearly over.

Professor Felicima's image suddenly formed in the dark computer screen. *Help him, Nathan. He needs someone to set things right.*

Shaking his head, Nathan snorted. "He was a thief. Do you really want me to help a bad guy?"

Do you believe everything you see?

"No, not since special effects were invented. That whole Muppet thing confused me for a while, but I got over that."

Get his story before you make up your mind about him.

Nathan leaned forward again. The noise level out in the hallway increased. He had to get moving soon or he was going to be majorly interrupted.

"I've already got his story." Nathan waved at the computer. "It's right there. In black and white."

You may learn something new or different if you take the time to find things out for yourself. Her features grew stern. *I won't accept this kind of laziness. No son of mine will ever—*

"That's part of the problem, isn't it? I'm not your son. You didn't raise me." He ignored the look on his mother's—*Professor Felicima's*—face, shut down the computer, and turned off the monitor. He'd had enough guilt trips for one day. He wasn't going to take one from a parent who wasn't even part of his life.

He got up and grabbed his trash. When he turned around, he discovered he wasn't alone. A pretty girl stood uncertainly in the doorway.

"Dude, do you always talk to the computer?"

"Skype connection."

"Seriously?" Showing real enthusiasm, the girl brushed her lank brown hair out of her face. "You bypassed the security network so you could make phone calls? That's massive."

"Totally." Nathan had done exactly that. Months ago. He gave her one of the cracks he'd set up and left the room. He couldn't wait for school to be over.

□—□—□

Nathan skateboarded home, the grinding noise made by the wheels passing over the rough sidewalks filling his head so that it was almost hard to think. And that was a blessing, because he had way too much to think about.

When it came to skateboarding, he had real skills. He coasted effortlessly, dropping his foot every now and again to propel himself along. He wove around rough areas on the sidewalk, other kids walking home, and outran dogs that took an interest in him. The faster he went, the less he smelled the leftover fresh-pine scent still clinging to him.

When he got the skateboard up to full speed and was really zipping along, he almost felt like he was flying back in Kukulkan's world. He closed his eyes a couple times and tested to see if he could fly here. He couldn't. He ended up taking a nosedive onto a driveway and then scrambling up before anyone could come out and check on him.

The day had warmed up a little, and the sun was out. As he coasted around a corner past a bodega, a Hispanic grocery store, someone was suddenly in front of him, reflected in the window showing all the SPECIAL signs. He'd cut the turn too close, leaving himself no room to maneuver.

Nathan threw up his arms to shield himself as he tried desperately to avoid the coming collision. He recognized the policeman's uniform in the reflection only a split-second before hitting him.

Braced for the impact, Nathan expected to get thrown backward because the guy was a lot bigger than him. The policeman didn't have time to move either, but he didn't look surprised. Then a terrible coldness closed in on Nathan, and he felt like he was going to freeze solid.

He passed through the coldness almost immediately and ended up out of control. His body reacted too slowly, and he slammed into the bodega's graffiti-covered wall. He dropped to one kneepad and looked back at the police officer.

Only no one was there.

Cautiously, Nathan stood and picked up his board. He could still feel the terrible cold. He was scared enough to take off running, but he couldn't move without looking back at the window to see if the man was still there.

The officer's reflection was still in the window. Now Nathan knew his name was John Montoya. The man looked troubled and somehow faded. Sorrow etched his face.

Nathan.

"Yeah?" Nathan watched the man but kept his distance. More than anything, Nathan wanted to run.

I want you to talk to me.

Nathan shook his head. "I don't want to talk to you."

You're the only one who can hear me. I need help, and I don't have anyone else to turn to. Someone killed me. Set me up.

"Why not ask your friends from the burglary ring for help?"

Montoya's face hardened. *I busted bad guys. I never worked with them.*

Nathan saw the pain in the man's face and the anger in his voice and wanted to believe him. "That's not what it says in the newspapers."

The newspapers got it wrong. I need to clear my name for my family's sake. I never asked for help in my life. But I'm asking now.

Overcome by confusion—and for some reason, a feeling of guilt—Nathan grabbed his board, sent it shooting along the sidewalk, and jumped aboard. He leaned into the next turn.

He paused at the next corner and waited on the light. Shivers ran through him, and he kept glancing all around for the policeman.

Don't freak out. Everything's going to be all right. Just get home. Take a deep breath and get home.

He wished that he believed it.

14

A small crowd gathered around the open pit that had been cut into one side of South Jefferson Street. Nathan stopped his skateboard in front of Manny's Deli and looked at the crowd. This was unexpected.

After talking to John Montoya, he'd wanted to see the murder site for himself. The newspaper article had mentioned the tunnel, but Nathan had assumed he'd have to figure out a way in. He hadn't expected it to be open, especially two years after the murder.

Looking at the crowd thronging around the opening in the street, Nathan had the creepy feeling that Officer John Montoya had found a way to alert dozens of mediums and spiritualists and draw them to the spot.

Right away, he dismissed that theory. First of all, he didn't believe in spiritualists and mediums. Of course, he hadn't believed in ghosts, the "frequency-challenged," before this morning.

Yellow earthmoving machines and guys in hard hats labored behind sawhorses marked: DANGER—STAY BACK. A guy in an orange jacket waved neon-orange batons at the operator running the big machine clawing earth from beneath the street. The roar of the diesel engine and the whine of the machine's hydraulics filled Nathan's hearing.

Maybe they found more dead bodies. Nathan looked around but couldn't see any reflective surfaces. For all he knew he was surrounded by the non-living right at this moment. He wondered if his mom was there too, and if she was happy about the fact that his curiosity was making him risk Alyssa's wrath by being late for the party.

Nathan tucked his board under his arm and turned to a guy about his age who was trying to peer through the crowd.

"Dude. What's going on?"

The guy turned around and shrugged. His nose and cheeks were red from the cold. He kept his hands tucked into his pockets.

"The streets and sanitation guys discovered something."

"Like what?"

"Some kind of Native American relics. Bones. Pots. Arrowheads. Like that."

"Oh." Nathan felt relieved and disappointed all at the same time. On the way here he'd gotten himself used to the idea of looking into the policeman's death. He actually convinced himself that doing some investigating might be cool—especially if he could find out more than Alyssa. After all, he was in a position to actually talk to the murdered policeman. Not that he wanted to. But he didn't kid himself about his chances of finding out what had gone on. Whatever evidence there had been to be found, the Chicago Police Department crime labs had already gotten to it.

"Isn't this where that cop was found shot a couple of years ago?" Nathan shifted around in the crowd and tried to find a clear view of the site.

The earthmover lifted another jawful of dirt and deposited it on a growing pile. Then it returned for another bite of the street.

The kid shrugged and wiped his nose. "Beats me."

Nathan checked his phone and saw that he was running out of time to get home. Stupid party. He took a deep breath and let it out. Gray fog twisted away in the wind in front of him. Still, he was right here, and he couldn't just walk away.

"Do the police have the tunnel completely shut down?"

The kid's face went still. "You want to get into the tunnel?"

Nathan hesitated, giving that question serious consideration. "Yeah. I really wouldn't mind getting a closer look."

The kid held out his hand. "Gimme five bucks."

Nathan stared at him for a moment and then pulled out his wallet and handed over the money.

"There're some access tunnels farther on." The kid worked his way through the crowd. "I'll show you."

Nathan followed at the kid's heels, hoping that he wasn't making a mistake but knowing he couldn't just walk away without trying to see where John Montoya died.

"The college archeologists and the construction guys are watching over the front of the tunnel where they found the artifacts, but you can still get in."

□—□—□

A few minutes later and a few blocks away, the kid led Nathan to a manhole cover in the middle of an alley. They looked around to make sure no one was watching and then levered the manhole cover up. The steel disk was heavy and awkward, but Nathan had slipped through sewers and tunnels under the city before and knew how to handle it.

"I don't suppose you brought a flashlight?" The kid looked at Nathan expectantly.

"No. Didn't plan on climbing through the tunnels."

The kid grinned and pulled a flashlight from his pocket. "Luckily I have one."

"Yeah."

"I'll let you rent it."

Nathan frowned.

"Five bucks."

Reluctantly, Nathan dug into his pocket again. "Kind of stuck on that price, aren't you?"

A look of serious contemplation filled the kid's face. "Do you think I'm too cheap?"

"No." Nathan passed over another five dollars and took the flashlight. "This does have batteries, right?"

The kid looked a little unhappy. "You think I should charge for batteries, too?"

Nathan flicked the light on. Without another word, he clambered down into the yawning mouth of the manhole. The flashlight barely kept the darkness at bay.

Inside the tunnels, Nathan built a mental map of his path and the direction he needed to go. He was good at keeping his sense of direction from all the video games he played. Remembering twists and turns was a breeze, as was maintaining an overall idea of his progress.

The tunnel was as dank and nasty as he figured it would be. He breathed through his mouth so the stench wouldn't be so bad. His tennis shoes stuck to the ground as he walked.

After only a few minutes, he arrived at the tunnel where the construction workers had widened the entrance to reveal the hidden artifacts. A lot of people were already working in the dig site. Several areas were marked off with tape and barriers.

"So, you decided to take a more active role in the Game?"

Recognizing Kukulkan's voice, Nathan looked back over his shoulder. Kukulkan stood there in the shadows in a suit and long coat. He didn't look like the cold touched him.

"You can come here? To this frequency?"

"Yes."

"I didn't know that."

"I can go anywhere I wish. I'm not limited." Kukulkan smiled. "Soon you won't be either. If you work at it." Kukulkan stared at the mouth of the opening. "What are you doing here?"

"Checking up on something."

"What?"

"You don't know?" The idea of Kukulkan not knowing what was going on surprised Nathan.

"This is your move, Nathan. I've got my own agenda." Kukulkan nodded at all the activity. "I'm interested in listening to what you've got going."

As concisely and quietly as he could, Nathan outlined the story of John Montoya.

"So you're here to help this man?"

"No."

That earned a raised eyebrow from Kukulkan. "No?"

"Look, the papers said the guy's a bad cop." Nathan glanced around as he realized he was speaking out loud and that his voice might carry to the archeology team and construction workers.

Kukulkan waved that away. "Don't worry about them. They can't hear us."

"Romulan cloaking device?" Nathan grinned.

Teeth flashing, Kukulkan nodded. "Something like that."

"Cool."

"It's very cool. I do stealth better than ninjas."

Nathan cracked up at that.

"So you don't want to see what they're looking at in the excavation area?"

Nathan wanted to say no, that he didn't. But he did. He was curious.

Blowing out a breath, Nathan nodded. "But it sounds like this is something my dad would be interested in more than me."

"The Native American artifacts are there too. But don't you want to know what happened to the police officer you've been seeing?"

Nathan thought for a moment. If he was honest with himself, he had to admit that he wanted to see the evidence. But it was hard to dismiss the idea that the case had already been investigated and the police had reached a conclusion based on the facts.

"Good cop or bad cop, it doesn't make a difference. The Game has to be played."

"The Game is involved in this? I don't understand."

"The ghosts, the *frequency-challenged* as you've been thinking of them, are part of the Game. They define goals or raise questions you have to answer."

Nathan still didn't understand. "About what?"

"Yourself. Them. Other things in life that make your people important."

"You know, you're starting to sound like a Chinese fortune cookie."

"Okay. Let's keep it simple. According to the media, everyone assumes John Montoya, one of Chicago's Finest, was a member of a burglary ring. If that is true, then who killed him?"

"Why should I care?"

"Nathan, when you play video games, does it really matter if you win?"

Nathan thought about that. Beating the game did matter. It felt good.

"Sure, it matters."

"Then maybe it matters who killed John Montoya."

"He's kind of dead. It's not going to matter much to him." Nathan felt bad stating it so baldly.

"Perhaps it does matter to him."

From everything the ghost had said so far, Nathan knew that it did matter.

"And maybe it matters to John Montoya's family." Kukulkan's dark gaze locked with Nathan's.

Okay, major guilt. Nathan rebelled against the unfamiliar feeling. He wanted to walk away, but he didn't want Kukulkan to be irritated with him. He didn't want to lose contact with the big man.

"So what do you say?" Kukulkan jerked a thumb at the excavation site. "Want to take a look?"

"Really." Nathan couldn't completely turn off his belligerence. "They're going to just let us walk in?"

"Yeah."

"How?"

"Romulan cloaking device, remember?" Kukulkan walked forward, and the workers seemed to shift to let him through. "Stay close."

Nathan followed Kukulkan, staying within arm's reach. Walking past people without getting touched or jostled—or even noticed—was totally cool.

Unable to resist, he touched the shoulder of a guy as he walked past. When the guy turned around with a mad look on his face, he couldn't seem to see Nathan.

"Can you teach me how to do this?"

"If you want to learn." Kukulkan strode past the construction warning line fearlessly. "If you listen." He glanced over his shoulder as Nathan started to tap another guy on the shoulder. "And if you don't taunt the people who can't see us."

Nathan couldn't help thinking what it would be like to pass through school completely unnoticed, and be able to do anything he wanted.

A moment of panic wound through Nathan's stomach as he stepped past the warning tape. Above him, the big jaws of the earth-moving machine opened and started to reach into the hole again.

"Watch out." Nathan jerked backward.

Kukulkan waved a hand. In response, the earthmover suddenly let out a metallic shriek that sounded a little like a cow getting kicked.

The operator halted the jaws, which had closed like an arthritic fist, and stepped out onto the platform beside the cab. "Blew a pressure hose. Gonna be an hour or so until we can replace it."

One of the construction workers with a clipboard walked over and surveyed the earthmover. He cursed and made a notation on the clipboard.

"Shut it down, Pete. By the time we get the hose replaced, we'll be done for the day."

The operator nodded and clambered back inside the cab. The diesel engine died a moment later, and Nathan was immensely thankful for the silence.

Kukulkan walked into the dig site. Lights hung all along the underground. It was a maintenance tunnel for the sewer and utilities, electricity, phone, cable, and gas lines. Nathan thought the area looked like a primitive science fiction set on a cheap movie budget. He'd explored a few of the tunnels himself in the past, and it hadn't proven as exciting as he'd hoped it would be.

It's a lousy place to die.

"It is, isn't it?" Kukulkan shook his head. "I don't care for underground places. Give me the openness of the forest or the beach. Even cities are barely tolerable because everything is locked down and closed away from everything else." He glanced at Nathan as they walked along the tunnel. "Why was John Montoya down here?"

"Probably receiving stolen goods from the guys who killed him." Nathan walked easily at Kukulkan's side. He tried to fly and actually lifted himself up a couple inches and sort of floated along but that looked weird and creepy all at the same time. It reminded him of the floating men on that one *Buffy the Vampire Slayer* episode where no one could talk.

"Is that what he said?"

"No. That's what the papers said."

"What did he say?"

"I didn't actually ask him," Nathan admitted. "He just wants my help. I bet he would tell me anything."

"Really?" Kukulkan glanced around. "Don't the police keep records of where their officers are? The logs wouldn't lie, would they?"

Memories of television cop shows flooded through Nathan's mind. Every time the cop got out of the car, he checked in and told the dispatch people where he was. With GPS on all the vehicles, though, they'd already know that. But John Montoya might have radioed in and said why he was somewhere.

"There should be records." Nathan shoved his hands in his pockets, but it was awkward while carrying the skateboard. It seemed colder in the tunnel, but he didn't know if it really was colder underground, or if it was only his imagination.

"Maybe you could ask."

"Yeah. They'll probably give that kind of information to a kid just as a reward for asking."

"There are public records, and there were other people around at the time."

"I'm not exactly Sherlock Holmes, here."

Kukulkan grinned. "One of the things I always loved about Sherlock Holmes—"

"You're kidding me, right? You don't really read Sherlock Holmes stories."

"I wouldn't kid about that. And I do a lot of things you might not expect, Nathan."

"Of course. Of course you do."

"Sherlock always regarded the solution to a crime as a challenge. Part of a game."

"Yeah." Nathan shifted his skateboard. "I see that. Just saying, you know." He paused. "Is this part of the Game? Because if it is, I don't see it on the game board or in the pieces."

"The pieces and game board are symbolic. This Game is all about the decisions you make, Nathan. And why you make them. You don't get to play the Game without risk."

"Sure. But what's the reward?"

"Reward?"

"Yeah." Nathan shrugged. "If there's risk, there's gotta be reward. So if I play, if I win, what do I win?"

Kukulkan smiled. "The chance to play me again."

"And if I lose?"

"You don't want to lose."

Panic swelled within Nathan. He didn't want to lose because he didn't like losing but now he also didn't want to lose because it might mean not seeing Kukulkan again. That was something he didn't want to lose.

"Okay. I don't want to lose." *I also don't see what John Montoya has to do with this. Or even why I have to put up with ghosts.* But if he had to put up with the frequency-challenged to hang out in all the cool places Kukulkan took him, it was worth it.

Kukulkan stopped and looked down at the floor. "This is where it happened."

Nathan started to ask, *Where what happened?* Then he stopped himself. He knew what Kukulkan was talking about.

"How can you tell?"

"Because all you have to do is sort through the frequencies. You can see through the frequencies if you want to."

"What do you mean?"

"Just look here." Kukulkan pointed at the ground. "Search for what happened here."

Hesitantly, Nathan stared at the ground. He concentrated and focused his gaze. "Nothing's happening."

"Don't force it. Just relax. The frequencies are tied to emotions. Anything of consequence, anything that generated strong feelings in one person or many, anything that is symbolic of your people or their history, can be found all through the frequencies. Even if it no longer exists in this frequency."

Nathan stared a while longer, even crossing his eyes like he did when he'd learned to stare at those pictures that hid other images. He started to shake his head and tell Kukulkan that he didn't see anything.

Then he did.

There, facedown on the ground, laid the body of John Montoya. Three bullet holes marked his back.

15

For a moment, Nathan thought he was going to be sick. Seeing the dead man there was even worse than the monkey skull at breakfast. It felt more painful and more real.

Covering his mouth with his hand and fighting the retching sensation, Nathan stepped back involuntarily and dropped his skateboard. Kukulkan caught the board before it clattered against the rough rock.

As fascination pushed away the *ewwwww* factor, Nathan stared at the body. Now that he looked at it, he realized it was gray, just like the . . . *frequency-challenged, that was a good name for it* . . . people he'd already seen.

But this body wasn't animated. Though that didn't stop Nathan from wondering if John Montoya was going to jump up and yell at him. That would have been too much.

Not real. Not there.

"What was he doing in the maintenance tunnel?" Nathan's mouth felt dry.

"You said it yourself." Kukulkan held the skateboard and regarded it with more interest than he did the body. "Although I would be careful about jumping to conclusions. As you learn the Game you will find that things are always more complicated than they look at first."

Looking down at the body, Nathan felt sorry for John Montoya.

For the first time, he didn't see the man as a bothersome ghost or a bad cop. Someone had taken a coward's way out and hurt him.

No. He wasn't hurt. He was murdered.

And no one should get away with that.

Nathan squatted down on his knees and ran his fingers through his hair. "Nobody knows who did this?"

"You know more about John Montoya's death than I do."

Glancing up at Kukulkan, Nathan shook his head. "Then I don't get it. How was he chosen to be part of the Game?"

"Everyone's a part of this, Nathan." Kukulkan's voice was gentle. "All of this? It's part of something that was written down a long time ago."

"You mean the Game."

"The Game is part of it. What you're doing, what you're learning, it affects all the frequencies. That's why you alone of all the people in this world have been given the power to navigate between those frequencies. You were born to play the Game. The stars, the universe, all aligned to bring you to this moment."

That sounded incredibly weird—and scary. Nathan tried to wrap his mind around it. All his life he'd figured the only one he really mattered to was himself. He was happy with that. He could deal with that.

Nathan rubbed his face with his hand as he stared at Kukulkan. "I don't know what I'm doing." He hated admitting that because he didn't want to look small in front of the big man, but he had a strong feeling it was important to say it out loud.

Kukulkan shook his head and smiled. He dropped a hand on Nathan's shoulder and squeezed reassuringly. "Patience. You'll learn. All will be explained. No one expects you to know everything at this point. The Game offers a lot of room for discovery, and it is free-flowing. The goals aren't always what you think they are."

"Then tell me what I'm supposed to do now. Tell me how I'm supposed to find out what happened to John Montoya."

"I cannot say whether or not you *should*."

"What do you mean? Why else would you bring me down here, show me a dead body, and guilt-trip me?"

"I didn't bring you here, Nathan," Kukulkan said calmly. "I found you here. And I didn't show you anything. I merely told you how to look."

Nathan's eyes blazed with frustration.

"Think of it this way," Kukulkan continued. "Good choices and bad choices. Good moves and bad moves. If this man is truly innocent, and you can help him—"

"That would be a good move," Nathan nodded. "But what if it's like the news says? What if he was involved in stealing?"

"Then wasting your time helping him would be a bad move. Some of these things, you'll have to figure out yourself. Merely deciding to do something will set you on a path of the Game."

"That stinks, and I'm not going to do it." Nathan kicked stubbornly at a loose rock and sent it skidding across the floor. Some of the construction workers that had entered the tunnel after them watched the rock.

"What was that?" One of them shined a light in the dark corners of the room that the overhead lamps didn't reach.

"Probably a rat. I've seen 'em big as my arm down here. And I tell you, you never want to come face-to-face with any of those."

Nathan was embarrassed by almost revealing their presence. At the far end of the tunnel, men and women prowled among the freshly turned earth.

"We're good." A gray-haired man that looked vaguely familiar at this distance waved a hand. "We're still well clear of the actual dig site, but the larger opening will give us plenty of room to excavate the ruins."

"That's good to hear, Professor." One of the construction workers surveyed the top of the tunnel. "Looks like everything here should hold up just fine. But you're gonna upset a lot of the locals while you and the university sift through everything down here. Traffic's gonna be a bear for a while."

"I know. But it's going to be worth it." The professor walked around with a powerful flashlight. "Judging by what we've found already, this dig is going to give us more information about the Beaver Wars that were fought across Illinois and the Great Lakes area."

Although it couldn't possibly be right, Nathan couldn't help imagining armed beaver platoons battling each other around Chicago. If not armed, did the beavers sneak around and try to chew through trees and drop them on each other? For a moment, he was lost in his imagination and didn't realize Kukulkan was speaking. He focused on Kukulkan and quickly figured out what he was saying.

"Playing the Game is your choice." Kukulkan spoke without inflection. "You can quit at any time you want to. If you quit, you'll lose, but you can quit."

Nathan sighed. He didn't want to quit. Everything was way too interesting, and the frequency-challenged didn't look like they were going to leave him alone any time soon.

"I need to know more."

Kukulkan nodded. "You will."

"I need to know more *now*." Nathan waved a hand at where he had seen the dead body. "I need to know what I'm supposed to do about this. Or even if I'm supposed to do anything about it. Because I really don't want to, and I don't know how I could possibly make a difference."

"If someone tells you the moves, you aren't truly playing the Game. If I tell you, I might as well be moving all the pieces."

"And it would be boring." Nathan understood what Kukulkan was saying, but understanding it didn't make it any less frustrating. "Okay, I get that."

"It's more than that." Kukulkan eyed Nathan. "The Game demands a balance be kept between the Players. We can know each other, we can even be friends, but we can't shortchange the Game by collaborating on the play. We must play for ourselves, and we must play our best to defeat the other."

Well, since I don't know what we're doing here and I've never played a game with real dead people in it, I don't see how I'm supposed to beat you. Hope you enjoy the victory. Even as those thoughts ran through his head, Nathan was thinking about how to go about spotting some trick, some way to turn events around if it became possible. He was the Loophole King. If there was a way to bend a rule into a pretzel without breaking it, he was confident he could do it.

"But how are you playing against me?"

Kukulkan shook his head. "There's only so much I can tell you. The rest you have to figure out on your own."

"Are there any rules to this Game?"

"Yes. There will be a Winner and a Loser. And there is no cheating."

I'd have to understand the Game to know how to cheat. "Not a big help."

Kukulkan suddenly squeezed the skateboard from both ends. At first, Nathan thought he'd somehow made Kukulkan so angry that he was going to break the board. Then, as he watched in fascination, the skateboard shrank down and turned shiny silver before disappearing in Kukulkan's big hands.

When Kukulkan opened his hands again, a silver bracelet with Nathan's name on it lay shiny against his dark palm.

"Great. You made a bracelet." Despite the sarcastic response, Nathan was totally in awe. But what was he supposed to do with a bracelet that used to be his favorite skateboard? "It's a cool trick, really, but I really would have preferred the skateboard."

Kukulkan smiled and winked. "The bracelet is a lot more than it seems." He dropped it to the floor. By the time the bracelet hit, it had changed into a skateboard again, only it was a much improved, much more expensive skateboard that Nathan had been eyeing for months. "I figured making it be more portable would be a good thing."

"Wow." Between the cloaking effect, the dead guy and the skateboard, and his imagined concept of the Beaver Wars, Nathan felt like he'd stepped into an episode of *The Twilight Zone*.

Kukulkan stomped on the back of the skateboard and caused it to flip up into the air. On the way up, it shifted back into the silver bracelet, and he caught it easily. He handed it to Nathan.

"Now you can carry your board anywhere you want without freezing your hands or having to make room for it. I thought you might like that."

"I do. Seriously."

"One other thing: the bracelet won't change into a skateboard and the skateboard won't change into a bracelet, if you're trying to show it off."

Blown away, Nathan examined the silver bracelet. He saw his reflection in it and then spotted the reflection of John Montoya standing behind him. Quickly, Nathan dropped his arm.

"Okay, I think you've seen enough." Kukulkan's voice was suddenly all business.

"What do you mean?"

"You came here to see where Officer John Montoya was murdered. You have."

"But I didn't learn anything," Nathan objected.

"What did you expect to learn?"

"I don't know. Something."

"If there was anything to learn here, don't you think the police forensics people would have learned it by now?"

"Then why did you come here?"

"This is where I found you." Kukulkan looked at him. "I just met you and tried to be helpful."

"Well, you didn't really help."

"I kept you from wasting time. I allowed you to exercise your curiosity. Hopefully, I helped you move into a better position to understand the Game."

"I understand it even less now."

Kukulkan smiled that knowing smile and slipped on his sunglasses as they walked toward the open end of the tunnel. "You understand more than you think you do. The Game isn't just cerebral, Nathan. There's an emotional complexity to it. You have to make choices, hard choices, about what you're willing to risk. And to learn."

"What if I don't want to risk or learn anything?"

"Then you won't play the Game."

"What about the dreams I've been having?" Nathan asked.

"You can still have those dreams."

"I can still fly?"

"Whenever you want. As I promised."

"Will we still hang out?"

"Sure. Take care of yourself. Talk to your mother. Let me know what you decide about the Game."

"Okay."

Without another word, Kukulkan faded into the shadows.

Nathan took a step forward and started to head back the way he'd gotten into the tunnel. A heavy hand fell on his shoulder and pulled him around.

"Hey, kid."

Barely maintaining his balance, Nathan peered up at a grizzled construction worker's face. Busted. Evidently Kukulkan had taken his Romulan cloaking power with him.

"What are you doing down here?" The construction worker's grip remained tight. "You aren't supposed to be down here." He turned around and raised his voice. "Anybody here know this kid?"

"Better call the police," someone suggested.

Great. Wonder if Alyssa will forgive me for being late if I'm being held at the police station? Unhappily, Nathan searched for a way out but kept coming up empty.

"I know him." A man stepped out of the gathering crowd of construction workers and archeologists and looked at Nathan with an expression of curiosity and surprise.

"Dad?" Nathan couldn't believe it was his father. "What are you doing here?"

"The university secured the rights to work this dig site." His dad took off his dusty glasses and cleaned them on his shirt. "What are you doing here?"

Nathan thought quickly. "I heard about the artifacts on television."

"You know this kid, Professor?" the construction worker asked.

"He's my son." He scratched his head, looking a little pleased. "I didn't know you had any interest in the kind of work we're doing here, Nathan, but I'm glad to see it." He sighed. "I just wish you had chosen a different dig in which to become interested, Nathan. We're keeping a tight lid on everything here, and I'll have to get special permission to have you on site. That is, if you want."

Nathan couldn't bring himself to say no, even though that was his first reaction. His dad seemed kind of hopeful that he might really be interested. So he nodded. Part of him thought maybe it wouldn't be so bad. Maybe something really cool would be found in the dig. And maybe getting a close-up look at what went on would give him a chance to understand what his dad found so fascinating about history.

"Sure, Dad."

Professor Richards beamed a little uncertainly. "Very well, Nathan." He glanced up at the construction worker. "Thank you, I'll take it from here."

The construction worker paused just a moment and then nodded and left.

Nathan walked with his dad and listened as he talked about the artifacts they'd found so far. Though he was trying to hear what his dad said, Nathan kept thinking about John Montoya's body lying on the floor of the tunnel.

At the tunnel entrance, Nathan asked his father a couple of questions about the dig before one of the students helping with the excavation called to him.

"Sorry," his father said. "I've got to go."

"Sure," Nathan said. "It's cool."

"I'll try to push through the necessary permissions to get you back down here real soon." Nathan said an awkward good-bye and headed down the street. When his phone rang, he didn't even need to look at the screen to know it was Alyssa calling. He decided not to answer, but he knew she would just keep calling and changed his mind.

Dreading what was coming, Nathan tapped the ANSWER button on the touch screen and raised the phone to his ear. "Hello?"

16

"Where *are* you?" Alyssa demanded.

"On my way. There was—" Nathan stopped, realizing he didn't really have a story to tell.

"What?"

"Never mind."

"I got you out of detention this afternoon so you could *be* here. On time."

Nathan sighed and looked back at the dig site regretfully. He couldn't decide whether coming here had been worth it. Jogging to the sidewalk, he slipped his bracelet off and tossed it onto the pavement. The bracelet became the skateboard somewhere on the way down and landed on its wheels, already in motion. He hopped aboard with practiced ease, shoved off a few times, and zipped along the sidewalk faster than he'd ever gone. The board was excellent. "I'm on my way. I'll be there soon."

"You should already be here."

"It won't be much longer. Geez." Nathan took the next corner perfectly and shot across the intersection just as the light turned yellow. Nathan hung up and pocketed the phone.

Alyssa tried calling back two more times. Then she began a series of abrasive texts, which Nathan ignored. Finally, she gave up, and by that time Nathan and the board were one, and he was hauling faster than cars could speed along the streets.

Despite knowing that he was hurrying home just to go to that stupid party, he couldn't help grinning. The board made him feel like he was flying, just like in the dreams. He was Chicago's answer to the Silver Surfer.

□—□—□

Less than thirty minutes later—that had to be a personal best—Nathan arrived in his neighborhood. Two more turns along alleys put him back on a direct course to his house. He wasn't looking forward to the birthday party, but he was enjoying the idea of hunkering down in his room after the day he'd had. Even the speed on the skateboard hadn't been able to keep his thoughts from Officer Montoya's body in the maintenance tunnel.

Questions popped into his mind faster than a bag of microwave popcorn exploding into a feast of fluffy goodness. Why had Montoya been there alone? Who shot him? Why the maintenance tunnel? Why would anyone kill him?

Finally, Nathan made himself push the questions away. Game or no Game, he didn't know how to investigate a murder. He didn't know the first thing.

But you know someone who does, don't you? Nathan thought of Officer Montoya immediately. The man would know how to start an investigation. He'd know the right questions to ask.

Nathan hated it that he'd come up with the answer so quickly. Nathan could talk to Officer Montoya. Except that the idea left him completely creeped out.

Zoning out by playing a video game sounded much better than talking to frequency-challenged police officers who might have been bad guys.

What if Professor Felicima was wrong and Officer Montoya was—

Nathan stopped that line of thought. He had no idea what his mother—Professor Felicima—thought about Officer Montoya. She hadn't said.

On the other hand, Nathan didn't have to play the Game. He focused on that. If the Game meant talking to dead people, then he didn't want to play.

Of course, that didn't mean the weirdness would go away. And really, he didn't want all of the weirdness to go away. Just the parts that kept overlapping into his world.

My primary frequency, he reminded himself.

A familiar deep voice interrupted Nathan's thoughts. *You ride that thing pretty good, kid.*

Uncertain, Nathan dropped his foot to the pavement, swiveled, and came to a stop. He stomped the end of his board and caught it when it flipped up into the air. Dumpsters lined both sides of the alley between back doors to businesses that fronted the streets at either end of the block. The cross street was only a short distance away, closer than turning around and going back into the alley.

"Thanks." Nathan's heart thumped so hard he thought it was going to explode.

You got real style. Smooth and easy.

The words sounded familiar and Nathan finally recognized the voice—and the man who'd given him those very same compliments on other occasions. Then he realized how impossible it was that he was hearing the words.

I ain't seen you in a long time, kid. Seems like a month of Sundays.

"A couple months, Mr. Dewar," Nathan whispered, and the wind whipping through the alley suddenly seemed colder. "You're not supposed to be here." *Really* not *supposed to be here.* Nathan looked at the glossy surface of his new skateboard to find the reflection he knew was going to be there.

A figure stepped out of the shadows of the wall, almost looking as if he'd emerged from the bricks. He was a tall, lanky old man with hollow eyes, blue lips, and black skin. Short salt-and-pepper hair ringed his mostly bald head and draped over his upper lip.

He wore a T-shirt under a Chicago Bulls tank top. A stained fry cook's apron that would never be white again wrapped his midriff. A folded white hat stuck out from the front pocket of his slacks. His red Chuck Taylors showed considerable wear and tear, and a host of stains.

Told you that you don't have to be so po-lite with me, kid. The man waved a hand. *Just call me Eddie. Ever'body does. You know that.*

"Eddie." Nathan spoke quietly, but glanced around, feeling trapped.

Eddie grinned at him and shook his head. *Ain't no need for you getting nervous, kid. Ain't nobody in this here alley gonna hurt you.* Sadness pulled at his face. *I sure ain't gonna hurt you. We always been friends.*

That was the truth. Eddie Dewar had been a short-order cook at the Easy Times Diner for years. The diner had been one of Nathan's favorite stops on his way home from school. Sometimes, before Uncle William had moved in, Nathan would get there and read the latest *Game Informer* or a comic or a book, take advantage of the Wi-Fi bleed-over from the upscale coffee shop next door, or play his DS or PSP.

But that had been before—

You want an eggnog shake, kid? Eddie lifted a hopeful eyebrow. *Be glad to fix you one.*

"Not today, but thanks." *Can frequency-challenged people still make shakes?*

Got places to be, huh?

"Yeah."

Eddie took a cigarette pack and a lighter from his pants pocket. He shook out a cigarette, lit it, and waved the smoke way with a hand. He inhaled and immediately had a coughing fit.

Don't look at me like that, kid. Eddie recovered slowly. *I know these things are bad for me. Got a doc that keeps telling me that. Tells me they're gonna kill me one day.*

"They did." Nathan couldn't believe he'd just said that, but he wasn't feeling as generous with the frequency-challenged as he had been at the start of his day. "I went to your funeral."

Eddie looked confused and then shook his head. *You're gonna have to speak up, kid. I didn't hear that. Traffic noise is loud this time of day.*

Nathan didn't have the heart to repeat himself. It seemed too unkind. The funeral had been two months ago, not long after Uncle William had moved in. Eddie Dewar had died from throat cancer. Uncle William hadn't understood why Nathan felt the need to go to the small funeral, so Nathan had sneaked out of the house. Uncle William had threatened to ground him when he discovered he had gone without permission, but Nathan's dad hadn't enforced the punishment.

"What are you doing here?" Nathan focused on the man. This was the first of the frequency-challenged he'd known as a flesh-and-blood person. His mom didn't count.

A smile spread across Eddie's face. *I work for a living, kid.* He said it proudly. Nathan knew a lot of people looked down on the kind of work Eddie did, if they bothered to look at all, but Eddie had always taken a lot of pride in his cooking and serving.

"I know." Nathan had always liked the old man. Eddie had told stories Nathan hadn't understood about playing baseball for farm teams, but he'd understood Eddie's love for the game.

Came to work today 'cause I don't miss work. Eddie knocked on the back door of the diner. Nathan didn't hear any sound. *I'd miss this place. Got good work, good people. Ain't nothing a man needs more.* He nodded at Nathan. *That's what you been missing in your life, kid. Work. Something you really love.*

Nathan didn't know what to say to that.

So while you got the chance, maybe you should look around. Take a good look at this new thing you got going on. Could be you'll find something you want to do.

"What new thing?"

Eddie smiled. *Kukulkan, kid.*

Suspicion warred with surprise in Nathan's mind, and he didn't know which was winning. "What do you know about Kukulkan?"

More'n you do. Right now. You just gotta figure things out.

Nathan took a few steps forward and then caught himself. "What things?"

You'll know soon enough. Just be watchful. You was always a watchful kid. Most folks don't know that. Eddie ground out his cigarette butt under his shoe. When he lifted his foot, nothing showed on the ground. *I gotta get back to work. But you think about what I said about everyone needing work. Kids your age, you especially need things to do. Things that matter to more'n just yourself. See you.*

"See you." Nathan waved, like he always did when he left the diner.

Eddie turned toward the door and started walking.

"Wait." Nathan broke through the astonishment that had held him motionless. Even though he'd been seeing dead people all day, he hadn't expected to see one he'd known so well.

But Eddie didn't wait. He slid right through the door.

K nowing his uncle, Nathan was a little surprised that no one had put out a big birthday banner or tied balloons to the door. He hadn't wanted anything, but he'd expected *something*. Alyssa had given him this big buildup of what was going to happen, and there was—nothing.

Feeling a little bummed, he told himself firmly that it was just because of the weird day he'd had, and because he'd seen Eddie in the alley and still didn't know why. Nathan used his key and let himself into the house. He stepped into the living room and waited for everyone to jump out and yell, *Surprise!* like they would in any one of a dozen sickly sweet family shows.

Instead, the house was silent, which was kind of creepy.

Maybe they got tired of waiting and went somewhere. Nathan could imagine Uncle William loading up Alyssa and her friends and going somewhere to have Nathan's birthday dinner. Couldn't break too far from routine, could they?

One person wouldn't have gone with them, though. Nathan headed back to his father's study. His dad probably still didn't know it was his birthday.

Something erupted from the shadows under the stairs and came straight at Nathan. A shrill honking sound shredded his hearing, and for one insane moment he thought that was exactly the sound a soul vulture would make when it swept in for the kill.

Before he knew what he was doing, Nathan drew back his fist and popped his attacker right in his big, red nose. Nathan saw the pasty white face, the red fright wig that framed it, the blue stars over the eyes, and the red lips. When he realized what a horror his attacker was, Nathan panicked and hit him again.

17

"**N**athan!" Alyssa yelled from somewhere nearby. "What are you doing?"

"C-c-clown!" Nathan yelped. He didn't know if the awful thing had thrown itself on him or if it was just unable to get away. Nathan lost track of how many times he pushed and hit it, trying to get it off of him.

"Nathan! Stop! Stop hitting Mr. Chuckles!"

Alyssa appeared behind him and grabbed him by the arm. Panic shattered Nathan's insides. It had been years since he'd been up close and personal with a clown. He struggled against Alyssa as she pulled him off the clown.

The clown lurched back a couple of steps and then pirouetted and sat down hard. In the next second, the clown flopped backward and lay still with his arms thrown out to his sides. His bulbous red nose honked sadly and deflated with grim finality.

"Oh my goodness!" Uncle William dashed out into the hallway and leaned over the clown. "Mr. Chuckles? *Mr. Chuckles?* Oh dear. I don't think he's with us anymore."

"What?" Alyssa asked.

"What?" Nathan squawked.

"Nathan killed Mr. Chuckles!" squealed one of the half-dozen girls who had flooded into the hallway.

"No, I didn't." Nathan pushed himself away from Alyssa in case she decided to start hitting him in retaliation. "I didn't kill him. And I was just protecting myself."

"He killed Mr. Chuckles? Oh my God!"

"Why would you kill a clown?" Another girl glared at Nathan angrily. She had tears in her eyes, but they didn't stop her from taking pictures of the fallen clown with her cell phone. "That's just . . . just . . . *horrible!*" She continued taking pictures and shot a few of Nathan as well.

"They should lock you up," another girl yelled. "Clown murderer!"

"What in blazes is going on?" Nathan's dad walked in the house.

"It's Nathan." One of Alyssa's friends pointed an accusing finger at him. "He killed Mr. Chuckles!"

"A clown?" Nathan's dad took his glasses off, cleaned them, and put them back on as if he were peering at the most impossible thing he'd ever seen. "It is a clown. What is a clown doing in my house? No clowns are allowed here," Nathan's dad said in disbelief, as if he'd just discovered a particularly vicious rodent had plopped into his soup.

"Missed the *clown-free zone* posting," a girl said sarcastically.

Nathan's dad turned on Uncle William. "What's this clown doing here? Clowns are like vampires. They can't come into your house unless you invite them." He pointed at Mr. Chuckles. "Did you invite this clown?"

"I hired Mr. Chuckles to come over—"

"Great Caesar's ghost! Why would you do something like that?"

"For Nathan's birthday." Uncle William seemed to wilt, and Nathan almost felt a little sorry for him. His dad could be intimidating when he got wound up about something.

"Nathan doesn't *like* clowns!"

"He doesn't? But Mr. Chuckles has been at every one of Alyssa's birthday parties."

"Nathan is *scared* of clowns!" his dad said.

Nathan wanted to argue that point. Clowns at a safe distance didn't bother him, but when they came boiling out from under the staircase—or chased him around in his nightmares—they bothered him. A lot.

"Scared of clowns?" Uncle William looked aghast. "I didn't know that. You should have told me that when we were going over the birthday plans."

"What birthday plans?"

"Nathan's birthday. I told you about this weeks ago."

Nathan's dad massaged his temples. "I distinctly remember telling you that this isn't how Nathan and I celebrate birthdays."

"You don't celebrate anything with the boy, Peter." Uncle William snapped back. "That's why Alyssa and I wanted to have Mr. Chuckles here. To liven things up and surprise Nathan. Birthdays should be fun."

Nathan silently agreed with that. So far, this birthday had totally stunk.

His dad, however, crossed his arms over his chest. "Well, you can certainly see how well that's worked out. I suppose a dead clown on the floor is your idea of a party. Maybe it's just me, but Nathan doesn't exactly look like he's having the time of his life."

Everyone looked at Nathan.

Not knowing what else to do, Nathan looked back.

In the tense silence that followed, Mr. Chuckles's red nose bleated sadly as he let out a breath.

"He's alive!" One of the girls clapped in delight, and the others joined in.

Nathan felt decidedly nauseated.

Mr. Chuckles stirred on the floor, and Nathan couldn't help remembering the way monsters came back to life in most horror movies. He took a few steps back, thinking that maybe Mr. Chuckles wasn't going to feel much like laughing when he woke up. There might be that whole matter of Clown Revenge to deal with.

□—□—□

Nathan sat in his bedroom and played a video game. He was loaded up with weapons but the undersea world had a lot of enemies that kept dropping out of the shadows. Kind of like clowns at birthday parties. Staying alive was a challenge, and solving the puzzles made the experience even more difficult.

"So this is where you went." Alyssa stood in the doorway and looked at him.

After a brief glance at her, Nathan nodded. "Yep."

"Can I come in?"

"Why? Did the Centers for Disease Control ask for a preliminary scouting report?"

"I'm supposed to plant a GPS tracking device in your room so they can hit it with a long-range anti-biological tactical weapon. Less risk to their people that way."

"Great."

"You didn't say if I could come in."

"If I say no, are you going to go away?"

"No."

"And you can't just say whatever you're here to say from the door?" Nathan raised a sarcastic eyebrow.

"I'm not going to."

"Then why are you even bothering to ask permission?"

"I'm trying to be polite." Alyssa frowned and folded her arms. "And courteous. I suppose you know what that word means."

"Something along the lines of, gee, I won't bring clowns to your surprise birthday party? Because if that's not what it means, I need to learn the word for that."

"I'm really sorry about the clown. I didn't know you were scared of them."

"Not scared of them. Don't like them."

"Sadly, I think Mr. Chuckles's view of kids may change from this point also. He kind of flinched every time we got close to him. He's never done that before. Do you know he told my dad that he would never do a birthday party for you again?"

"Win-win." Nathan punched buttons and flamed another pair of attackers. "I can live with that. And is it still in the house?" The idea of Mr. Chuckles still lingering around creeped him out.

After he had recovered from his initial beating, which had been more shocking than painful, Mr. Chuckles had stayed to entertain Alyssa and her friends with balloon animals, magic tricks, and lame jokes more suited for first graders. But Alyssa and her friends had acted like Mr. Chuckles was the greatest thing ever. Nathan had kept his distance.

"Yes. Mr. Chuckles is gone." Alyssa walked over to Nathan's bed, cleared a space by pushing some dirty clothes on the floor, and sat. "Anyway, I just wanted to apologize for what happened. Dad is beside himself."

Nathan shrugged. "No big. I'm not emotionally scarred or anything."

"You're sure?"

Thinking he'd answered too nonchalantly and inadvertently hurt Alyssa's feelings—which he actually didn't want to do—

Nathan nodded. "I'm—"

Alyssa curled her forefinger and mimed getting a big hook in her mouth. She yanked her head around.

"Terrific." Nathan returned his attention to the game, but he was playing on autopilot. His mind was totally locked onto Officer John Montoya and what had happened to him. The mystery just wouldn't leave him alone. "I'm going to head out in a little while. I'm meeting up with my friends."

"Oh, really?" Alyssa arched a disbelieving eyebrow. "So what are you and your friends going to do for your birthday?"

Nathan shrugged and lied casually. "The same as we always do. Grab some pizza and Cokes and play laser tag at the mall."

"You're right. That's way better than having a party." Alyssa's words dripped with sarcasm.

Nathan saved the game and tossed the controller onto the bed. "It's almost seven. I gotta get going if I'm going to catch up with the guys."

Alyssa studied him for a moment. "Is that what you want to do? It's your birthday. You should be with family."

There's not much of that, is there? Nathan thought, but he didn't say it. Instead, he mimed juggling scales in his hands and frowned in mock indecision. Alyssa rolled her eyes but turned sharply and left the room.

Nathan let out a sigh and sat back down on the floor. His eyes glanced around the room as he debated between playing more video games or getting out of the house. Then his eyes caught sight of the board game. He had almost forgotten about it after his encounter with Mr. Chuckles.

He moved closer to look at the board and saw that all of the visions he was having translated to the board. His hand reached out, lightly touching the pieces but not daring to move them. *The board hasn't changed. That means it's still Kukulkan's turn. What is he waiting for?*

Nathan thought about the Game, then decided to find out more about Officer John Montoya. And the Beaver Wars.

18

S eated in a Starbucks with a big cup of hot chocolate, Nathan downloaded the files he'd lifted from Alyssa's website onto his netbook and then logged onto Wikipedia and searched for Beaver Wars. He quickly found out his imaginary strife between warring beaver clans was a lot more interesting.

As it turned out, the Beaver Wars were part of the friction between tribes of Native Americans caused by the arrival of European settlers and traders. The Iroquois Confederation joined up with the Dutch traders and tried to seize control of the beaver fur trade. Their main opponents were the Algonquian Indians, who fought with the French.

To Nathan, it sounded like another variation of the Coke and Pepsi wars. Or the Xbox 360 and PS3 conflicts. It would have been much more interesting if the Beaver Wars had involved shape-shifting shaman troops or aliens.

He settled back and sipped his hot chocolate and then set to work on Alyssa's files. He opened up a Word file for compiling the information he found.

Putting his ear buds in, he opened a link to a local television news story that Alyssa had linked. A pretty African-American reporter stood in front of Manny's Deli in a trench coat and started talking into her microphone.

"A police spokesman has just confirmed that the dead man is a highly decorated and loved member of the Chicago Police Department. Thirty-seven year old patrolman John Montoya was found shot to death in this maintenance tunnel just behind me."

Nathan paused the playback and pulled up the obituary of Officer Montoya. The man in the picture looked a lot happier than the gray ghost that Nathan had met. He saved the obituary column into the folder he was building.

Maybe he slacked on the schoolwork he found boring, but when Nathan found something that interested him, he could do very detailed work. He hoped his teachers never found out.

He went back to the news byte.

"This maintenance tunnel was one of those flooded back in 1992 after the pilings near the Kinzie Street Bridge were installed the previous year. This section of tunnel has been undergoing repairs in anticipation of installing new telecommunications lines in the area."

Nathan paused the playback again and opened another Internet window. He searched for the Chicago Flood of 1992 and marked it as well. A quick read through the information revealed that the flood had been officially termed a "leak" so that insurance companies would have to pay off on the millions of dollars of damages suffered by downtown businesses.

Most of the underground tunnels throughout the downtown area had been underwater for days, including the abandoned Chicago Tunnel Company railroad tunnels. Nathan spent some time browsing through the history of the freight tunnels that were used to move packages, mail, food, coal, and sometimes people between stores, office buildings, warehouses, and factories, forty feet below the streets. It would have been easy to get distracted by this fascinating piece of Chicago history, but he returned to the news piece.

"No witnesses have come forward, but the department is giving this case its highest priority." The camera panned in closer on the news reporter.

Ah man, you missed one of the most obvious connections. You're going to have to pay better attention.

Nathan backed up the playback until he found the reporter's name. He Googled her and found out she was still part of the local news scene. He copied down her information and email address.

News reporters couldn't always tell or write everything they knew or thought. And they sometimes followed up on stories.

He hit play again.

"Detective Sergeant Bonnie Lane—"

Nathan paused, took down the information, performed a quick Google search that only netted several other news reports of murders and burglaries where Detective Sergeant Lane served as police spokesperson.

"—can only tell us that the department considers the death of Officer Montoya a great loss to the city and the police force. Their condolences go out to his family.

"We will follow this case closely, and update you as new information becomes available. This is Giavonna Tate, reporting live."

Nathan played the story a few more times, a couple of times with the sound off just so he could better pay attention to visual details. He did that sometimes with video games because he'd discovered sound could be a distraction.

There was a follow-up report on the "Tragedy in the Tunnel," as it had been dubbed. The same reporter, in the studio this time, gravely read a report provided by the police department stating that irregularities found in Officer Montoya's duty logs had led to an internal investigation. The findings in that investigation were not made public, but anonymous sources inside the department confirmed that the Montoya family had been denied death benefits. The reporter left it to the viewer's imagination to decide what that meant, though it was clear she believed he was guilty of some wrongdoing.

The whole thing seemed cut-and-dried. He felt disappointed. He hadn't expected a clue to jump out and yell, Aha! But it would have been nice.

He glanced at the time in the corner of the netbook and realized he'd been at the coffee shop longer than he'd intended. As he threw away his empty cup and pulled on his coat to face the weather, he spotted movement in the window glass and avoided looking directly at it. He didn't want to deal with that any more today. He just wanted to get to the mall and lock into some video games before they shut down.

Outside, he tossed the bracelet toward the ground and it shifted into a skateboard. He pushed off and got rolling, trying to maneuver against the strong, chilling winds.

So, are you playing or not? Nathan grinned into the cold wind. He knew he couldn't back away, but he didn't know how he was going to handle everything that was going on. *One move at a time. Just one move at a time.*

☐─☐─☐

Nathan sat in the back of the elevated train car and stared out at the city. He rested his hands on the seat in front of him and couldn't wait until he hit the mall. He had his PSP in his pocket. He was only seconds away from an online community. Players were out there waiting to be friended.

In the meantime, he would let his subconscious mind sift through everything he'd learned about Officer John Montoya.

One of the things Nathan really wanted to know was what had gotten Alyssa and her brainiacs interested in John Montoya and how whoever had assigned them had chosen the cases.

The rail car jerked and jostled as it rattled through downtown Chicago, the Loop. The familiar motion lulled Nathan into a stupor, and the city lights took on a surreal quality that was almost hypnotic.

Nathan Richards.

Hearing his name jarred him alert. A cold wind ghosted through him despite the jacket he wore. He wrapped his arms around himself as he looked around the car.

Only a handful of tired-looking adults rode the car, probably on their way to work or just getting off. Most of them were reading or listening to something through headphones.

Nathan Richards, are you listening?

Shivering a little against the cold that howled outside the window, Nathan stared around the car and hoped he was just imagining the voice. Then he hoped that he wasn't because that might have meant he was finally losing it.

Movement reflected in the window beside Nathan caught his attention. When he glanced at it, he saw the gray reflection of an old woman standing beside him. Panic flooded him as he whipped his head around to find out what she was doing there.

But when he looked—no one was there.

Feeling trapped, he made himself breathe. He wished there was some way to turn off seeing dead people in every reflective surface he passed.

Think it through, he told himself. *There's a way to handle this.*

You just haven't figured it out yet.

Then the lights went off inside the car, and night filled the space. Now he was panicking. Nathan looked through the window. Chicago was still there, swathed in neon and bright illumination. Traffic hummed through the streets.

Just chill, dude. The mall's not that far away. Drop a few tokens, get into the groove of a game, you'll be fine.

Instead of looking through the window, he looked at it. The old woman was no longer alone. More pallid gray people stood behind him, and this time there were dozens, an impossible number to fit into the elevated rail car.

And they were all fixated on him.

They can't touch you. Nathan told himself that, but he was afraid to find out if it was true. The air turned colder around him.

He felt the mass of them closing in on him. He sensed them more strongly this time and could feel the weight of their attention. Staring at the reflections, he saw that they were of all ages, male and female. Some of them were strangely dressed, looking like they'd stepped off a movie set or something.

Nathan.

He recognized the woman's voice. Nathan turned to look for her in the reflection.

Professor Felicima Diego Barrera Richards stood in the middle of the car. *You can't hide from them any longer. Your power has grown too strong. No matter where you go, no matter what you do, they're going to find you.* She held a hand out to him. *Please. Let me help you get through this. If you don't let someone in, this is going to swallow you up.*

In the reflection, the horde of gray people moved closer to Nathan.

19

Nathan's panic at the sheer number of the frequency-challenged hovering around overwhelmed him. He felt like he couldn't breathe. He watched the reflections in the window press forward.

"Stop!" Nathan's voice cracked and the word felt jammed in the back of his throat. But the crowd took a step back.

He turned back to Professor Felicima.

"What are you doing here?" Nathan hated the frightened edge he could hear in his voice.

His mother smiled at him. *I wanted to see you. I wanted to apologize for lecturing you at our very first meeting. I want to start again, and find a way to help you learn the things you need to know.*

"Help me how? Like the way you put that big cop onto me? John Montoya?"

I didn't send him to you, Nathan. He approached you on his own. I just encouraged you to acknowledge him, to talk to him. There's more at stake in helping him than you realize.

"I didn't have anything at stake. I was normal until my birthday."

Nathan. His mother's voice was gentle. *You've never been normal. I know it's not something you want to hear from your mother, but the fact is that you have a grand destiny ahead of you. You must embrace it.*

"Let someone else have it. I want my life back."

You do have your life. In fact, you're going to have more of a life than you could ever dream.

"Am I? Or are you just pushing me to be more because I'm not *living* up to your expectations? Maybe I should remind you that I'm the only one *living* here." Nathan couldn't help himself from lashing out. Hurting the people around him was his first and best defense to make them leave him alone.

A hurt look crossed his mother's face, and she stared out the window for a moment. *I know how you feel. I know this is all very confusing.*

"Really? You know how I feel? You got haunted by ghosts when you were my age? Had your dead mother popping up in your school locker when you'd seen her exactly . . . oh yeah, *never?*"

Nathan, I grew up believing that I would be the one to play the Game. My grandfather taught me how to play, and he prepared me to do my best against Kukulkan. We were both wrong. It is your destiny— but I have knowledge that I can share with you to help you prepare.

"Yeah, you were wrong big time," he said bitterly.

Blame me if you want, Nathan. But I do care about you, and I can help you. But I need you to trust me.

His mother sat down in the seat across the aisle from him and folded her hands in her lap. *I know you have a lot of questions.*

Nathan did, but he didn't utter a single one of them.

I did die, his mother said. *But death isn't the end of things. There are many changes, many beginnings.* She sighed. *I know that I must sound like a broken record, but you have so much to learn and so little time to learn it in.* She shook her head. *Even though I prepared to play the Game, when it comes right down to it I'm as lost as you are. Kukulkan chooses what he reveals. I'm trying to find out more for you, and there are others who are helping.*

Enough. One of the crowd of dead people surged forward angrily. *You cannot take all of his time, woman. We need him as well.*

Need? The man's tone scared Nathan. It had the same dangerous, obsessed quality of Gollum's voice in *The Lord of the Rings*. Nathan opened both eyes and looked at the window to better see the man.

He was heavy-set and moved like he believed in his own importance. His black suit had a strange look to it, like something Nathan imagined would be worn to a funeral. His gray hair fell to his shoulders, and he had a full beard. He leaned on a cane topped by a roaring bear's head.

Whatever problem you have can't be as important as mine. An old woman shoved to the front of the group. *I still have relatives living. People who need me. You're not even a memory.* She wore a long dress and reminded Nathan of the harsh first-grade teacher for whom he remembered feeling an intense dislike. This woman had thick glasses, and her hair pulled back into a bun.

Other angry voices joined the first two, and the spirits suddenly became an unruly mob. He drew back in his seat and kicked out at them, which was weird because once he looked away from the window he couldn't see them, and his foot went through the air without touching anything.

"No!" Nathan yelped. "Get away! Leave me alone!"

Several of the rail car passengers turned to face him, looking concerned and frightened. A couple took out their cell phones and started dialing.

"There's a crazy kid on the train."

"We need help."

"He might be dangerous."

Now Nathan was truly afraid. Security would surely be waiting at the next stop, if they weren't already on the train and making their way to his car.

Much to his shock, something seized him and yanked him from the seat. So far the ghosts hadn't been able to physically touch him. Now they were doing a lot more than touching.

He broke free, but when his gaze fell on the window, he watched the reflections with growing horror.

The dead reached for him, hands grabbing at his head, his clothing, any piece of him they could get. He fought them, but somehow his hands passed through them when he tried to push them away. He rolled across the seat, and the ghosts lost their grip.

Nathan's mind raced frantically. *Think! They can touch you. You gotta be able to touch them back. Figure it out.*

Then his mother grabbed the closest of the spirits and heaved them away like they weighed nothing. She looked like a WWF wrestler working her way through a high school cheer squad.

When they hit the train walls, they passed through instantly, yelling and cursing. Even though she effortlessly got rid of them, more of them kept coming.

Concentrate, Nathan. His mother seized a big guy and heaved him through the wall. *You're giving them the power to touch you. Block them from using it. Concentrate on what you feel going on around you. Focus your senses.*

Nathan closed his eyes to block out the sight of the ghosts and stopped struggling for a moment. Feeling vaguely ridiculous, like he was pretending to be the Green Lantern, he took a deep breath and imagined that he was surrounded by a force field. For just a moment, it seemed like there were fewer hands touching him. But when he opened his eyes, the dead were still coming at him, and now there were even more.

A passenger wearing dark blue coveralls and baseball cap leaned toward Nathan.

"Are you all right, boy?" the man asked. He was oblivious to all the gray people around him. "Are you hallucinating? Are you sick? Are your parents on this train?"

There are too many of them. Professor Felicima had obviously reached the same conclusion he had. *I can't hold them back, and they're not going to stop.*

Nathan pushed against one of the ghosts and managed to force the man away.

"What are you seeing?" The man in coveralls reached for Nathan and closed a strong hand around his wrist.

Nathan struggled to get free, but couldn't. The dead swarmed over him and crushed him down into the seat. He couldn't breathe.

"Just relax, boy." The man leaned into Nathan, pinning him to the seat. "We're going to get you some help."

Then Professor Felicima shoved her head and one arm through the man's chest. The effect was chilling. The man didn't even know she was there. *Nathan, take my hand.*

Nathan didn't move.

Take my hand! You don't know how to resist them, but I can teach you. Take my hand!

Flailing weakly, Nathan caught her hand. She felt cold at first, like she'd just stepped out of a refrigerator, and then she started warming up. The man in the black suit grabbed Nathan's free hand and tried to pull it away.

Hold tight. His mom smiled reassuringly. *Everything's going to be all right.*

Nathan wanted to believe her. The world spun around him, and he plummeted with dizzying swiftness.

20

When Nathan opened his eyes again, he tried hard not to panic. He could tell he was falling. But he hadn't expected to see the elevated train hurtling along the tracks over his head.

Falling! Panic filled him. *You're falling!* He twisted in mid-flight and looked over his shoulder at the street coming up fast.

It's all right. His mom still held his hand and smiled at him.

What does she care? She's already . . . already frequency-challenged.

Nathan wanted to scream at her that things weren't all right, that in fact he was about to die, which was something he didn't want to do. The dying mostly, but the screaming like a girl would look bad too. He tried to speak, but nothing came out.

Right before he smacked into the street, a hole opened up in midair and swallowed him. For the briefest second, he thought the hole looked like the gaping mouth of a catfish. Then he blinked, and he stood in the middle of a forest again. He felt the solid ground beneath him.

"It's okay. You're safe here." His mother kept a hand on his elbow and helped steady him.

Nathan glanced down at the large rock he stood on. It gleamed white in the moonlight.

He wished Kukulkan was with him instead of his mother and then he felt guilty almost immediately. That wasn't fair, and he knew it. His mom had just saved him from . . . from . . . well, he didn't know what for sure, but it was definitely bad.

"Nothing here can harm you." His mom straightened his jacket and brushed her hand over his hair.

"Not even soul vultures?"

She took a quick breath. "Well, maybe not nothing, but only a few things."

"The spirits from the train aren't here?"

"They can't come to this place. They don't know the way. They're lost. Couldn't you see that?"

"They didn't act lost to me. They looked like they knew exactly what they were doing."

"They are lost," she repeated. "That's why they're drawn to you. You're like a light in the darkness."

"Why me?"

"It is part of the Game. You need to help them find their way," she explained.

"And if I don't?"

"They will remain lost. So will you."

"I'm not lost."

"If you weren't also lost, you wouldn't be able to see them. The fact that you are a little like them is part of what allows you to play the Game effectively."

"Maybe you're wrong about that."

His mother started to argue and then stopped. "Perhaps I am."

"Except that there are frequency-challenged people everywhere," Nathan conceded.

"I call them lost souls."

Nathan looked at her. "Do you feel lost?"

Sadness showed in her dark eyes. "I didn't get to raise my baby.

What do you think?"

Nathan took a deep, shuddering breath. He stepped off the rock and remained standing in midair. Realizing he had the ability to fly made him smile in spite of the terror of the past few minutes and the sadness that clung to his mother.

"Kukulkan told me you were a natural flyer. There are actually very few of those."

She seemed proud of that, and he couldn't think how weird that was. How many moms took pride in the fact that their sons were "natural flyers?"

"I can't fly." She stepped down off the rock and stood on the ground. She smiled up at him.

"Really?" Nathan grinned. It felt good to know that he could do something she couldn't. "Too bad. You're missing out."

"Perhaps. But I prefer to stay firmly grounded, thank you."

Only then did he realize he was actually seeing her face to face and not in some kind of reflective surface. And he was actually hearing her voice with his ears, not in his head. "I can see you and hear you."

"I know." She smoothed her clothing self-consciously. "Away from our home frequency, you can."

"You're shorter than I thought you would be." Unable to resist the urge, Nathan reached out to touch his mom's shoulder. She felt solid. Real.

"I don't understand." His voice came out as a strained whisper. "How you can see me? And touch me?"

He nodded.

"We're out of the primary frequency." She waved at the forest around them. "Since I was . . . *lost* to the primary frequency, I can have more of a presence here. And in other places. But I thought you might be most comfortable in this one."

"Maybe. Except for the soul vulture."

Shapes moved through the trees. Nathan couldn't quite make them out, but he didn't feel threatened by them. The canopy blocked out nearly all of the night sky as effectively as it had blocked out the sun during the day. He smelled water somewhere in the distance.

Nathan focused on his mom. "What happened on the train? Why did all those people try to bum-rush me?" Now that he was away from them, the fear had faded and he could think rationally again. "Why were you able to touch them? Why can't I?"

"Let's take it one step at a time, Nathan. There's a lot to learn, and you can't learn it all at once. But know this: everything I can do, you'll be able to do and more."

Nathan took a deep breath and let it out. "All right." It was hard being patient, but he liked the fact that she was talking to him like an adult, not a kid.

"Your power awoke on your thirteenth birthday. And it will keep growing stronger as you use it."

"What power?"

"You can recognize and travel the frequencies. *All* of the frequencies. Some of the people here can travel through a few of them, as can some of the creatures."

"Kukulkan mentioned the frequencies."

"I suppose he did. After all, he created them."

That took Nathan back. "Kukulkan *created* the frequencies? But that . . . that's impossible." Nathan tried to imagine how there was once upon a time *nothing*, then something. A lot of somethings as it turned out.

"You do realize that you're saying that as you're standing in midair."

Not liking the obvious answer to his own question, Nathan descended to the ground and stood a few feet away from his mother. "Frequencies are like . . . *worlds*, then."

"Not exactly. The frequencies are like flawed doppelgängers of the real world. Or sometimes like a photocopy of a photocopy. Details, except for those that are strongest and truest, sometimes get lost. The farther you get away from your home frequency, the less that world shows up. Only the most meaningful things—and persons—show up that far out." She waved a hand. "This place doesn't recognize modern buildings, but there are some buildings here that still exist in your home frequency. And some that don't."

"Wait. You're trying to tell me that Kukulkan not only created the frequencies, but he created the world?"

"He did."

"So he's a god?"

"The Mayans recognized him as such. One of several. Perhaps, in time, you'll meet others."

Nathan didn't know if he should take that as a threat or a promise. He tried not to think about that at the moment. "Those people on the train weren't there when I first started riding."

"Of course they were. You just couldn't see them."

"Then how did I suddenly start seeing them?"

His mother shook her head. "I don't know. I haven't quite figured out how your powers work. But gradually you became *attuned* to them. Either you reached out to them or they reached out to you."

"Don't you have powers too? You pulled me out of that train and brought me here."

"I didn't use my power." She nodded at him. "I used yours."

"How?"

"Because you don't know how to keep me from doing that. Not yet. That's why the lost souls on the train were after you. To them, you represent raw power, a resource, a conduit, a way for them to contact and communicate with your frequency. Until you learn to control it, they'll feed on you in an effort to try to do things they feel they must in that frequency."

Nathan shivered. He didn't want anyone *feeding* on him. "My frequency?"

"I suppose I shouldn't call it that." His mother paused to think for a moment. "The frequency isn't yours alone, of course. It belongs to a lot of people. At one time, it belonged to the people riding the train tonight. They think they could come back to your frequency if they could control your power."

"Why would they want to come back?"

She gave Nathan a pained expression. "Because they're not settled. They've left unfinished business behind. Some of them want their lives back." She paused. "And some of them, like me, left things undone."

Nathan wasn't yet ready to deal with what his mother had left undone.

"I know this isn't easy for you." His mom looked at him, and he heard the truth in her words. "It hasn't been easy for me either." She took a deep breath. "I had planned on being there for you." Tears glimmered in her eyes. "I had so many things I wanted to show you. So many things I wanted to share with you. Good things, Nathan. Not the things I must show you now."

Sadness tightened Nathan's throat and tears burned the back of his eyes. He pushed the feelings away. He couldn't be sad over something that had never happened, could he? That was just stupid. He was fine. He didn't need anybody hovering over him.

Especially not a ghostly mother or motherly ghost—whatever Professor Felicima thought she was missing out on.

He wasn't missing out on anything.

He forced himself to speak calmly. "If there's something Kukulkan wants me to learn, then that's what I need to do." He paused. "I'm not going to let anyone use me."

Her eyes widened in surprise. "I'm not using—" She stopped herself.

He forced himself not to respond. "If I'm going to play the Game, I need to know how all of this works."

"Then that's what we'll do."

A sudden blast of cold rolled toward him, a sensation so intense he almost stepped back.

"The world," his mom said, "is like a rainbow. Seven colors make up the rainbow: red, orange, yellow, green, blue, indigo, and violet. And those seven colors make up what we think of as white light."

"White light is created by combining all the colors," Nathan said. "I got that in first grade."

"Then you know what creates the color black?"

"The lack of reflection of anything." Nathan shrugged. "Earth looks colorful because we have an atmosphere and lots of particulates floating around in it that reflect the light. A lot of those particulates reflect the color blue."

"There's that fine mind that your schoolwork doesn't reflect," she teased him. "A prism can split that light into the original seven color wavelengths."

She seemed pleased with him, and he surprised himself by feeling a little proud of that.

"You are like a prism, Nathan. You have the power to separate out the frequencies that layer the world. You're not trapped in one frequency as are most people and things."

"What things?"

She frowned. "There are things that prowl the frequencies."

"Like the soul vultures?"

"Yes. Although they can't yet reach your frequency."

"What do you mean, *yet*?"

"Kukulkan created the world, Nathan, but he didn't create it to last forever. Humanity's time on this world—your home frequency—draws to a close. Soon the barriers separating the frequencies will weaken and fail. The soul vultures and other creatures will be able to move between all frequencies. But that won't last long. The world will end as suddenly as it began."

Nathan thought about that. The end of the world was a popular theme in video games, comic books, and spy movies. But real people didn't talk about it like it was a fact. Especially not moms. That she clearly believed what she was saying frightened him.

"When?" His voice came out as a croak.

"The world as you know it is going to end December 21, 2012."

Nathan felt like he'd been hit between the eyes with a sledge-hammer.

21

"Can't something be done to stop that?" Nathan couldn't believe he had just asked that question so calmly. *Can you really just ask someone if the end of the world can be prevented?*

"I don't know." Distracted, his mother looked up at the tree canopy.

"Does Kukulkan know?"

"The Game is his creation, his measuring stick of this world and humanity's place in it. This is all by his design." Her head turned, tracking something through the trees.

This time Nathan spotted the movement as well. Something big and incredibly quick moved through the forest. The thing hid in the shadows. Then Nathan spotted another shadow to his left. An instant later, he noticed a third and fourth. All of them closed in on their position with precision and skill.

The movements reminded Nathan of a National Geographic episode he'd seen where a pack of raptors had closed in on an iguanodon. They were predators closing the circle for the kill.

"I made a mistake bringing you here." His mom kept her voice soft and flat, and that was somehow even scarier than if she'd been screaming. "It's not as safe here as I'd believed."

"What are they?"

"Bears, but these are twisted by the soul vultures and the darkness of the frequencies." She backed away a little.

"What do they want?" Nathan looked around hopefully. He wouldn't wish the twisted bears on anything else, but he didn't want them coming after him. Judging from their movements, they were big.

"I think they're hunting us."

Fear spiked through Nathan. *Is there anywhere that something isn't out to get me?*

Branches shook as the bears gathered in calculated precision. The creatures had surrounded them in seconds, and there were at least a dozen of them. Chuffing growls broke the stillness of the night.

Nathan thought maybe they were cheering each other on. The sounds were terrifying.

"They're wary of us for the moment," his mother said. "But they're not going to stay that way." She reached for his hand, but this time her hand slid across him like smoke. Something had changed, and he wasn't clear what it was. Fear tightened her face. "Nathan! You've got to get out of here!"

"How?" Nathan backed away from the nearest bear.

"You can move through the frequencies."

"You did it last time."

"I reached into your subconscious."

"Maybe you could do that again."

His mother took his hand and looked at him for a long moment.

Nathan had a sinking feeling in the pit of his stomach. "Nothing's happening."

His mom shook her head. "I can't do it."

Nathan glanced up at the dark shadows filling the trees. "So you're saying I'm stuck here?"

"No. You're not stuck here. You have the gift of travel, Nathan.

You just have to use it. Think of a place, make it real in your mind, and go there."

Nathan thought of his room, but nothing happened.

A flash of movement tumbled through the trees and landed with an earthshaking thump only a few feet away. The bear stood to its full height of eight feet and growled. Corded muscles stuck out like rocks. Black fur covered the thing except for the bowling-ball sized head equipped with sharp teeth. The bear opened its cavernous mouth and growled louder. Other bears stepped in behind it.

The closest one lunged at him and raked at him with a fistful of claws. Nathan jumped up to fly, fell backward, and found himself awkwardly upside down when one of the bears caught his ankle. The sudden realization that he was dangling over more bears like a birthday piñata struck him just as two of them leapt at him simultaneously.

Nathan dodged, jerked free of the bear that had seized him from a nearby tree, and flew to one side. Helplessly, he watched as the predators closed on his mother. Can they touch her?

One of the creatures lashed out at her and knocked her to the ground. She screamed in fear and pain, and the sound raked his senses like fingernails on a chalkboard. He'd never dreamed of hearing his mother's voice, much less her frightened cries.

Nathan focused on his mom and flew toward her as one of the bears leaped forward and tried to grab him. He narrowly avoided the creature as he shot forward.

"Mom!"

She looked up at him, saw him coming toward her, and shook her head. "No!"

"Give me your hand!" Nathan reached for her hand and caught

it as he zoomed toward her. Somehow she was more solid; his fingers closed on her wrist, and he lifted her just as the bears rushed in for the kill.

The extra weight of another person slowed Nathan, and for a moment, he thought his mom might drag him to the ground. When she understood what was happening, she tried to squirm free, making it even harder to hang onto her.

"Don't." Nathan tightened his grip even more.

"Let me go. You can get away."

"We're both going to get away." Nathan concentrated harder, flipping through images of places he'd been, and then managed to gain altitude. For a moment he thought they were going to get free. Then one of the bears grabbed his ankle.

The creature's huge weight pulled Nathan back toward the ground and the waiting pack. He held onto his mom's arm despite her efforts to get away as he watched the ground come up at them.

Gotta go somewhere else! Nathan concentrated on that. Dorothy had ruby slippers that took her back home. But was that where he wanted to go? And would the bear climbing up his leg come with them? He didn't even know how to go between frequencies. Were they like light waves, as his mother suggested?

Hollow clicking sounded in his ears and made him remember how the rattling of the game pieces had woken him. Suddenly, fast as lightning, he made the connections.

As he dropped, he listened. At first, all he could hear was the growls of the bears waiting to tear him to pieces. But when he'd crossed frequencies to meet Kukulkan, Nathan was sure he remembered hearing the man's voice calling to him. And when he'd moved between frequencies during Mr. Lloyd's class, he'd distinctly heard the noise of the river before he'd seen it.

Another bear grabbed hold of Nathan's leg, but now he could hear the clacking of the el on the tracks. He closed his eyes and concentrated on the sound as he felt another bear grab hold of him and his mother cried out in pain. The clacking grew louder and louder, and—holding tightly to his mom—he went toward it.

22

When Nathan opened his eyes, he discovered he was standing on the el tracks looking out over Chicago's Loop. But the downtown district looked different somehow. The buildings didn't look the same, and there was a lot of empty space. No cars sped through the streets, and even the streets themselves looked different. With only the moon beaming down, the city looked dark, not lit up the way it usually did.

Wind buffeted him and rocked him back on his heels. He could barely feel his mother's hand in his. He looked over at her in shock. She was still visible, but just barely. She almost looked like she was made out of fog.

Chicago. His mom peered down into the streets.

"This isn't Chicago." Nathan released her hand and turned in a circle to look around him. "Not the Chicago I know. There aren't any cars. No lights. And not even many people."

You're right. But this frequency is very near yours.

"So you're *almost* a ghost?" Nathan asked with a hint of sadness in his voice.

But this is good, Nathan. His mom smiled at him. *This is really good. The transition was faster and easier this time. We came through together.*

"Yeah, about half a second before getting chomped by the bears."

But this is Chicago, only a few frequencies removed from the actual city.

"That's possible?"

Of course. Cities are important to people. Maybe they look different in different frequencies—smaller, or less industrialized, or larger—but they almost always exist in multiple frequencies. They only disappear at the very distant perimeters from the home frequency.

Nathan struggled to imagine a world filled with emptiness. "Nothing exists out there?"

Only the most important things. Things that have real value.

"Things that are worth a lot?"

Not necessarily, though some of those things exist as well.

Nathan took a few steps along the el track. He'd always wondered about walking along it. The wind hit him again and nearly knocked him over.

His mom watched him. *Be careful.*

With a smile, Nathan shot up three feet into the air. "No sweat. Natural flyer, remember?"

Showoff. There was no irritation in her tone.

Nathan dropped back to the el. "Are the people who live here lost souls too?"

Some of them. But others are native to this place.

"Can they cross over into other frequencies?"

Not usually.

"What does that mean?"

He could faintly see his mom sit down on the edge of the track and dangle her legs over the side. *The rules of the frequencies seem to prevent natives of one frequency from moving into others, but changes are coming. If things go badly, I don't know what's going to happen.*

"You mean me learning the Game."

Yes, this is mostly about you. Nathan, this is without a doubt the most important thing you'll ever do. You can't just float through this. You've got to care about what you're doing. You've got to realize how important this is. She paused. *And the place you have to start is by helping the lost souls in your home frequency.*

"Officer John Montoya."

There's a reason he came to you, though I don't know what it is. He's tied to you in the Game.

Nathan sat down beside her. He took a deep breath and let it out. "Okay. So what do I need to do?"

Practice seeing and moving between the frequencies. As your skills improve, so will your ability—and capacity—to help people.

Nathan sat there for a moment and watched people going under the el. They drove wagons pulled by strange-looking beasts that looked like giant guinea pigs.

"Why are the streets still here?"

Paths and trails have always been important. His mom waved her hand across the cityscape. *People have always traveled from one place to another. Paths and trails marked the way. Most rivers will be in all of the frequencies as well.*

"Because people traveled on them?" Nathan guessed.

Exactly. And because rivers are like living things, always in motion, going from one place to another.

"Like the lost souls."

Yes. Only the ones you're going to be helping have become stuck. You've got to give them a nudge or a push—

"Or a swift kick?"

His mom laughed. *Possibly. I won't deny that sometimes they'll fight you. But John wants your help. He'll listen to you, and he'll teach you things as well.*

Nathan was silent for a long time, considering how to ask his next question. "What happened in Palenque?"

Do you mean, how did I die?

"Yeah."

It was his mom's turn to sit quietly. *I kept a journal on every dig. Before I answer your question, I'd like you to read my journal from Palenque. Start there, and if you have more questions, I'll answer them. If I can.*

She seemed to shake off her somber mood. *In the meantime, we have some serious work to do, young man.*

Nathan grinned. He turned his head, listening. "I can hear them now."

Hear what?

"The frequencies. Each one sounds different, like individual notes. Some are closer, some are far away. Some are strong and some are weak. I can hear them all."

Can you tell which frequency is which?

"Not yet. But I'll be able to as I travel through them."

23

"It's going to take time to learn them all because it sounds like there are a lot of them. But it'll be like ring tones on my phone after a while—a lot easier to remember than trying to build pictures in my head."

He thought about it for a minute.

"The frequencies have to be organized according to some kind of logic, and logic usually involves math. Pythagoras discovered that music is based in math, and it's an easy math to work with. So maybe the logic of the frequencies is musical—at least for me."

Pythagoras?

"Yeah, he was this Greek philosopher—" Nathan stopped himself and looked at his mom suspiciously. "You know about him already."

About Pythagoras, yes. I just like knowing you know. I'm proud of you, you know. She reached over to tousle his hair, but she had started to fade, and was barely able to ruffle a few strands. *If you applied yourself a little more at school, your teachers would be proud of you too.*

"Yeah—really don't want to have this discussion. We were getting along really well."

We still are. I'm just trying to point out that you already have the skills and abilities you need to learn the Game, and that I'm here to help you when I can. She tried to put her hand on his shoulder, but it just slid through. *I'm just reminding you that you're not alone, Nathan.*

For some stupid reason, Nathan felt about ready to cry. He turned away from his mom to blink back tears.

I've got to be going. His mom tried to touch his cheek. *There's more I can do to help you, but that research has to be done elsewhere. Anyway, you need to get back home. You've got school tomorrow.*

"Yeah, but time doesn't pass the same when I'm in the frequencies. I can stay here as long as I like."

You still need to sleep.

"I don't sleep much."

She looked at him and shook her head. *Promise me you're going back home now and not playing around out here.* His mom shimmered as her image grew less distinct.

"Why are you disappearing if you're not ready to go back?"

It's hard for me to stay away from my home frequency. Kukulkan has given me the ability to be elsewhere if I'm helping you, but I can't stay too long. She gave him a reassuring smile. *Go home. Get a good night's sleep. Talk to John Montoya, and see if you can help him. Find the tie that binds you. I'll see you soon.*

Nathan nodded. Then his mom reached out to give him a hug, only her arms moved right through him and his moved through her. Before either of them could say anything, she was gone.

"Bye Mom." Nathan's voice was a weak croak drowned out by the clacking of the train coming down the track.

□—□—□

S harp pain bit into Nathan's cheek, and he struggled to turn his head away from the source of the pain. He realized someone was holding him down, and it took a second for him to realize he was back in his own frequency, and back on the train.

A man, the man in the blue coveralls, flesh and blood and not one of the lost souls, grasped Nathan's upper arms. "Kid? Are you okay?"

Fighting his instinct to struggle, Nathan made himself take a deep breath and relax.

"Yeah." Nathan nodded. "I'm okay."

The man held on a little longer. "You're sure?"

"Yeah."

Still wary, the man released Nathan and stepped back. He swayed with the train's movements as it rattled across Chicago. "What happened?"

"Forgot my meds." Nathan moved deliberately, trying not to spook the man, and pulled a package of Reese's Pieces from his backpack.

The concerned look on the man's face deepened. "Kid, those aren't meds."

"I've got low blood sugar. Diabetes. I took too much insulin at dinner. I've gotta get my sugar back up. I get hallucinations sometimes." Nathan crunched some of the candy. The story was believable. There was a kid in his class who had to carry candy around for just that reason.

"Sugar must have been really low to hallucinate like that."

"Weird, huh?"

"Seriously weird."

Nathan looked embarrassed, which he found wasn't as hard as he'd thought it would be. Not with everyone looking at him. He tried a half-smile. "You should have seen it from this side. I thought the train was filled with ghosts that were trying to get me."

"Yeah. That's what it sounded like. You need to call someone?"

Nathan shook his head and crunched more candy. "Nope. I'm fine now. I'm almost at my stop. My dad's at home if I have any more problems. I appreciate you helping me."

"Sure, sure. No sweat." Obviously concerned that Nathan might have more trouble, the man returned to his seat, but he kept a close eye on him.

A few minutes later, the train rumbled to a stop. Nathan got out and nodded good-bye to the man. He tried not to feel offended when the other passengers getting off the train stayed away from him.

Police Officer John Montoya stood waiting as Nathan stepped out of the car. Nathan sighed, shifted his backpack, and went to meet him.

24

Nathan stood in front of John but had to use the reflection in one of the plastic-covered advertising boards to see him. "How did you find me?"

I'm good at finding people. The man tapped the badge pinned to his shirt. *That's kind of what I do. To serve and protect.*

And burgle? Nathan thought to himself.

"Yeah, I get that. Maybe we could talk somewhere else." Nathan turned and walked toward the exit. "The mall's just a couple of blocks."

"You mind if I get a pretzel?" Nathan tried not to think it was weird that he was asking a ghost for permission to get something to eat. He checked for John in the display window of the arcade.

Fine by me. John Montoya glanced along the mall like he was looking for snipers. Then he realized Nathan was watching him. *Kid, I have to tell you that you kind of creep me out.*

"Me? But I'm the only one of us who's alive."

The man frowned. *Yeah, but you seem to attract a lot of bad karma. Until I started following you around—*

"You're an undead stalker. Tell me that's not creepy." Nathan stood up straight and faced the police officer. "You can't go around talking about bad karma unless you include yourself."

John Montoya lifted his hands. *Calm down, kid. I get your point. If I was you, I'd probably count me as one of the creepy things in your life too. As I was starting to say, until I started following you around, I didn't realize there were so many creepy things out there.*

The pretzel shop didn't have a lot of business at that time of night. It was less than an hour till the mall closed. After everything that had happened to him, Nathan couldn't believe it was still so early. He felt like he could sleep for a week.

He bought a pretzel with salt, a small bucket of nacho cheese, and a Coke. He turned to the police officer. "You want anything?"

Montoya just smiled. *Ghost fries. Side order of spirit sauce.*

"Oh. Right." Nathan couldn't believe the guy could be so cavalier about his condition, but it made him laugh. When Nathan turned back to the woman who was ringing up his order, she was staring at him. He remembered that she couldn't see the man standing beside him. "Headset phone." Nathan tapped the side of his head and gave her the money.

"Sure, kid." The woman dropped his change into his hand. "But if you start hearing dogs talking to you, telling you to do things? I'd have that phone checked out."

"Sure. That'll be the first thing I do. Thanks for the advice." Nathan turned to John. "I keep talking to you and they're going to lock me up."

Maybe we should find a quiet place to sit.

Pretzel and Coke in hand, Nathan walked to the fountain in the center of the mall and sat on the edge. People walked by, and a few young kids ran over to toss coins into the fountain. The sound of the water drowned out conversation.

Several lost souls lurked in the mall, in doors to businesses and in the hallways. Nathan saw them in all the display windows, and even in the skylights. Some of them rode the escalators to the next floor and then immediately rode them down again. Normal people always made room for the gray people, but Nathan was willing to bet they didn't know why they left the empty spaces on the steps.

Panic rose in Nathan. He didn't want another scene like the one on the elevated train. He didn't want to get mobbed again.

Don't worry. John Montoya spoke calmly and confidently. *They're not going to bother you right now.*

"How do you know?" Nathan looked at Montoya's reflection in the water as he sat down.

Because I told them not to.

"You can do that?"

Apparently it's one of the rules of the Game, kid.

"You know about the Game?"

The officer frowned and looked at Nathan. *Not much.* He slid his hand into the fountain water and didn't even leave a ripple. When he drew his hand out, it was perfectly dry.

Nathan took a sip of his Coke. "I'm still learning about it too. There's a lot to figure out."

Hey, eat your pretzel before your cheese gets cold. I hate it when the cheese gets cold.

Nathan hated that too. He tore off a piece of the soft pretzel and dabbed it in the nacho cheese. When he ate it, his stomach rumbled in satisfaction.

Guess the birthday cake didn't hold you long, did it? John smiled. *I can remember being your age. Seemed like I was hungry all the time.*

Nathan tore off another piece of pretzel and ate it. "How did you know about the birthday cake?"

I was there.

"I didn't see you."

I think that was because you were freaking over the clown. That kind of tuned you out to me and the others like me. He waved at the lost souls.

"Yeah . . . the clown really surprised me." Nathan felt incredibly embarrassed and shivered again when he thought about the clown. The fact that remembering Mr. Chuckles could still weird him out meant something, but Nathan wasn't exactly sure what that was. He didn't want to explore that.

John waved his hand dismissively and grinned. *Don't worry about it. I don't like clowns either. There's something really out of whack with those guys.*

"My uncle doesn't get that."

Your uncle seems like a good guy. Maybe just overcompensating for everything that's going on. He'll settle down. Just give him some time.

"Sure." Nathan didn't agree with that. It had already been a few months. He was beginning to suspect that Uncle William had always overcompensated.

Nathan felt better with food in him. He took a sip of Coke. "So, what do you need from me?"

John's face turned hard and emotionless. *I want you to find out who murdered me.*

25

Shocked, Nathan turned to look at John Montoya eye to eye. Which did no good at all because he couldn't see him like that. He returned his gaze to the water.

"Whoa." Nathan was surprised by how calm his voice sounded. "Just hold on. Nobody said anything about me solving your murder."

John shrugged. *What did you think I was going to ask you to do?*

"I don't know." Nathan tugged on his hair. "Maybe give your loved ones a message? Let them know you're still thinking about them? Something like that."

Yeah, that would be great, kid. Of course, it won't help them get my pension.

"Your pension?"

Yeah. You know, the money you put away for when you retire? Or when you die, so that your family has something to live on? John sighed and took a deep breath. *Look, I'm sorry. This isn't your fault. None of it. You're just like me: in the wrong place at the wrong time. I'm sorry you got caught up in all of this.*

I wish it was that easy, Nathan thought. *Apparently, this is my fate.*

"Officer Montoya, I'm willing to try. It's just that I honestly don't even know what I can do. Whatever abilities I have, I've had them for less than twenty-four hours."

I know.

"Um . . . maybe you could just skip over those parts where you were watching me and I didn't know."

John nodded and looked sheepish. *Creepy, huh?*

"Skip it." He thought for a moment, trying to figure out what questions to ask. "Okay, say we decide to try to figure this out. According to everything I've read, no one knows why you were in the maintenance tunnel that night. Figuring that out seems to be a good place to start. Do you remember?"

John shook his head, but he didn't answer.

The newspapers didn't give out the whole story.

One of the most important things I did as a cop was keep my eye on the kids. So many kids end up on the street through no fault of their own, and it's hard for them to find a way to survive. There's a whole class of scum that takes advantage of kids in that situation.

It doesn't take long for a cop to learn the street handles of every kid on his beat, and I worked at it harder than most. Finding a way to help street kids turn their lives around was important to me, and I was lucky enough to be good at it—even if the numbers didn't look that way. I found good foster homes for a dozen boys and girls in the first couple of years, and helped more than that break away from gangs. I cared about them, and they trusted me.

When one kid found the courage to tell me about a burglary ring being run in my part of the city, I took it personally. The more I investigated, the worse it looked; someone was running nearly a hundred kids in an operation that spanned the entire south side and a couple of suburbs. I had no hope of saving every kid in the gang, but I had to take a shot at breaking the organization—but I didn't want to take down the kids who could be saved along with the real bad guys. So I made the investigation official department business but kept my eye on a couple of kids I knew were ready to break away. It was too dangerous for the kids—and me—to communicate much, but I started paying a few of the kids for stolen goods and keeping the evidence at my house.

Nathan snorted, but he didn't interrupt.

I know, it sounds crazy. But my reasoning was that the kids had money to take back to their boss, the stolen goods were out of circulation, and I was gathering evidence that I could put together with the official investigation when the time came—and the kids were out of the evidence trail.

When I got killed, the police investigating the murder followed my work, and they couldn't make my log match the part of the investigation that I kept off the books. They found the evidence, followed the money, and drew the logical conclusion.

The tunnel where I was found was a good place for skells—sorry, means bad guys, street people, like that—to hang out and do business. At the same time, that tunnel was starting to draw the urbex guys.

Nathan wasn't familiar with the term. "Urbex?"

It's short for urban exploration. They also call it infiltration. Guys creep into abandoned buildings, railways, sewers, storm drains, any kind of tunnel they can fit into.

"What's the appeal?"

The same reason me and some of the guys I used to hang with when I was a kid would go into condemned houses. Just to see what was there. To see if there really were ghosts. John chuckled. *Anyway, I could have been checking the tunnel that night for bad guys or the urbex, but I could also have been meeting one of the kids from the burglary ring. I talked to a telecommunications guy running wire for upgrades in there a few nights earlier, and he said he'd noticed a lot going on down there.*

Nathan furrowed his eyebrows. *If he's lying, he's really good.*

Nathan. I know you don't know much about me outside of what you read in those newspaper stories and maybe saw on YouTube, but I was a good patrolman. I may have been guilty of bad judgment, but I was not on the take. I didn't know whoever killed me, so it wasn't a falling out among thieves. When you're out there on the street, you don't trust anybody outside your own skin.

"I guess you're real trusting now." Nathan smiled at his joke.

John just stared at him.

"I mean, because you're dead, and you're obviously out of your—" Nathan cleared his throat. "Never mind. Go on."

The point is, whatever I was doing that night, no one could have snuck up on me. If I'd thought there was any danger, I'd have had my weapon in my hand.

"Somebody shot you in the back."

I know. For the last two years, I've tried to remember that night. But I can't.

"Why not?"

Can you explain why you can fly when you're in those other places?

Nathan thought about that for a moment. "Point." He thought for a moment. "What can you remember?"

I think I can remember getting out of the car at Manny's. John rubbed his jaw. *I'm pretty sure I remember that. It's a good place to go. They make corned beef sandwiches there that are to die for.* He stopped himself when he realized what he'd said. *It wasn't one of the sandwiches that killed me.*

"Kind of figured that. Manny's has a lot of sandwiches, but I haven't seen any of them packing guns."

You're a funny guy.

"Not everybody appreciates that about me."

John gazed at the water. *But after that, I can't remember a thing. Everything else I just got from the papers and the television news. Just like you. It isn't a very pretty picture. And there wasn't anything I could do about it.* He looked at Nathan. *Until today.*

Nathan lifted his hands in front of him. "Hey, I still don't know that we can do anything about this. I'm not exactly Mr. Teen Detective here. In fact, this is my first day of being a teenager and . . . whatever else I am, and I don't think that's come off really well either." He thought about all the FaceSpace pictures of him with the swirly from school. That was going to be hard to live down.

I feel guilty about going to a kid with my problems because I know you have a lot of your own already. John sounded really tired. *But I don't have anywhere else to turn.*

"What's the first thing you remember after . . . after that?"

I came to in the hospital. When I heard all the medical equipment beeping and buzzing, I figured I was in the ER. I just didn't know how I'd gotten there.

"You were still alive at the ER?"

No. John shook his head. *When I looked down, the doc was marking the time and zipping up the body bag. Next thing I knew, I was toe tagged and in the morgue.*

The image gave Nathan goose bumps. Thinking about being in a morgue—especially with his own body—was scarier than being chased by the bears. He shook off the idea. "Do they really say toe tagged?"

John smiled grimly. *I do. Too many cop movies when I was growing up.* He paused. *After that, I looked for my family. They were there at the hospital for a long time. My captain got someone to take them home.*

John eyed him squarely. *Nathan, I'm laying it out for you. If I was guilty, I'd say so. But I'm not, and my family needs your help.*

Nathan just sat there, thinking.

John tried to stay calm, and the effort showed up in the tension in his shoulders and the deliberate way he spoke. *I'm gonna tell you something. As a patrolman, the people I helped weren't always innocent. You don't always just get to help innocent people. Sometimes you help the bad ones to, because someone else needs them, or maybe you're the last chance they need to finally get their lives straight. Do you hear what I'm saying?*

"Yeah."

John hesitated. *Look. I used to be a lot like you. You're not happy. You cruise through life—*

"You've been watching me what? One *day*?" Anger swept through Nathan and he tried to control it, but it got away from him. "And you think you know me?"

It's the truth as I see it, John shot back. *I don't know everything about you. But I know about being lost. I grew up in bad homes and swore I'd never raise kids that way. Then I got on the police force and found work I liked doing. I loved it.*

Guilt washed away Nathan's anger. The police officer had lost everything, and he wasn't giving up. He was trying to find a way to do the right thing.

I felt the same way when I met Maria, my wife. John's voice softened and tears gleamed in his eyes. He looked away from Nathan and took a deep breath. *Everything I ever wanted in my life, I had. I was so much different than I had been when I was a kid. I got up every day with a purpose, with a world to conquer and a family to raise. I did my best.* He looked back at Nathan. *Somebody took that away from me.*

Nathan shook his head. "I don't know how to find your answers."

What do you mean? You've already been doing it. Looking up the stories. Doing the research.

"If that was going to catch who killed you, the news people would already have done it."

Maybe they missed something.

"And the police department forensics people, too?"

John looked at Nathan. *Whether you think I'm a bad cop or good cop, somebody killed me. And no one's been arrested for it. Something's been missed.*

Nathan couldn't argue with that.

I can help you, Nathan. We can be a team.

"Like Batman and Robin?" Nathan intended the question to be sarcastic, but it didn't quite come out that way. He'd almost sounded like he was looking forward to it.

John nodded. *If you want to think of it that way, sure.*

Nathan kind of liked the idea, but he was also old enough to know it sounded pretty stupid. "I'm not a martial artist or an acrobat and I don't have any Batarangs."

It's okay. We'll go with your strengths. I'll cover your back with the ghoulies hanging around until you can do it for yourself. And I'll help you with the investigation. You can be the legs of the operation.

The offer sounded tempting, almost like one of the story-driven video games Nathan liked to play. But it also sounded dangerous.

As long as you've got me around, it'll be like having eyes in the back of your head.

That didn't sound too reassuring.

But now he was curious. And there was the whole business about how helping John Montoya was part of playing the Game.

He didn't have much choice, and somehow he didn't mind.

Partners? John held up a clenched fist.

Nodding, Nathan touched his clenched fist to the image in the water. "Partners."

In his periphery, Nathan saw the game board reflected in the surface of the water. He saw one of his black pieces enter the center of the board. *Good move.*

26

The next morning was Saturday. Usually Nathan slept in until noon, even though Uncle William tried to get him out of bed. But then usually Nathan stayed up all night Friday playing video games or watching television.

After he'd gotten home from the mall the previous night, he'd fallen into bed without even getting undressed. He'd slept like a rock, and he was pretty sure he'd dreamed, but he couldn't remember much of it. Everything was jumbled.

Nathan, c'mon. Time to get up. We're wasting daylight here.

Wasting daylight? Groggy, Nathan pulled his head out from under his pillow. A glance at his computer told him the time was 7:48. Way too early for a Saturday morning.

Seriously. You've got to get up if we're going to get started.

We? Nathan glanced around the room and blinked at the bright morning sunlight splashing against his windows.

Reflected in the computer monitor, Officer John Montoya stood in the middle of the room. He looked sharply dressed, especially against the chaos that ruled Nathan's personal domain.

"It's too early for this."

Crime never sleeps.

"Not even on Saturday morning?"

Nope. Get up. I've been here an hour already.

"Doing what? Watching me sleep?" Nathan didn't even want to

think about it because it was too weird. And that made him start wondering how many lost souls were going to be hanging around in his bedroom until he figured out a way to lock them out.

Had to be here in order to keep all the . . . lost souls away.

"I thought you had an agreement with them."

Not all of them listen. Lawbreakers are everywhere. Just because you're dead doesn't mean you're going to stop breaking rules or putting yourself first.

"Terrific. Some bodyguard."

Hey, I kept them away, didn't I?

When Nathan looked around, he had to admit that the room appeared to be ghost-free. He yawned and stretched. "What are we supposed to do today?"

I thought we'd do what every good investigator does: return to the scene of the crime.

"I thought the criminals did that."

Criminals do too. That's why investigators go back.

"I was there yesterday."

You looked at the crime scene. You didn't canvas the neighborhood.

"The detectives had to have done that already."

They did. Actually did a pretty good job of it, too. But there's an avenue that they neglected.

John crossed the room and stared down at the game board and pieces. *Is this the Game? The physical representation of it, I mean?*

"Yeah. I don't exactly understand everything about it yet." Nathan glanced at the board and discovered that more pieces had been moved. Reluctantly, he stood and surveyed the board, trying to make sense of everything that was taking place. A lot of moves had been made since yesterday, but he had no idea what he'd done that had moved his pieces.

He was frustrated enough to want to dump the pieces onto the floor but couldn't bring himself to do it. He was curious to see what happened next, and he was afraid to disrupt what had been done. If he interrupted the Game, he was certain only bad things would happen.

He picked up his phone and took a picture of the board. Maybe if the pieces moved again before he got back, he could figure out what had gone on.

Are you going to get dressed? In the reflection on the computer monitor, John looked at him expectantly.

Nathan grabbed underwear and jeans and headed for the bathroom. John followed him.

"Whoa. A little privacy?"

Oh. Sure. John hesitated then pointed back the way he'd come. *I'll just be in your room.*

"Don't touch anything."

John looked over his shoulder and shook his head. *That was a joke, right?*

Nathan grinned. "Yep."

Wiseacre. John stepped through the door and vanished inside Nathan's room.

"You're talking to yourself." Alyssa poked her head out of her room. Her hair stood out wildly from her head.

Nathan raised his fist and moved the thumb up and down like a lip as he spoke in a high-pitched voice. "Is all right?" Then he answered in his regular voice. "Is all right."

Alyssa rolled her eyes. "You are so beyond weird." She closed her door.

Despite the early hour, Nathan felt better for having irritated Alyssa before she'd gotten her act completely together. He went into the bathroom and turned on the shower.

□─┤─┤─□

"**N**athan? What are you doing up?" Uncle William sounded shocked.

"I had some things I wanted to do. Thought maybe I'd hang out with some friends. Maybe hit the comic shop." Nathan hung his computer backpack on a chair and then walked to the refrigerator and peered inside. He found a quart of Sunny Delight and took it out. He stopped himself short of drinking from the container while his uncle was watching him and took a glass down from the cupboard.

You almost got busted. Reflected in the glass Nathan held, John leaned against the breakfast bar and gazed around the kitchen. *Nobody likes the guy who drinks from the containers in the refrigerator. That's just sick.*

"I'm working on some breakfast here." Uncle William waved at the stove.

"Yeah." Nathan put the Sunny Delight back in the refrigerator. "I figured that out all by myself."

Uncle William frowned. "Don't you think it's a little early for sarcasm?"

"Not really, no. Kind of gets me primed for the day."

"He's a grump." Alyssa entered the room fully dressed and groomed. "I noticed that this morning. He was talking to himself. I think he's suffering from post-traumatic clown scarediness."

"Your hair this morning caused a severe clown flashback."

Wow, you don't take any prisoners, do you?

"But my hair now looks perfectly wonderful. Thank you very much." Alyssa hugged her dad and gave him an affectionate peck on the cheek. She snatched a few grapes from the bowl on the table.

"How about some breakfast?" Uncle William looked at Nathan.

"Do we have any Pop-Tarts?"

"You're not eating Pop-Tarts when I'm cooking breakfast."

"I like Pop-Tarts. And they're breakfast. Says so right on the box."

You better eat a good breakfast. We're going to be covering a lot of ground today. You don't know when you're going to eat again.

"You need something more substantial than that." Uncle William shook his head.

"Okay." Nathan sat at the table.

Surprised, Uncle William stared at him and had to make three attempts to press the intercom button by the refrigerator. "Peter, come to breakfast. Everything is ready."

Alyssa helped her dad put all the food on the table. Despite the early hour and the fact that Nathan wasn't prepared to be in anything that resembled a good mood, he had to admit that everything smelled fantastic. He picked up a piece of bacon from a plate and crunched off a bite.

A few minutes later his father entered the room carrying an orange and brown ceramic cup and a notepad. He put the cup down on the table with exaggerated care and plopped his notepad beside it.

"New coffee cup, Uncle Peter?" Alyssa asked brightly.

"No. A Mayan drinking vessel." Nathan's dad poured himself a cup of coffee and took a plate from a stack on the table.

"Hoping for matching silverware?"

John laughed.

Score: 1 for Alyssa.

His dad chuckled. "That would be too much to ask for, I'm afraid. That, however, is a very special cup."

"May I look at it?"

"Of course. Just be very careful. It's irreplaceable."

Out of the corner of his eye, Nathan watched Alyssa pick up the cup and gently turn it around to look at the figures carved into the ceramic. Nathan felt a little jealous; his father would never have agreed to let him handle something *irreplaceable*.

"The pictures are carved and painted." Alyssa ran her finger over the images.

"Yes. It's called slip paint." His father buttered a piece of toast.

"That's clay diluted with water, and they used crushed minerals to color it."

His father looked at Alyssa in surprise. "That's right. How did you know about slip paint?"

Alyssa shrugged. "Mr. Tolliver's history class. He's an artist and always mixes history with art techniques. We actually made slip paint during one of the units. But this is really cool."

"Glad you think so. It was recently found in a K'iche' burial pit. I think it was used in rituals of human sacrifice."

Alyssa froze, looked at the cup, and grimaced. "Oh. Really." Carefully, she set the cup down by his father's notepad again and then got up and washed her hands in the sink.

When John laughed again, Nathan snickered and drew Alyssa's death stare.

His father chuckled as he sat down at the table. "The cup's been cleaned. I did it myself."

Alyssa shivered. "I'm sure it has. And I'm sure you did a good job. But still. Sacrifices? Ewwwww."

"This from the young lady that handled a monkey skull without flinching only yesterday morning?"

Wow. We never had breakfasts like this when I was a kid.

"A monkey skull doesn't quite seem as dirty as something robbed from a grave. And there was no thought whatsoever of drinking from the monkey skull." Alyssa sat back down.

"There was no grave robbery involved with the recovery of this cup. Nor with the burial urn I have in my workroom. They were gifts donated to the museum."

Uncle William leaned back in his chair in exasperation. "We have a burial urn in the house? Peter, what are you thinking?"

"*I* have a burial urn in my workroom." His father sat the cup aside and turned to his breakfast. "And I'm thinking that I have to clean up that artifact, authenticate it, and document it for the museum so we can exhibit it properly."

That caught Nathan's attention. He loved the Field Museum. Since his dad worked there, Nathan had spent a lot of time wandering the rooms and the exhibits. There was major coolness about the history on display that most kids he knew didn't get. With his imagination, it was like stepping into a time machine each and every visit. Nathan's mind seized on the idea of checking out the Mesoamerican exhibit, wondering if there might be some mention of the Game or Kukulkan at the museum that could answer some of his questions. It was something worth checking out when he wasn't playing Boy Detective.

Finished with breakfast, Nathan picked up his plate and headed for the sink.

"About the burial urn." Uncle William wasn't going to let that go. "You don't still have the body that came with it, by chance?"

"No. I tried." His father looked disappointed. "We could have probably gotten more viewers at the exhibit if we had. There's something about a dead body that just draws people in."

Ain't that the truth. John's voice held a lot of disgust. *Anytime you find a dead body or there's a traffic accident, the rubberneckers line up around the block hoping to get a peek.*

Nathan couldn't help remembering the footage he'd seen about the discovery of John Montoya's body. People had been everywhere.

His dad sipped his coffee. "Of course, then we might have had a Mayan ghost hanging around the house, and you wouldn't like that."

Uncle William looked uncomfortable. "You know I don't believe in ghosts."

Well, you should have been hanging out with me yesterday. That would have made a believer of you. Nathan thought, drying his hands and pulled on his backpack. He checked the pantry and found a box of strawberry-flavored Pop-Tarts. He shoved a couple of packages into his backpack.

Alyssa laughed at her father. "Since when do you not believe in ghosts? You still don't like horror movies. And you have all kinds of problems with the sounds this house makes."

The whole idea of ghosts haunting the house suddenly wasn't funny to Nathan. He looked at the reflection of John in one of the kitchen windows, certain the police officer wasn't going anywhere until he had answers or knew he wasn't going to get them. In effect, they were already haunted.

And when John Montoya was gone, would other lost souls come along to take his place when they were no longer held back by the rules of the Game? He got tired just thinking about it.

Nathan cleared his throat. "Can I get a few bucks?"

His father looked up at him. "For what?"

"Thought I'd go out. Movie. Some comics. Maybe lunch somewhere later."

His father took out his wallet and held out twenty dollars. "Is your cell charged?"

Nathan took the phone out and showed it to his father. "Yep. And I've got the charger with me."

He reached for the cash.

Uncle William cleared his throat. "It was his birthday yesterday, Peter. You didn't get him a present. You could be a little more generous."

"Oh. That's right. Birthday."

Alyssa and Uncle William seemed surprised that his father had forgotten so quickly, but Nathan wasn't. His father reached into his wallet again and took out another twenty and then looked at Uncle William.

Uncle William rolled his eyes. "Comics are expensive these days."

"Right. I knew that. Let's make it an even hundred." His father handed the money over and smiled absently. "Happy birthday, Nathan."

"Thanks." Nathan shoved the money into his pocket and headed out the door.

John followed after him.

Outside, Nathan slipped off his bracelet and tossed it to the sidewalk. His next step put him on the skateboard, and he zipped out into the neighborhood.

"So what's your big plan?"

There weren't any reflective surfaces around for him to see how John kept pace without a skateboard, but he did. He sounded like he was talking directly into Nathan's ear.

The investigators and detectives talked to all the adults in the neighborhood, but they didn't talk to all the kids. Like I told you, when I patrolled that area, I got to know a lot of the kids, the good ones and the bad ones.

Nathan pushed off again, gaining a little speed and paying attention to the grinding sound of the wheels. The ride was so smooth. But it also made him think of Kukulkan; he wondered where he was and when he'd be coming back. There were a lot of questions Nathan wanted to ask. He turned his thoughts away from that and focused on the task ahead of him.

"Why didn't they talk to the kids?"

Because they didn't know the kids that hung around there. I do. Even if they'd known the kids, they might not have talked to any police officers besides me. Those kids don't trust anybody.

"Then they're not going to trust me."

You're a kid. You'll fit right in.

"You know, you've got a lot to learn about being a kid. We don't just 'fit right in' with each other. Sometimes it's incredibly hard."

You'll find a way. I got faith in you.

Nathan gave the skateboard a couple of pushes to get back up to speed. "It's been two years. They may not still be the same kids."

Some of them were pretty young. Most of them are still there. I walked through the neighborhood yesterday afternoon—

"You mean there was a time you weren't stalking me?"

I took a break from that while you were at school. I figured I'd freaked you out enough for a while.

"Then you missed the swirly."

I saw the pictures posted in the hallway.

"Terrific."

Life's not easy for anybody at any age.

"Those kids, if we find them, are going to have a hard time talking to you now."

Actually, I hadn't thought about that.

"That's okay. We'll see if we can find a way around it." Nathan was surprised to find he was looking forward to the challenge.

By the time Nathan reached the Loop, it was after ten-thirty. He picked up his board and put it on his wrist as a bracelet, then started making the rounds as directed by John Montoya.

He walked up to a pawn shop only a few blocks from Manny's. The shop was long and narrow. Hand-lettered signs in the window advertised CASH FOR JEWELRY, COMPUTERS, AND VIDEO GAMES.

"Who are we going to see here?" Nathan pushed through the door. A bell overhead tinkled loudly.

Kid named Aristotle. Four years ago, he was in a bad way. Living with an abusive father, but he didn't have any family but his old man. When I busted his dad for child endangerment, I arranged for Aristotle to get a foster family. I was tempted to take him in myself, but there just wasn't room, and things were already complicated enough with my son.

A middle-aged man stood behind the counter. He was bald and wore a goatee. He also wore a Hawaiian shirt with big red flowers that didn't match the season. He placed his hands on the glass display case containing laptops and cameras.

"If you've got something to sell, I'm going to tell you right now that I'm not buying it." The man nodded at Nathan's backpack. "I've got a policy not to buy from kids. Too many complications. If you want to buy a video game or a DVD, I'll be glad to help you out."

"I'm not here to sell anything. I just wanted to talk to Aristotle if I could."

"You a friend of his?"

"No. A friend sent me to talk to him."

"Why?" Suspicion gleamed in the man's eyes.

Sal's really protective of Aristotle. He's a good guy. You're going to have to sell him on something.

Nathan thought hard and then caught sight of a PSP sitting beside a lunch cooler on one of the shelves. A case with Aristotle's name sat beside it on top of a half-dozen electronic gaming magazines.

Gamer geek. Cool.

"I'm playing one of the new video games, and I'm stuck on a level. A mutual friend said Aristotle had played it and could maybe help me."

Sal shook his head and grinned. "He probably can. Ari is a wizard when it comes to gaming. He can do things I hadn't even thought of doing." He nodded toward the back door. "He's in the back sorting inventory. Go on through."

"Sure. Thanks."

Good job. You're a natural at this.

Nathan swallowed and headed for the back door. *Sure, except for the whole knee-knocking thing.* He'd gotten past the pawnbroker, but he had no idea what he was going to say to Aristotle.

28

The storeroom contained a lot of stuff but looked pretty organized. Musical instruments sat together. Video game hardware and games occupied a couple of shelves. Televisions and DVD players sat in stacks. Furniture, from sofas to baby chairs, took up space as well. Bicycles, skateboards, MP3 players, and sports gear covered one wall. The combined smell of mustiness, leather, and cleaning fluid clogged Nathan's nose.

A boy stood at the back of the room using a box knife to slit open a cardboard box. He was short and skinny, with dark curly hair and dark eyes. He wore jeans, a Bulls T-shirt, and a black windbreaker.

"Hey." Aristotle turned to face Nathan. "You're not supposed to be back here."

Nathan jerked a thumb over his shoulder. "Your dad said it would be okay."

Not bad, kid. A half-truth.

Nathan knew how to get around rules and people.

"Why?" Evidently Aristotle wasn't inexperienced. "I don't know you." He looked ready for trouble. He raised his voice. "Hey, Pop?"

"Yeah?"

"Did you tell this guy he could come back here?"

"Yes. He said he wanted to talk to you about a video game."

Knowing he was about to be exposed, Nathan decided to lay all his cards on the table. "I actually came here to talk to you about John Montoya."

"John?" A pained look flashed across Aristotle's face. "What about him?"

"I'm trying to find out who . . . hurt him."

"Is something wrong, Ari?"

Aristotle hesitated for a long moment. "No. Everything's cool, Pop. You mind if I take five out in the alley?"

"Go ahead."

"Thanks." Aristotle nodded Nathan to the back door, opened it to let him walk past, and then stepped out after him.

Panic rolled uneasily in Nathan's stomach as he watched Aristotle sizing him up. Nathan was out of his depth, and he knew it. Getting into a fight at school was one thing. Teachers were everywhere and could be counted on to stop it pretty quickly. But in an alley, there had to be a cop around. And the only one with them that morning was dead.

Be easy, Nathan. Everything's going to be cool. He's a good kid. Just closed in. You know what that's like.

Nathan kept his eyes on Aristotle, but he saw John's reflection moving in a pool of water on the asphalt.

"Who are you?" Aristotle glared at Nathan, as if daring him to try lying again.

"My name is Nathan."

"I don't know you, Nathan." Aristotle paced restlessly, like a tiger in a zoo. He was wiry strength and determination in motion, and Nathan knew the older boy could hurt him if he chose to. "That means I got no reason to talk to you."

"I'm trying to clear John's name."

That stopped the pacing for a moment and then Aristotle shook his head angrily. "Lot of people think John was a bad cop. But he wasn't. He was one of the best, and he was my friend. Anybody come around here saying otherwise, I'm gonna mess them up.

"Anyway, the cops couldn't clear John's name. What makes you think you can?"

"I don't know if I can, but I have to try."

"Why?"

"Because I'm . . . I was friends with him too."

Aristotle looked at Nathan with open disdain. "You ain't no street kid. John knew street kids. He wouldn't know somebody like you in this neighborhood."

"I met him at school." Nathan figured that one might fly. Police officers always showed up for career day and other programs.

"So you wait two years to come poking your nose into this?"

"Two years ago, I was eleven. I wasn't old enough to do anything."

"And at thirteen you figure you are?"

"I just figured maybe you'd want to help me find out who killed John. If that's too much to ask, I'll let you get back to what you were doing." Nathan let himself get angry. He didn't like getting shut down on something he wanted to do, and it looked like Officer Montoya's great idea was blowing up in his face. The problem was that he couldn't come up with a quick alternative.

"You don't come down here and diss me like that."

Nathan waved him off, turned around, and walked away, stepping through the pool where John Montoya's face looked up at him.

Don't give up on him, Nathan.

"Forget it. He's not going to listen. This was just a waste of time."

Find a way to talk to him. He can help you.

"He's not interested in helping anybody. Frankly, if somebody like me came to me with the same story, I wouldn't listen to him either."

Nathan—

A hand grabbed Nathan's shoulder and spun him around. Aristotle hung onto Nathan's arm and cocked his fist. "You always go around talking to yourself? Are you crazy or something?"

Nathan resisted the urge to fight back. That would have been the easiest thing to do, but it was obvious that Aristotle was hurting over losing John.

"Something like that. I haven't quite decided myself." Nathan held his hands up in front of his face.

"Answer me straight, or I'm gonna throw you a beating."

Nathan stared into the other boy's eyes and knew he meant what he said. "John. I'm talking to John."

"John's dead."

"I know, and he won't shut up. You can only imagine how frustrating this is for me. I didn't even know him."

"You said you did."

Nathan shrugged. "I lied. I was trying to get you to talk to me."

"That was stupid. I knew you were lying."

Meeting Aristotle's gaze full measure, Nathan took a deep breath. "Am I lying now?"

For a moment, Nathan was certain Aristotle was going to hit him, and he braced himself for the pain. Then Aristotle dropped his clenched fist and pushed Nathan away.

Stumbling for a few steps, not believing he wasn't getting pounded, Nathan regained his balance.

"Go away." Aristotle headed for the back door to the pawn shop.

"You didn't know John. You got no business talking about him."

"I'm trying to help him."

"You can't help the dead."

"Actually, I can."

Aristotle wheeled around and cursed.

Nathan kept talking. Usually if he kept talking, he could make trouble go away or at least delay it. "At least, I think I can. John's the first dead guy—I call them lost souls—I've tried to help. But you don't really need to know that, do you?"

For a moment, Aristotle stood his ground. "You can talk to John?"

"Yeah, man."

"He can hear me?"

"Yes, but he can't talk to you. Only I can hear him."

Aristotle shook his head. "Kind of convenient for you, huh?"

"Not really, no. Guy keeps yammering. Constantly. Like a machine gun. 'Help me find out who killed me.'"

Hey!

Folding his arms over his chest, Aristotle smirked. "You ask John what was the first hat he ever gave me. You get it right, I don't pound you."

John told Nathan, and Nathan repeated it. "Cubs, but you didn't take it. You told him you wanted a White Sox cap or nothing. Then he took you to your first baseball game. It was after he'd got you set up with your foster parents."

The fight went out of Aristotle as he stepped forward uncertainly and gazed around the alley. "John?"

Yeah, kid. I'm here.

Nathan relayed the message.

Tears glittered in Aristotle's eyes. Nathan was stunned by how much the boy had obviously cared about someone who wasn't even family. Taking a deep breath, Aristotle shook his head and focused on Nathan.

"Tell him I'm sorry for everything that happened to him."

"He can hear you." Nathan didn't like all the raw emotion coursing through him. It felt uncomfortable. But he couldn't turn away from it. John's voice was husky with his feelings, too. "You can talk to him."

Aristotle nodded. "John, I miss you. Every day, man. I appreciate what you did, finding me a family and all. Things are really working out."

I'm glad, buddy. Nathan mouthed the words for John.

Aristotle wiped his eyes on his sleeve. "What do you need me to do?"

29

"How do you know so many people?" Nathan sat at a back table in a Mexican café and picked at the remains of his lunch.

John Montoya sat across from him, reflected in the shiny napkin dispenser and the window. He looked worn. *I spent years on this beat. I got to know people.*

It was after two o'clock in the afternoon. Aristotle had gotten the day off so he could walk Nathan around the neighborhood and introduce him to some of the other kids who had known the police officer. All of them had stories to tell, but none of them had any real information. Nathan was ready to give up, but John had urged him to stick with it.

"Why?" Nathan glanced toward the bathroom, waiting for Aristotle to come out. Throughout the several hours they had spent finding and talking to other kids, Nathan had seen Ari glancing around, as if he might catch sight of John.

Aristotle had told his own stories about the things John had done to help out the neighborhood. John Montoya had helped a lot of kids get out of the drug scene and back in school. He'd taught self-defense classes at one of the local gyms. And he'd let every kid know that if they had a problem, they could come to him.

According to Aristotle, John Montoya also had made a lot of local enemies of drug dealers, thieves, and other people who tended to use or hurt kids. But none of them had ever confronted John. Ari only pointed that out because it meant they were unlikely to find strong suspects at the local level.

Why did I get to know people?

"Yeah."

John rubbed his jaw and sat back in his seat. *Because that's what we're supposed to do, Nathan. We're supposed to get to know other people. That way, we can help them. Having friends keeps the world simple.* He smiled ruefully at that. *Or it makes it incredibly complicated. You don't usually get one without the other.*

"Yeah, but I like being alone."

All the time?

Nathan shrugged.

Some people do need more alone time than others. I usually took mine after my night shift. I'd find a diner I like and then sit outside in the car with the radio turned off for a while. But being alone isn't normal for people.

"Maybe I'm not normal."

John grinned. *You're normal. Every kid your age feels like they're not normal, but you are. I didn't feel normal at your age either.*

"Normal usually means not being stalked by lost souls."

That's just your mutant power kicking in. John looked more serious. *Or your destiny.*

Nathan hesitated. "Kukulkan tells me my destiny is to play the Game."

From what I understand, you are playing.

"My mom tells me the fate of the world depends on me learning to play."

John looked troubled. *I don't know anything about that.*

"Figured maybe it was in the *Lost Souls Gazette* or something."

A grin spread across John's face.

"What kind of mom would tell her kid something like that?"

Maybe one who cares enough to keep things square between you. Something like that isn't easy to lay on someone, Nathan. Especially someone you love.

"If it's true."

I've met your mom. If she told you that, she believes it's true. And I know she loves you. Trust me, I've learned to tell parents who really care from those who don't. She does.

Nathan thought about that. "But what if I'm not the guy for the job? I mean, how am I supposed to know something like that?"

Nathan, every cop, every person who has to do something scary, worries about that. Police officers are afraid they won't stand up during a gunfight. Firefighters wonder if they'll run into a burning building the first time it becomes necessary. Emergency room nurses hope they don't freak out during their first crash cart. Nobody gets through life without being afraid that they're not going to measure up at some point.

Nathan nodded. "Are you still going to feel that way if I can't help you find out who killed you? Or are you going to think I didn't measure up?"

Hey, you're out here trying, Nathan. That's all I asked. That's all anyone can ask. I feel like you already measure up.

That declaration made Nathan feel good, but he turned away and didn't let it show.

Aristotle came back from the bathroom and looked at the table. "John still here?"

"Yeah."

"Cool. He got any ideas?"

Look for people who spent time in that maintenance tunnel. Kids who went there to crash or to party. Let's stay with that now. Ask him if he knows Tommy Mertz.

Nathan relayed the message.

Aristotle looked like he'd swallowed something bitter. "Yeah, I know Tommy. Not a nice guy, generally, but I heard he cleaned up his act. You sure you want to do this?"

"Yeah." Nathan was surprised at how much he wanted to. He felt like he was getting close to something too.

"Let's roll."

Seventeen-year-old Tommy Mertz worked in a mechanic shop only a few blocks away. Nathan followed Aristotle through the alleys, and they'd had to jump out of the way to avoid getting splashed by low riders filled with dangerous-looking men.

Nathan had rarely been through the dicey sections of the Loop. Nathan was wary and a little experienced, but he was scared too. Aristotle acted like he was at home.

The mechanic shop was sandwiched between a laundromat and a tax accountant's office. Across the street were a cheap hotel, a bar, and a video store. It wasn't the kind of area that inspired a feeling of neighborhood.

"You sure this is the right place?" Nathan looked at the graffiti and gang signs spray-painted on the building's brick walls and garage doors.

"Yeah. This is it." Aristotle looked at Nathan. "You want, you can wait out here."

Don't let him do this by himself. John Montoya stood beside Nathan with his arms folded. Two strips of gray duct tape held the broken window and his reflection together. A faded Santa Claus poster hung at the top of the window.

"I'm coming with you."

"Okay. Just stay close. And don't say anything. The work these guys do in here isn't always legal."

Chop shop operation. I kept putting them out of business; they kept going back into it. John's image disappeared as he followed Nathan and Aristotle into the building.

"Something I can help you guys with?" The guy behind the counter was covered in tattoos and wore biker leathers. His unruly beard masked the lower half of his face. Biker posters hung on the wall behind him.

Aristotle nodded. "We're here to see Tommy."

"You're the kid works down at the pawn shop."

"Yeah."

The man's gaze bored into Nathan. "But I don't recognize your friend."

"Just a friend. Nothing to tell."

The guy hesitated a moment and then glanced back at Aristotle. "Tommy's in the back salvaging parts. Don't waste all day with him. He's got work to do."

"Sure." Aristotle led the way through the door into the main shop.

Several men labored on cars, laughing above the constant throb of hip-hop blasting from a stereo in the corner. They looked up as Nathan and Aristotle walked through but didn't say anything. The room reeked of gasoline, oil, and sweat.

Nathan followed Aristotle through a maze of tool chests and spare parts. They walked around a rack of tires and then headed out the back door.

The lot was muddy from a recent rain, surrounded by a high

wooden fence that no longer hung straight. Nearby in an artistic stack, four cars and a pickup sat in different stages of decomposition, as if they were being eaten slowly by vultures with a taste for metal.

Covered in grease and wearing shapeless coveralls and a zip-front jacket, Tommy Mertz looked at them from under the hood of a car that had been sideswiped on the driver's side. He had a wrench in one hand and used the other to hold his cigarette.

He was bulky under the coveralls, but it wasn't fat. There was a lot of muscle, and he was broad shouldered. He looked like he could take the wrecked cars apart barehanded. A watch cap covered his head, and several piercings stuck out from his lips, nose, and ears. A purple dragon tattoo hugged his neck just under his jaw.

"'Sup, Ari." Tommy nodded.

"'Sup, Tommy." Aristotle stopped on the other side of the car and leaned on the fender. Nathan stayed a couple of steps back.

"Ain't seen you down here . . . well, *ever*."

"That's 'cause I don't come. Better off not coming this way."

Tommy grinned. "I understand. But what brings you down here today?"

"Wanted to talk to you."

"What about?"

"I heard you were out of the business."

Tommy cut his eyes to Nathan.

"He's cool." Aristotle waved a dismissive hand. "He's with me. Anything gets said here, he forgets about."

They talk like gangsters, Nathan thought. He was fascinated because it was almost like watching a crime movie.

Kids around here learn to grow up fast. John's reflection showed in the cracked windshield of the car. *They fall into crime or away from crime at an early age.*

"I ain't in the business no more." Tommy reached for another socket and attached it to the wrench. "I been legit almost two years."

Good for you. John smiled and looked pleased.

"That's good, Tommy. Real good. I was worried about you."

Tommy shook his head. "Yeah." He fitted the wrench onto whatever he was working on. "There at the end, I was worried about me too. But I was able to cut loose and get away from those guys who had me stealing. It helped that the police busted them while they were investigating John's murder." He looked up. "I still miss him, you know."

"Yeah. Me too."

"For a cop, he was an all-right guy. He rode me a lot, gave me a hard time, but you knew he cared." Tommy shook his head. "I can't believe they never caught whoever killed him."

"I know. That's kind of what I'm here to talk about today."

Tommy straightened up. "What are you talking about?"

Aristotle jerked a thumb at Nathan. "My friend here is trying to see if he can learn anything about who killed John."

Suspicion knitted Tommy's brows. "Why?"

"When the police department decided John was a bad cop, they suspended his pension. His wife and son could use the money." Nathan shrugged. "I'm trying to help out."

"Who nominated you to help do anything?" Challenge rang in Tommy's voice.

"Look, I've just got some questions about the stolen goods they found in John's house."

"*What?* You think I had anything to do with that?" Tommy sounded like he was ready to explode, and he came around the car with the wrench in his hand. "Get out of here!"

30

"Hey." Aristotle lifted his hands and stepped in front of Tommy, going chest to chest with the bigger boy to get him to stop. "Just chill out a minute, Tommy. Nobody needs to get hurt here."

"I ain't worried about getting hurt by a couple of punks." Tommy pointed the socket wrench at Aristotle. "I want you and your little friend out of my face. Now. Comprende?"

Aristotle walked slowly around the car. "We're trying to help John. All right? You liked John."

"John's dead."

"Then we're trying to help John's family. They need to know the truth about what happened to him."

Tommy shook the wrench and didn't stop staring at Nathan. "So you came down here to try to hang something on me? Is that what this is?"

"No." Nathan's voice sounder calmer than he thought it would under the circumstances, especially with the way his knees were threatening to buckle. "We're just trying to figure out what went down that night."

Keep talking, kid. Sell this. John told Nathan what to ask.

Nathan swallowed and kept talking. "We need to know about the stolen goods they found at his house."

"I didn't have anything to do with that."

"John knows—knew that. He—I just want to try to follow the trail, see if we can figure out why he was in the tunnel that night—who he met."

Still angry, Tommy stalked off, stomping his heavy work boots through mud puddles. He looked at Aristotle as he clomped back. "I quit the gang after John was killed. I stepped away from all of that. Did you know that?"

Good for you, Tommy.

"Do you know how hard that was?" Tommy's face was full of pain and anger.

Aristotle lowered his hands and stood quietly in front of Tommy. "No, man, I don't."

Suddenly, Nathan didn't feel like he was playing Batman anymore. This was too real, too dangerous.

Hang in there, Nathan. This is what it feels like when you're doing work like this. It's always scary. If you get to where you don't feel a little scared, it's time to get out.

"I understand that you have a situation to handle." Nathan's voice broke a little, and he coughed to cover it. "But we're trying to help John's family. We know John was not on the take."

Tommy took out another cigarette and lit it. "No. He wasn't. But he made a lot of enemies—and he was going up against people who didn't even know his name. They just knew he was messing with their business."

"You got names for us, Tommy?" Aristotle spoke quietly but remained between Tommy and Nathan.

"Nah, no names. But there were a couple of guys who showed up on the scene a couple of months before John died. They were strictly small-time, hassling kids who were already working for someone, intercepting them before they could drop off their score and taking stuff to resell through their own network. They were just starting to become a real danger to themselves when John was killed."

In the cracked windshield, John looked startled.

"You're saying they were cops?" Nathan asked.

Tommy shook his head. "No. Not cops. Nothing heavy like that. These guys were private security guards. They flashed their badges around like they were the police, but the kids weren't fooled. Nobody wanted to call them on it, though, because they jammed up a couple of kids right away. Almost put them in the hospital."

I didn't know about that. This is the first time I've heard about them.

Nathan focused on that. "Nobody told John?"

Tommy shook his head in disgust. "This happened right before he was killed. John was a cool guy and all, but nobody wanted to run to him with every problem. John couldn't control everything that happened." He was quiet for a moment, like he was remembering bad times. "And sometimes kids got beat for ratting out their parents or friends."

Tommy's right. Sometimes a kid ended up worse off. For a while. Couldn't be prevented. There was only so much I could do. But I had a chance to help. I had to take it. Things always worked out better in the end.

"The other reason we didn't run to him for everything was because we were worried about him. We didn't want John to get hurt because of us. The people out there on the street?" Tommy pointed toward the front of the mechanic shop with the wrench. "A lot of them are bad people. We live with them every day. We know the rules. These two security guards working their re-sale hustle? They were small-timers. But even small-timers can be dangerous if you crowd them."

"But you think they were the ones who killed John?"

Tommy shrugged. "I don't know, man. But when I heard what happened, I thought of these two guys. Everybody around here that sells stolen merch on the street knows what everyone else is selling. And stealing. But the stuff they found at John's house? That was from some job I hadn't heard of."

"Wait a minute. We're missing something." Nathan looked at John's reflection in the windshield.

"What?"

"Let's forget about who for a minute and think about why someone would frame John. I mean, if I was going to lose stolen goods that you could make money on in order to frame someone, I'd want to make sure I was getting something out of it."

Hey, kid, you're getting to be a natural at this. John smiled encouragingly.

That just made Nathan realize that he was in more danger than before.

Tommy scratched his chin. "Maybe John surprised them in a deal, and they hightailed it out of there. Maybe they got scared after they fought him and killed him."

No fight.

"There wasn't a fight." Nathan thought it through. "John was shot in the back. His gun was in his holster. If he'd seen trouble, or thought he was in danger, he would have had his gun out."

Good call, kid.

Reluctantly, Tommy nodded. "Sure. Whoever it was, they wanted to jam John up. I still think these two security guys were connected. Where else you gonna get a haul like that without someone helping you set it up?"

"Where did they get it?" Aristotle asked.

"From a middleman, like I said. Ain't no other way it could be. These guys kept busting kids, finally got one to roll over on his fence. You know, the guy that resells stolen stuff. They went to the fence's house, caught him with the mother lode, and ripped him off."

"Then why dump it, or even some of it, at John's house?"

Tommy cursed and shook his head. "I don't know, man. I've tried to wrap my head around that, but I can't."

"If you thought these security guards were involved, why didn't you go to the police?"

Tommy frowned. "I tried. They blew me off. Wasn't no secret that I was a thief. Nobody they'd want to trust. The police didn't want to listen to anything I had to say. But they investigated me like maybe I killed John for a while. I wasn't anywhere near the tunnel that night. It was my little brother's birthday and there were a lot of people who knew where I was."

"Nobody else went forward about the security guards?" Nathan tried to imagine what being involved in something like this would be like, then realized he was pretty involved in it now. It was scary, but it was exciting too.

"New kid." Tommy shook his head. "You got a lot to learn about the street if you want to stay alive out here. If you're doing criminal stuff and the cops don't know about it? The last thing you want to do is go tell them."

Can he identify the two security guards?

Nathan asked.

"No." Tommy stood and waved his arms, obviously trying to create more body heat against the chill of just standing there.

"I never saw them." He thought for a moment. "But I can tell you who might."

"Who?"

"Kid named Irby Dell."

He's one of the urbex kids I was telling you about. Belongs to a group that calls themselves the Night Spiders.

"I know Irby," Aristotle said.

Tommy nodded. "Thought you might. Irby's one of those guys that climb around abandoned buildings."

"Urban explorers," Nathan said.

"Whatever." Tommy waved it away. "Bunch of idiots if you ask me. Weird hobby."

"Why would they know about these security guards?"

"Because they had a confrontation with them one night. Irby and his peeps were in that tunnel. The security guards came up on them and told them they had no business there, and that next time they caught them there they'd lock 'em up. Evidently Irby and his homies didn't leave fast enough. The security guys took out their clubs and hit Irby. His mom took him to the emergency room, and they found out his arm was fractured. Irby didn't want to tell his mom what really happened, so he made up a story about falling."

When did this happen?

Nathan asked.

"A few days before John got killed."

Aristotle looked at Nathan. "Maybe we should go talk to Irby."

Nathan checked his phone. It was after three, but nobody had called. He slipped the phone back into his pocket and nodded. "Okay. You know where to find him?"

Tommy grinned. "It ain't dark, so he ain't out creeping through some building or tunnel. You'll probably find him at home in his cave. If he's awake."

"Cave?" Nathan tried to imagine where anyone would find a cave down in the Loop. Other than the maintenance tunnel. Of course, there were a lot of those.

"Irby made a deal with his building's super. If he helps around the apartment building, the super lets him keep his 'command center' down in part of the basement." Tommy shook his head. "It's pretty pathetic, actually."

"Thanks, Tommy." Aristotle held out his fist and bumped Tommy's.

"No big. You need anything else, gimme a shout." Tommy flicked his gaze to Nathan. "You, too, new kid."

Nathan nodded and adjusted his backpack straps.

Tommy hesitated before he went back to work on the car. His voice was soft as he spoke. "You know the one thing I regret about this whole thing, Ari? Other than John getting killed?"

"What?"

"That John never got to see me after I went legit." His voice was raw with emotion.

Ari looked at Nathan.

"John sees you now," Nathan said.

Tommy glared at Nathan. "Who asked you?"

Nathan held his ground. Just as he had in Ari, he could see the pain Tommy was carrying. "Ask me something only John would know about you."

"Is this some kind of game, Ari?" Tommy didn't take his gaze from Nathan.

"Naw, man. It ain't no game. Ask him."

After a brief moment to collect his thoughts, Tommy walked over and put his face right in front of Nathan's. "I'm going to ask you a question, new kid. And if you get it wrong, I'm gonna wreck your grill."

Nathan was scared, but he refused to let it show. "Gee. No pressure there."

Tommy ignored him. "First place John ever took me to eat."

John answered without hesitation.

"Turtle's Chinese Restaurant. It was Beatles Day, and the jukebox was stuck playing *Sgt. Pepper's Lonely Hearts Club Band*. You wouldn't tell John what your fortune cookie said."

Slowly, Tommy shook his head in disbelief. "Ain't no way you could know that. Only me and John went there that day."

"I know."

"Then how—"

"John knows, Tommy. He sees you and he's proud of you. He wants everything to turn out good for you."

31

Irby's mother, Mrs. Johnson, answered the door and looked at Nathan and Aristotle with a slightly annoyed expression. She was a fiercely intimidating woman dressed in lavender-colored nurse's scrubs. "Y'all are here looking for Irby, I suppose?"

"Yes, ma'am." Aristotle smiled so politely it looked really fake. Nathan just stared at him.

"Well, at least you got manners." Mrs. Johnson waggled her finger at Nathan and Aristotle. "Both of y'all got manners, right?"

Nathan caught an elbow in his ribs and knew he was supposed to respond. He smiled through the pain. "Yes, ma'am."

"Ain't gonna go creeping around no abandoned buildings or sewers with my boy, are you?"

"No, ma'am."

"Good. 'Cause I told him and ever'body else, I catch you with him, I'm gonna wale on you like you was my own. Understand?" Mrs. Johnson turned a hard gaze on both of them.

"Yes, ma'am."

Irby Johnson's "cave" proved to be an apt description. The basement held a lot of equipment, furnaces and furnishings and parts, but Irby had cleared space for himself and his work in a back corner.

Dim-wattage bulbs in the overhead lights made the surroundings barely visible, just enough to avoid colliding with them. In contrast, Irby's corner was brightly lit by a green-shaded banker's lamp and a computer monitor.

"Hey, Irby." Aristotle made the final turn around boxes of cleaning supplies that smelled of chlorine. "Got a couple of visitors, man."

Nathan saw that his assumptions about Irby Johnson were incorrect. He'd expected the guy to look like Wesley Snipes or the Rock, and definitely to be antisocial. Instead, Irby was quiet and intelligent-looking, wore black frame glasses, and kept his hair cut short. He had on jeans and a *Star Trek* shirt.

He sat at a desk that had been battered and mishandled, something someone had thrown out and he'd managed to reconstruct after a fashion. Street maps, drawings, and photographs covered the two corner walls near his desk.

Irby's dark face split into a quizzical white smile. "I know you guys?"

"Not yet. I'm Ari. This is my friend Nathan."

Nathan took one of three folding chairs from the wall and sat. "We're looking for information." Then he decided that sounded way too cop-speak. "Basically, we're trying to help John Montoya's family."

"John Montoya? Wasn't he that police officer who was shot down in front of Manny's? In the tunnel?"

"Yeah." Nathan nodded.

"How are you planning to help him?"

"We want to clear his name."

"Cops tried to do that."

"We think maybe they missed something. We're trying to follow the trail of the stolen goods they found in his house."

Irby leaned back in his chair. "Way I heard it, he was managing a ring of street-kid thieves."

"No." Aristotle's voice was quiet but firm.

"If he was framed, who could walk away and leave that money on the table?"

"That's what we're trying to find out." Nathan's eyes roved over the maps. They were well organized, decorated by notes neatly handwritten in different colored markers.

Irby shook his head. "Doesn't make sense."

"I know." Nathan gazed at Irby again. "But we're trying to make sense of it."

"If there was anything to find out, don't you think the police would have found it already?"

"Not if there was something they didn't know to look for." Aristotle shifted on his seat.

"Why wouldn't they know?"

"Well, the police might not know certain facts about stolen goods for the same reason they didn't know about the two security guards that busted your arm." Nathan watched the boy for any kind of reaction.

Suspicion pulled Irby's face tighter. "Who have you been talking to?"

"Tommy Mertz."

Irby scowled. "Man, Tommy don't know nothing. Guy's a loser."

You gotta sweeten the deal for him, Nathan. Make him realize there's trouble available, and offer him a way to back out of it. Even if the police don't care that he was at the tunnel that night, his mom might.

Nathan decided that angle was uncomfortably close to blackmail, but he also suspected it would work.

"Tommy knows you were in the tunnel that night." Nathan held

Irby's gaze. "We could let your mom know what you were up to."

"Why would you do that?"

"Because we think the two security guards might have been involved with John's death, and we want information."

Irby grimaced. "Dude, that's even more reason not to tell my mom. She wouldn't want me to have anything to do with that."

"Yeah. She'd probably ground you. Maybe close up your command center here." Nathan gazed meaningfully around at the desk. "Look, I don't want to come across as mean or ugly or something—"

"Yeah, well you're flirting with it for sure."

"—I'm just looking for some answers. I need to know if you can help me."

Contemplating the situation, Irby stared at Nathan. "You ain't from around here."

"Not this neighborhood, but close by."

Irby looked around Nathan. "You got a laptop in there?"

"Netbook."

"Cool. Can I see it?" Irby smiled and stuck out his hand.

Nathan hesitated just a momentand then took the netbook out and handed it over.

Irby sat the netbook on the desk and powered it up. He rubbed his hands together enthusiastically. "This is awesome. I haven't gotten my hands on one of these yet." His gaze flicked across the screen as he opened the contents. "You got hacker files on here."

"Cracks. I got some cracks on there."

Irby looked at him and smiled bigger. "Only serious guys know the difference between a hacker and a cracker. You got any skillz, baby?"

"I do okay."

Turning back to the screen, Irby shrugged. "You must be raw, because this stuff you're working with is weak."

"I don't make a habit out of cracking code."

"Some of us do. It's a lot like the urbex thing. Slip in. Look around. Leave everything like it is. And get out. It's a trip, man."

"The sooner we know about the guys who broke your arm, the sooner we're out of here." Aristotle tapped a rhythm on the desk.

Sighing, Irby returned his attention to Nathan's netbook. The whole time he talked, his hands roved over the keyboard as he searched through Nathan's files and games.

"Those guys were dangerous. Really hardcore creeps. They did not bat an eye when they broke my arm."

"Why did they chase you out of the tunnel?"

Irby shrugged. "Don't know. Maybe John Montoya caught them."

No. John stood reflected in the monitor and looked thoughtful. *But if those guys were down there, they were there for a reason.*

Nathan thought about that. "What if they weren't down there because of stolen goods? Tommy said they were already running a gang of kids. Could they have been looking for something else?"

"Well, could have been dropping off a body." Irby remained focused on the netbook. "These two guys looked like the type that would do that." He turned to Nathan. "I'm just saying. But one thing's for certain, these guys were for reals, baby. They ordered me out, I hesitated and they whacked me with a nightclub hard enough to break my arm. They either ain't afraid of nothing, or they were that night."

Ask him if he can describe them.

Nathan did.

"Do you one better than that, home fry. I got pictures of them.

Before they discovered us, me and the rest of the Night Spiders was watching them." Irby reached for a thumb drive and slipped it into one of the USB ports on the netbook.

"What were they doing?" Nathan was growing frustrated. Every time they seemed on the verge of a breakthrough, it slipped away.

"That night, they were standing around."

"Waiting for someone?"

"Could have been. They found us. One of my guys got nervous and slipped in loose dirt where someone had been digging."

That caught Nathan's attention. "Digging? For what?"

"Don't know exactly, but the phone company was running new telecommunications line through there. Upgrades. Could have been related to that. We got John on tape talking to the guy that did the upgrades. Thompson? Thomlinson? Something like that." Irby sorted through the pictures on his thumb drive. Most of them showed dark buildings, tunnels, sewers, and guys and girls Nathan assumed were the Night Spiders.

Then the photos concentrated on two guys.

Nathan looked more closely.

32

Both guys were older, but not as old as Nathan's dad or uncle. He thought maybe they were in their thirties. One guy was baby-faced and wore a moustache and long sideburns. The other had red hair and hooded eyes that made him look mean. They wore matching security guard uniforms.

Some of the pictures showed the guys in the tunnel, but a couple of them—from farther away—showed them standing in front of Manny's. They looked even more dangerous in daylight.

"Do you know these guys?" Nathan glanced at John's reflection in Irby's monitor.

I've never seen them before, but guards from a lot of security firms eat at Manny's.

"I don't know these guys." Irby thought Nathan had been talking to him. "If I'd ever gotten their names, I'd have turned in complaints on them. Not using my name, of course, but I could've caused them grief."

"Can I have those pictures?"

Irby nodded and hit a few keystrokes. "They're yours." The thumb drive cycled, and the netbook's hard drive churned.

"Thanks. Do these guys still hang around?"

Leaning back in his chair, Irby put his hands on his head and thought for a minute. "After they broke my arm, I watched for them. Figured I'd catch them doing something wrong so I could report them, but I never did. After a few days, they stopped coming around."

"Before or after John Montoya was killed?"

Irby pointed at one of the pictures of the security guards in front of Manny's. "That time/date stamp is correct. I always make sure the cameras are up to date. That was taken two days after the police officer was killed, according to your news reports."

Nathan tried to control his impatience. "Do you have anything for the night John Montoya was killed?"

"Man, I was grounded. My mom found out about an abandoned building I scoped out the night before. We were seen by a security guard, and he identified me. Ended up seeing juvenile services that time. Got put on probation for trespassing, but that passed." Irby shrugged. "I'm just better at not getting caught these days." He grinned.

"Did you ever find out who these guys worked for?" Nathan was sure he anticipated John's question.

Irby turned his attention to the computer and magnified the photo of the men. "They work for a security service called Wright Guard." As they watched, the shoulder patch on the red-haired guy became legible. The name WRIGHT GUARD was plastered over a round Roman shield.

Aristotle cracked up.

Nathan smiled at that too.

"Yeah, I know. Bad name." Irby shrugged and smiled. "For a service kind of named after a deodorant, these guys really stink." He pulled up a website on his computer. "Wright Guard handles a lot of apartment complexes in rough neighborhoods."

I've heard of them. They're not exactly top of the heap when it comes to security services. John frowned in displeasure.

"But you don't know who these specific guys are?" Nathan studied the website. "There's no personnel listing?"

"They've got the big guys listed and profiled." Irby pulled up another page. "But these guys don't rate."

Nathan scanned the faces shown on the personnel page and reached the same conclusion. "And you say these guys haven't been back around?" If they would show up, he could follow them. That seemed like it would be right out of the junior detective handbook.

"Nope. Like I said, after a few days, these guys never showed up again."

"Coincidence?" Nathan didn't sound convinced.

It could happen, kid. But a patrolman in the field learns to check out coincidences all the same. They happen sometimes, but not often. John appeared thoughtful. *If they were the guys who shot me, there has to be some connection to the burglary ring case I was working.*

Irby snorted. "Looking at it now, I don't think it was a coincidence." He stared at the screen and shook his head. "You get lucky with those kinds of odds, you need to buy a lottery ticket." An alarm bell tinkled on the computer. He glanced at the time stamp in the lower corner of the computer screen. "Dinner time, guys. I gotta blaze or my mom will come looking for me. And she hates coming down all those stairs just because I won't check the time."

"Sure. Just one more thing. What about that Thompson or Thomlinson guy?"

"I asked John about him. But he died before he got back to me so I'm not sure."

Nathan put his chair away, but his mind kept churning. He nodded at the maps. "How many of these places have you been to?"

"Not enough. Chicago's full of interesting places that are basically abandoned. Buildings. Underground tunnels and sewers. Houses. You'd be really surprised what you can find. I'll take you boys some time if you want."

Aristotle shook his head. "No way, man. There's stuff down there in those sewers you can't get off your shoes."

Irby laughed. "Don't wear your good shoes. Get some at the Salvation Army. Boots would be best. Sometimes it gets deep."

Aristotle shuddered. "Gross, dude."

Nathan said, "You know, I may take you up on that."

"You should. It's a blast. Good times."

"Until your mom catches you," Aristotle said.

"Yeah. Until then." Irby's phone rang, and he answered it. "Hey, Mom. I'm on my way. Oh, really?" He looked at Nathan and Aristotle. "My new friends were really polite, huh?" He covered the mouthpiece with a hand. "Mom wants to know if you want to stay for dinner."

"Can she cook?" Aristotle asked.

"Oh yeah. The woman can cook." Irby uncovered the mouthpiece. "Oh, you heard that, did you, Mom? Yes, ma'am. No, ma'am. Yes, ma'am, I know it was disrespectful to refer to you like that. I'm sorry about that. No, ma'am. I won't do it again." He banged himself on the forehead. "Yes, ma'am, we're on our way now." He folded the phone and shoved it into his pocket.

At first Nathan was going to turn down Mrs. Johnson's dinner invitation, but everything smelled so good he decided to call home and ask for permission to stay. Uncle William answered and asked a lot of questions, but after he talked with Mrs. Johnson, everything was settled. Aristotle had no problem getting permission either.

Mrs. Johnson fussed over them at the dinner table, praising

their appetites when Nathan thought she should have been honestly shocked. They ate everything, lemon chicken, salad, homemade biscuits, twice-baked potatoes, and steamed vegetables. Then she brought out a huge key lime pie.

By the time he'd finished eating, Nathan was stuffed like he couldn't ever remember, and he didn't want to have to move. They sat in the living room and watched television for a little while and then broke out Irby's Xbox 360 and got down to the serious business of racking up the kills in Halo.

"Nathan."

He looked up at Mrs. Johnson. "Yes, ma'am."

"Maybe you should call your uncle and tell him you're going to be staying here tonight."

"I couldn't do that." Nathan pulled his phone out of his pocket and found it was after nine. He didn't know where the time had gone.

"It's dangerous to be out here late at night. I'd feel more comfortable with you staying than with you going home so late." Mrs. Johnson sounded firm. "Call your uncle, and I'll talk to him myself."

Nathan called home and handed over the phone. He checked all the reflective surfaces in the room but couldn't locate John Montoya anywhere. In fact, he couldn't remember when he'd last seen the police officer. But then again, there didn't seem to be any other lost souls in the area, so Nathan figured John was still holding up his end of their agreement.

Then he felt guilty for sitting there playing Halo with Irby and Aristotle when he could have been—doing what? He was stumped for the moment.

Mrs. Johnson came back a few minutes later to return his phone. "Everything's worked out. You can stay here tonight. Your uncle sounds like a nice man."

"Thanks." Nathan put his phone away.

"Don't mention it. I like to see Irby making friends with good boys instead of ones that like to traipse around where they ain't got no business being."

Irby grimaced.

"I know you didn't just make a face at me, young man."

Nathan couldn't believe Mrs. Johnson had seen Irby's expression. She was evidently good with reflective surfaces as well.

"No, Mom. It's this controller." Irby shook the device irritably. "It's sticky and keeps getting me killed."

"You keep getting killed because Nathan is better at that game than you are. I've been watching."

Nathan grinned at that, and Aristotle laughed out loud.

Irby's bedroom was small, so Mrs. Johnson let them make beds on the floor in the living room. Irby had a good selection of science fiction movies and zombie films, but they split the difference and settled on *Pitch Black* starring Vin Diesel. Nathan liked the movie, and the monsters were definitely creepy. It was bad, though, when they reminded him of the soul vulture.

As Irby and Aristotle settled into a discussion of movie monsters and Vin Diesel movies, Nathan got an idea.

"Hey, Irby. You mind if I borrow your computer?"

Puzzled, Irby looked at him. "Your computer's better than mine. Why would you want to use mine?"

"I need the Internet."

Aristotle grinned and sat up. "You got a girlfriend, Nathan? You been holding out on us?"

Nathan's face burned a little. "Ha ha. I need to email my cousin. Alyssa's got this class project where they're looking into cold cases. Murder investigations that have stalled out?"

"Dude, everybody knows what a cold case is." Irby waved a hand in circles. "Get on with it."

"I want to email her the pictures of the two security guys. Maybe she can identify them."

"How can she do that if you can't?"

"Her mom works in the district attorney's office, and Alyssa's actually working on this cold case as a class project. Maybe Aunt Jennifer can find out who these guys are."

Irby looked nervous. "Okay, but if I get the district attorney's office knocking on the door, I'm telling my mom you did it."

"We won't get caught this way." Nathan got Irby's laptop and quickly set up an email: whokilledofficerjohnmontoya@gmail.com.

"Kind of right out there with it, aren't you?" Irby asked.

"I wanted it to be something that would get instant attention."

"That would do it." Aristotle watched with interest.

After plugging in the thumb drive, Nathan composed a short email:

```
1. Who are these two guys?
2. Why were they in the maintenance tunnel
where Officer John Montoya was killed?
3. Did Officer Montoya catch them selling
stolen goods in the area?
```

Nathan hacked back into Alyssa's webpage concerning the cold case investigations. He brought up the email link and sent the email to everyone on the list. Then he pasted the pictures into the webpage of information on John Montoya.

He figured that it was also time to read the police report. He combed through a massive amount of information. They had interviewed everyone in the police department as well as anyone mentioned in John Montoya's notes. Nathan tried his best to find any clue he could about the security guards, but it seemed they weren't in the tunnels when John was on patrol. Instead, he found information on Thomlinson. Montoya had written his name down in his notes, and records showed a phone number listing for him. Nathan jotted it down. *In the morning, I should give him a call.*

The images of the two men stared back at him from the computer screen until he shut the computer down. He figured that the two men's faces would haunt his dreams, but they didn't. Kukulkan got there first.

33

"**N**athan."

Opening his eyes, Nathan was surprised to discover that he was on a sailboat in the middle of a huge body of water. All the sails were furled and stowed, and they sat at anchor. The waves rocked the boat, and he couldn't help but grin.

"It's been a long time since you've been on the water, hasn't it?" Kukulkan stood in the stern. He wore a red muscle tee, white slacks, and boaters. Wraparound sunglasses covered his eyes and his long black hair was lifted by the wind.

"Yeah." Nathan got up from the long seat where he'd been lying. "A few years." He inhaled the breeze. "I've missed it. I love sailing."

"I know." Kukulkan grinned. "I'm glad I got the chance to bring you."

"Me too."

Nathan joined Kukulkan in the stern. He spread his arms out and let the wind rush over him. It felt good.

"How's the skateboard working out?"

"The skateboard is fantastic. I think about you every time I ride. It's a drag that I can't show the trick to anyone, but I do have a rad board."

"It's important to keep some secrets to yourself."

"There's a lot of lost souls that seem to know my secrets."

"The spirits will all recognize you." Kukulkan reached into an ice chest and handed Nathan a chilled chocolate soda.

It felt chilly against his palm. He peeled the top and drank, relishing the rich flavor.

"Why do the lost souls know about me?"

"Because they have a tendency to wander the frequencies. Since you also now can move between the frequencies, they have an affinity for you."

"Mom says they'll try to use me if they can."

"They'll try." Kukulkan opened a chocolate soda for himself. "But they're going to teach you a lot too."

"What am I going to learn from dead people?"

"Some aspects of how to play the Game, for one. And for another, how to be a more complete person."

Despite how much he liked Kukulkan, or possibly because he did like the man so much, Nathan felt a little hurt. "You don't think I'm a complete person?"

Kukulkan grinned disarmingly. "You're young. You've still got a lot to learn. Of course, you're not complete. You should be grateful you're getting such a great opportunity."

"Okay." Nathan didn't necessarily agree with the assessment, but he didn't want to spoil the moment.

"You're investigating John Montoya's death."

Nathan nodded.

"Seems like you found a couple of suspects."

"Maybe." Nathan watched a gull glide through the blue sky. "I don't know if they had anything to do with it."

"What do you think?"

"I think it's too much of a coincidence for them not to have been involved in some way. What bugs me is that the police didn't find these guys. They should have."

"Sometimes people look for what they expect to find instead of what is there."

Nathan looked at Kukulkan. "Do you know who killed John Montoya?"

"No." Kukulkan smiled. "When you find out, I'm sure you'll tell me."

"Yeah. I suppose so."

"I do have a question though."

"What?"

"Why didn't you just ask Alyssa to help you instead of hacking into her webpage? She's already on the project, and she might have useful information."

Nathan shrugged. "I didn't want her involved in my investigation."

"Do you think that's the right way to go about this?"

"I thought I had to do this on my own."

"You involved Aristotle, Tommy, and Irby."

Feeling a little defensive and surprised at the turn in the conversation, Nathan broke eye contact. "I didn't have a choice."

"Agreed. If you were going to pursue this investigation, you had to involve them."

"Then what's the problem?"

"You're not using all your assets," Kukulkan said. "You have a lot of Game pieces to play, and you need to plan ahead to get them on the board."

"If Alyssa gets involved, if she figures out that I know all this stuff, she's going to try to take over."

"You don't know that."

"I sort of do. I think I know her better than you do."

Kukulkan was silent for a moment. "All right, Nathan. I see your mind is set in this regard, and I respect that."

"Thank you."

"But I also think you may be passing up on a great opportunity, and you may be risking more than you think."

"I'm doing okay so far."

"You are. You're learning the Game, and that's what I asked." Kukulkan smiled. "Enough talk about that. You've got your agenda in place."

Nathan didn't know about an agenda, but he had already decided he was going to have to go back to the tunnel and maybe sort through the frequencies again.

"We've got this beautiful boat and a great day ahead of us," Kukulkan said. "So do you want to sail or do you want to dive?"

Nathan looked into the deep water. "Is it safe?"

"As safe below as it is above."

"You know, that's not really a comforting answer."

Kukulkan grinned. "Your life has changed. You're going to be exposed to more danger, but you have powers that you'll be growing into. There is a balance, Nathan, between power and danger. You've just got to find it."

"And if I don't?"

"Let's just say that wouldn't be good."

"Great." Nathan looked at the water again. "How about we dive for a while and then go sailing?"

"All right."

Nathan looked around. "Do you have scuba gear?"

"Do you need wings to fly?" Kukulkan dove cleanly off the stern, changing into a swimsuit on the way, and hit the water without leaving a ripple.

Excited and scared at the same time, Nathan followed. He

immediately turned back toward the surface but still was amazed at how clear the water was. Fish swam by in schools.

"It's all right, Nathan." Kukulkan floated only a short distance away. "Haven't you ever dreamed of breathing underwater?"

Nathan stopped a few feet short of the surface. He had dreamed of swimming underwater without scuba gear. Then he realized that Kukulkan was talking underwater.

He nodded.

"Then breathe," Kukulkan said.

Scared at first, Nathan opened his mouth and was surprised that the water didn't rush in. Then he took a breath, sipping air instead of water. "Wow, I can breathe!"

Kukulkan pointed at Nathan's clothes. "Maybe you want to change into something more suitable."

Nathan thought about his swimsuit and was immediately wearing it. "Cool."

"Have you ever dived to a sunken city?"

"No. I've never even seen one outside of television and fish aquariums."

"Then come with me." Kukulkan dove deeper.

Nathan followed. Only a short while longer, he saw the pink stone the buildings lying scattered across the bottom of the sea. When Kukulkan stopped on top of a high tower, Nathan joined him.

"What is this place?"

Kukulkan shook his head. "I don't know."

"I thought you knew everything."

"No."

"But Mom said you created the world."

"I did."

Nathan couldn't believe how matter-of-factly Kukulkan said that.

"I got everything started, Nathan, but I don't try to control everything. I enjoy surprises, and sometimes things turn out much differently than I thought they would."

"Like what?"

"You."

Nathan was surprised.

"I'd planned you since before your birth, Nathan. And I knew that we would meet on your thirteenth birthday. I just figured you would be different."

"In what way?"

"I'd hoped you'd be more open to things, and to other people. I'd hoped that you'd be more driven."

Nathan felt a little hurt. "You make me sound like a bad person."

Kukulkan laughed and clapped Nathan on the shoulder. "Not at all. I think you're a good person. You've just got a lot to learn about the Game."

"This isn't about the Game."

A serious expression chased away Kukulkan's laughter. "Everything is about the Game, Nathan. Never lose sight of that."

Nathan didn't know what to say.

"Now, why don't we explore this sunken city?"

Eager to change subjects and get back to the cool stuff they could do together, Nathan nodded. "Haven't you been here before?"

"I have. But I haven't ever really explored this place. It was one of the things I was saving to do with you."

"Cool. So where do we go?"

"Why don't you choose, and I'll follow."

After a quick survey of the city, Nathan leaped off the tower and swam down to street level. He glided effortlessly through the water, like a fish, and it was one of the coolest things he'd ever done.

"**D**ude, how long have you been having these dreams about Sea-Monkeys?"

Nathan blinked his eyes and realized he was lying on his back in the middle of Mrs. Johnson's living room, no longer in the sunken city. He looked up at Aristotle, who stared down at him in amusement.

"Sea-Monkeys?" Nathan levered himself up on an elbow and looked around.

Mrs. Johnson was in the kitchen working on what smelled like pancakes and sausage. Irby tinkered with his laptop.

"Must have been Sea-Monkeys," Aristotle said. "You kept mumbling about exploring underwater cities."

"Sounds like a definite Sea-Monkey hang-up to me." Irby clicked the keyboard rapidly.

"Y'all leave him be," Mrs. Johnson called. "He was probably dreaming about hanging out with you two sea monkeys."

"Ouch," Aristotle commented.

Nathan laughed, but he felt a little uneasy about talking in his sleep. Feeling tired, he sat up.

"Or he could have been dreaming about this swirly." Irby held up his laptop and showed a picture of Nathan fresh after his dunking at school on his birthday.

"That's an awesome swirly." Aristotle hooted with laughter.

"Great." Nathan threw a pillow at Aristotle. "You guys go ahead and yuck it up. That happened on my birthday."

Irby tried to hold a sympathetic expression but couldn't do it. He cracked up, laughing even harder, and Aristotle joined in.

"Dude, you have got some seriously messed up birthdays."

Nathan decided not to mention the incident with Mr. Chuckles. That would have been too much to bear. "Thanks. Really, thanks."

Irby leaned closer to the computer screen. "You also got mail from your cousin."

Nathan scrambled to his feet and went to see.

34

A lyssa Richards to whokilledofficerjohnmontoya

You pose interesting questions · · · and
you chose an intriguing way to ask them· If
you are brave enough to reveal yourself,
let's meet and share resources·

"Sounds a little scary." Aristotle looked over at Nathan.

"Was that the response you were hoping for?" Irby said.

Nathan sat with crossed legs and stared at the screen. "Not even close. I figured Alyssa would at least be curious enough to send the pictures over to her mom. And I'm definitely not meeting up with her. That would be dangerous in the extreme."

Aristotle flopped on his back with his arms behind his head. "Maybe the direct approach would have worked better."

That echoed Kukulkan's sentiments too closely for comfort.

"You guys just don't understand Alyssa." Nathan took a breath. "Everything she does, she does right. She's Miss Perfect. She likes to run things and doesn't take orders. She lives for the glory."

"If you really want to help John's family," Aristotle said, "she sounds like someone you need on your side."

Feeling guilty, Nathan quickly searched the room for John and didn't see him. *That doesn't mean he doesn't know.*

"It's okay." Nathan took a deep breath and tackled the problem from a new angle. "There's someone else we can send the pictures to."

"Who?" Irby leaned forward, concerned as Nathan started composing a new email.

"Giavonna Tate. She's the reporter who covered John's murder. If we send her the pictures, maybe she can find out who these guys are."

"Are you sure that's the right move?"

Nathan shook his head in frustration. "What choice do I have?" He attached the photographs, then hovered the cursor over the SEND button. He hesitated.

"Maybe you could try to talk to Alyssa," Aristotle suggested.

"No. I can't explain to her what I'm doing, and I don't think she'd be interested in listening." Nathan hit SEND and tasted acid at the back of his mouth.

☐—☐—☐

So what are you going to do now?" Aristotle walked at Nathan's side as they headed back toward the Loop.

"Catch the el back home. Then wait and see what happens." Nathan shrugged. "I don't know what else to do."

"What's John say?"

Nathan looked up at the store windows beside them, but there was no sign of John Montoya.

"John doesn't seem to be around right now." Nathan wondered if the police officer was mad at him. But if that was the case, wouldn't he let the lost souls run over him? Nathan wished his mom was around. Maybe she could have made sense of some of this.

"Is that normal?"

Nathan sighed. "Dude, I think I gave up normal on my thirteenth birthday."

"Bummer." Aristotle was silent for a moment. "It's rough when you lose people, but you get through it. I remember my mom. She died in an apartment fire when I was five. She handed me to firemen right before the roof collapsed on her."

Immediately, Nathan felt like an idiot, totally self-absorbed. "That's terrible."

Aristotle nodded. "I know. I miss her every day. Irby and Mrs. Johnson—they lost Irby's dad a few years ago to a traffic accident. He worked on street construction." He shrugged. "No matter how much you want things to stay the same, they change. You just gotta roll with it." He bumped shoulders against Nathan. "You'll figure this out, dude. John will be there. So will me and Irby. You need anything, all you gotta do is call."

"Okay. Thanks."

"Stay in touch," Aristotle said. "Lemme know how it goes."

Nathan nodded and walked on. As he passed the pawn shop window, he checked for lost souls. John still wasn't around.

After getting off the el, Nathan skateboarded toward home. He tried to stop worrying about what he'd done and hadn't done. It bothered him that John Montoya hadn't bothered to put in an appearance. Nathan couldn't help wonder if something had gone wrong—if he'd made a decision so bad that John couldn't talk to him again.

He gave himself a little pep talk. "Take it easy. No one's going to leave you alone for long. That's not how these guys work."

As he rounded the corner to go down the alley to his house, it seemed like the wall of the garage next to him fell over on top of him. Except that walls didn't come equipped with arms and legs that punched and kicked.

Nathan turned turtle and pulled his head in. He caught two more punches to the back of his head before he levered an arm against his attacker's throat and managed to roll free. As he got to his feet, he realized the "wall" was Arda.

"What are you up to, Nathan?" Arda's face was beet-red with anger. "Thought after Friday you'd leave things alone for a while. Thought you'd get the message."

"You? Give me a message? You can't even write, you Neanderthal."

Arda swung at him, and Nathan barely got out of the way. The wind of the near miss whipped by his ear. He ducked down and came up throwing a punch that hit Arda in the stomach. Arda was too wound up to even feel the blow.

Using his size to his advantage, Arda stepped forward and swung again. This time he caught Nathan in the side of the face and sent him to the ground. Dazed, Nathan rolled over and tried to get to his hands and knees. Arda kicked him in the side hard enough to knock the air out of him.

"Get up." Arda shook his fist. "I've been waiting all morning for you to come home."

"I didn't know you had the attention span to stay with something so long." Nathan struggled to get up.

Arda cursed. "Why have you been asking questions about my dad?" He kicked at Nathan again.

This time Nathan caught Arda's foot, twisted, and managed to pull his opponent to one side because he couldn't shove him away. Arda yelped and fell, and Nathan managed to scramble out of reach.

"Your dad?" Nathan glanced around and saw that Chas and Barkley were there as well. "I don't know anything about your dad."

Arda jumped up. He bunched his fists. "Then why have you been asking people about how he died?"

Suddenly the last names clicked in Nathan's head.

John Montoya. Arda Montoya. And Arda's dad had died a couple years ago. Nathan hadn't bothered finding out the particulars at the time, and he hadn't known Arda's dad was a police officer. Nathan had been too caught up in his own world, and he and Arda weren't friends. He couldn't believe he hadn't made the connection when he started looking into the case.

"My dad is none of your business!" Arda roared with rage, but Nathan heard the pain in there too. He felt bad for Arda, and he felt bad for John too.

But not bad enough to stand there and get beaten up. He stepped to the side as Arda came at him again. Then Chas put his hands in the middle of Nathan's back and shoved hard. Nathan stumbled and went forward. Arda caught him in the face with his fist.

Agony shot through Nathan and spots swam before his eyes. Warm tears trickled down his cheeks and blurred his vision. He tried to get his bearings, but Arda hit him again, this time catching him behind the ear.

Staggering, Nathan managed to stay on his feet. Then Arda grabbed him behind his head, kneed him in the stomach, and brought his face down hard against his leg. Luckily Nathan's face hit Arda's thigh instead of his knee, but the impact still jarred his brain enough that he almost disconnected.

"Stay outta my life! If you don't, I'm going to put you in the hospital!" Arda kicked him again, but this time he only caught Nathan in the hip.

His vision partially clear, Nathan spotted his skateboard only a few feet away. He dodged over and grabbed it, then used it to block Arda's next kick. Flipping the skateboard, Nathan rammed it into Arda's stomach. When the bigger boy bent over, Nathan hit him with his shoulder and knocked him back into Chas.

As Chas and Arda went down, Nathan sprinted past them, threw the board out in front of him, and clambered aboard. He zipped to the other end of the alley before they could overtake him.

Arda leaped the low picket fence surrounding Nathan's yard and pounded after him. Nathan had his key in the door lock before Arda caught him. He slipped inside and locked the door, hoping that Arda wouldn't try to break in after him.

I'm sorry.

Nathan looked up, then looked at the nearest window for a reflection. John Montoya stood in front of him looking unhappy.

"You might have told me Arda was your son." Nathan pressed back against the door as Arda kicked or hit it in frustration.

I thought you knew.

"If I'd known, I wouldn't have been out asking questions about you. Arda is going to kill me."

No, he won't. He's a good kid.

"A good kid? Did you see the way he just jumped me?" Nathan blew out an angry breath and tasted blood.

John appeared shaken. *He's going through a rough time.*

Nathan dabbed at the blood in the corner of his mouth. "Well, this hasn't been easy on me either. If you ask me, I think we just hit a deal breaker."

What do you mean?

"I mean I'm done helping you. I've looked everywhere I can think of, and I don't know who killed you. And I mean that I'm not going to get beaten up by your son for trying to help you."

Nathan, you've made some headway. That's something homicide investigators haven't done. You can't quit now. We can still do this.

"I can quit. I am." Nathan peered out the window and saw that Arda had joined Chas and Barkley out on the street. He turned back to John Montoya. "And if you want to turn the lost souls back on me, go ahead. It can't be any worse than this."

You're scared. You're mad. Believe me, I understand completely.

"I don't want to be understood." Nathan's face and sides ached. "I just want to be left alone. Do you understand that?"

Sure, kid. Sure, I do. Without another word, John faded from the window.

Nathan sat hunched against the door for a while, waiting for his breathing to return to normal and his ribs to stop aching quite so much. Then he reached down for his skateboard, turned it into the bracelet, and headed up the stairs to his room.

Everything was impossible. Too many people were asking too many things of him. He couldn't do it all. He wished someone would understand that.

Later, showered and changed, Nathan choked down two ibuprofen tablets and lay on his bed to watch Cartoon Network. He remembered when he'd wanted to have cool powers like Ben 10 and Danny Phantom. Now he knew that was stupid. On television, cartoon heroes worked through their problems easily, usually within twenty-two minutes and commercials. They could even save the world in that time.

Or they got shot in tunnels for no apparent reason. That thought trickled into Nathan's mind, and he immediately felt guilty about the way he'd ended things with John Montoya. The police officer had been a hero to a lot of kids in that neighborhood. The fact that no lost souls had shown up in spite of his decision to quit looking for John's killer made Nathan feel even more guilty. John was keeping his side of the bargain anyway.

Nathan knew that he wasn't making a good decision, but all he had to do was move to remember why he was quitting. Pain shot through him, and his lip was huge. He could only hope it wasn't this big in the morning. It felt like he could pull it over his head. He looked over at the board game but knew already what he'd see. Kukulkan had two pieces in the center of the board. He's winning.

Alyssa came up the steps. He recognized the rapid staccato of her footsteps when she was angry.

Nathan pulled his pillow over his head and hoped she would just keep going. Of course she didn't.

35

lyssa opened the door without knocking and barged in. Nathan felt his cousin's glare through the protective padding of the pillow.

"You hacked my cold case website."

Nathan didn't move. His head throbbed even more. "Don't know what you're talking about. Go away."

"You're the only one outside of my group who knew I was working on cold cases for class credit."

"Someone in your group probably told someone else. Go away."

"You sent that message about those two security guards."

"Again, I don't know what you're talking about. Go away."

"How did you find out about those guards? Why did you send those pictures to me? Did they really have anything to do with John Montoya's death?"

For a moment Nathan was tempted to tell the truth. But telling part of the truth would lead to telling all of the truth, and he didn't feel like trying to get Alyssa to believe he was talking to lost souls. "Pay attention this time. I don't know what you're talking about. I didn't. I have no idea. Go. Away."

Alyssa yanked the pillow from Nathan's head and glared down at him. Anger turned into concern when she saw his face. "What happened to you?"

"I tried to catch a bus with my face. What does it look like?"

"Like someone else finds you as obnoxious as I do."

"You really should see the bus."

"Do you need to go to the hospital?"

"No."

"You're bleeding on your pillow."

"I think I'm almost done."

Alyssa almost looked sorry for him, and the beating was almost worth it for distracting her anger and questions. "Do you want me to tell Dad? Or your dad?"

"Do you really want to spend the evening in the ER? Because if your dad gets involved, that's what's going to happen. He may call in the police. Throw in Mr. Chuckles, and we could have a party."

Alyssa thought about that and shook her head. "Not really. I've got homework to do."

"Then go away." Nathan put the pillow back over his face.

"I'm going to grant you a reprieve right now, Nathan. But only because you're bleeding."

"Yay me."

"But if I find out you hacked my webpage and sent those pictures and got my study group upset, I'm going to haunt you."

Take a number, he thought. Nathan tried to sink into sleep.

N*athan?*

"Mom?" Nathan took the pillow from his face and looked up in surprise. When he didn't see anything, he moved so he could see his room reflected in the window.

His mom stood beside his bed. She smiled tentatively. *How are you feeling?*

"Like I got hit by a truck." Nathan swung his legs out of bed and sat up. It was weird having his mom here in his room. Behind her, the window showed the night. "I didn't expect to see you."

I've been doing my own investigations, as promised. She came to stand beside him, and he could see her run her fingers along his face, though he couldn't feel it. Almost immediately, he felt better. *I would have come sooner, but what I'm doing is a lot of work.*

"What have you found out?"

Nothing that makes any sense, yet. But I've still got some leads I can follow. A look of sadness he hadn't seen before was on her face.

"You know, I'm getting really tired of all the mysteries and secrecy." Nathan pushed her hands away. "The only one who seems to be telling me everything is Kukulkan. He takes me cool places, and we have a good time."

Yes, well, that's part of what he does. And for the moment, that's the part he's sharing with you.

"What are you talking about?"

She shook her head. *That's his business to handle with you. I just wanted to make sure you were all right.*

"I'm fine." Nathan tried to sound tough, but it still felt good to know that she cared enough to check on him.

I hear that you've decided to stop helping John.

"I can't help him. I've tried. And Arda sure doesn't want me to help. And look at me: really not working out for me, if you couldn't tell."

She walked away from him. *Look at all these half-finished models. The games you've started and haven't finished. The books and the comics you set aside without getting to the end.* She turned to face him. *You've learned to quit, Nathan. You've learned to just stop yourself, or to only halfway try at something. And you've learned to halfway care about yourself and everyone else.*

"Gee, I hope you didn't come here tonight just to give me this sterling pep talk."

No. I did want to make sure you were all right. But I also wanted to ask you not to give up on helping John.

"I don't know what I'm doing."

Then learn, Nathan. His mom sounded angry then, but kind of sad at the same time. *You've got a good mind. You've got a good heart. You just have to learn to risk them. You've been given this incredible gift and you need to figure out how best to use it. Instead you're just going halfway with it and giving up far too easily.*

The anger and sadness in his mom's voice surprised Nathan, but he felt a little angry and sad himself. He kept his mouth shut.

You need to apply yourself. His mom's eyes flashed as she regarded him.

"I've tried."

I know, but you have to keep trying.

"Who says?"

I do. She pointed at the game board. *Your playing is sloppy. You're not focused and you're not committed.*

Nathan studied the board. Kukulkan had gotten three of his five pieces into the center circle. Nathan only had two in the center, and two pieces were not even on the board yet. The Game was almost over, and he still didn't know what he was doing.

"I don't understand the Game." Nathan shook his head. "I'm not even moving the pieces."

Your actions are moving the pieces, Nathan. The Game is all about choices. You've made some good ones, but you've made some bad ones too.

"How can you tell?"

Because you're behind.

Nathan tried not to think too hard, because thinking too hard made his head hurt worse. "This is making me crazy. I have to figure out what I'm doing."

His mom came and stood over him. *For now, you need to get some sleep. I can help take away the pain so you can rest. But tomorrow you've got to keep thinking. You're close to helping John solve his problem.*

Reluctantly, Nathan lay back in the bed. He closed his eyes and thought he could nearly feel his mother's fingers stroking his forehead as she hummed. Then he slept.

☐—☐—☐

"Yo, dude, have you heard the news?"

Nathan took his books out of his locker, slammed it shut and locked it. Mitch Colfax, one of his fellow online gamers, stood behind him.

Mitch was cool and good looking, and he masked his geekiness well. Girls chased after him, and he remained aloof, which made him even more desirable to them.

"What news?" As Nathan looked around, he noticed that a lot of the students were huddled up in groups.

"About Arda Montoya's dad, man."

Nausea swirled in Nathan's stomach. He shook his head. He'd gotten up that morning, without ghosts, and had gotten ready in record time. Then he'd ridden Alyssa's vapor trail to school and actually arrived before the second bell.

"No."

"Somebody emailed a television reporter a picture of these two guys who might have killed Arda's dad. The reporter did a recap of the case on the news last night, reminding people that the case was never solved, and asking people to come forward."

Nathan immediately thought of Tommy, Irby, and Aristotle, but he didn't think any of them would come forward. Aristotle hadn't witnessed any of it, and Tommy and Irby had their own reasons to stay away.

At that moment, Arda came down the hallway with his entourage behind him. In fact, the entourage was even bigger this morning.

"Did you do this?" Arda roared. "You sent those pictures to the television reporter, didn't you? You were the only one poking around in this."

Nathan tried to back away, but the crowd wrapped around him too quickly. His face was still puffy from the fight the day before. Getting another beating was the last thing he wanted.

Arda didn't wait for an answer before he started swinging. He waded in and flailed at Nathan. Nathan ducked and dodged, managing to keep away from the flying fists.

Teachers quickly interrupted the fight and pulled Arda away. Nathan couldn't help feeling bad for him.

After a quick trip to the school nurse to check on the bruises he'd gotten the previous day, Nathan sat in the principal's outer office. He flipped through the Green Lantern graphic novel he'd brought with him, relishing again how Geoff Johns had put Hal Jordan back together with the power ring.

Hal Jordan had been turned into a villain, gotten killed, and served as the Spectre—one of the scariest jobs in comicdom—and still had returned as an iconic hero. Nathan loved the story, but he knew things like that didn't happen in real life.

At least Hal Jordan got instructions with his power ring.

Nathan had thought about slipping off into one of the other frequencies. But he wasn't ready to go there then and have to come back here and deal with Principal Masterson. That would have been a huge letdown and an even huger pain.

He turned a few more pages and watched the Green Lantern in action. Hal Jordan hadn't given up. He'd had a great destiny ahead of him, and he hadn't ever completely stepped away from it.

Was that all it took to be a hero? Just perseverance?

Or did you need a power ring?

"Mr. Richards." Principal Masterson summoned Nathan into her office with a crooked finger. She looked like she was ready to bite his head off.

Sighing, Nathan put his book into his backpack and headed for the execution.

36

Finally away from Principal Masterson and school, Nathan remembered that he had one more lead he hadn't followed up on. He pulled out his netbook and looked up Thomlinson's phone number, hesitantly dialing it into his phone.

The line rang twice before Nathan started thinking about what in the world he'd say if anyone picked up. Then he heard, "Hello?"

"Hey. Hi. I'm uh—a student, Nate. I'm hoping to talk to Marcus Thomlinson."

"Speaking. What do you want?"

"I'm in a class investigating—uhh—cold case files. I'm working on the case of Officer John Montoya. Our assignment is to follow up with all of the witnesses. It said in the file that you knew John?"

"For school, huh? And they're letting you investigate real case files?"

"It's an advanced class—to teach us about investigation techniques, question posing, and uhh—it's also supposed to teach us about community involvement."

"Well, the police already talked to me, kid, and that's all I have to say. I don't like people asking me questions. I find it annoying, and I get rid of annoying people."

Nathan felt a shiver go down his spine.

Thomlinson stopped talking for a long moment, then rushed on. "Look, kid. I just worked in the tunnels. I didn't witness any crime. I'd appreciate it if you wrote it that way exactly in your school report." Nathan heard a click, and Thomlinson was no longer on the line.

Nathan felt relieved that he wasn't on the phone anymore. He didn't like prolonging the amount of time he had to lie. He pulled out his PSP and thought about the little-to-no information he had received from his phone call with Thomlinson.

"I knew I'd find you here. You always come here when you don't want to go home."

Surprised to hear a human voice speaking to him instead of a lost soul, Nathan looked up from his PSP and saw Alyssa standing in front of him. He sat at a table in the café that was part of the comic book shop not far from school.

"What are you doing here?"

Alyssa arched a brow at him. "Maybe you could ask me to sit, and I could buy you a late lunch. You haven't eaten, have you?"

"No." As sore as his mouth and teeth were, Nathan didn't know if he could eat.

Impatiently, Alyssa nodded at the chair, on the other side of Nathan's table. He'd deliberately sat near the cardboard cutouts of heroes and away from the windows. There were no reflective surfaces around him, and so far the PSP hadn't betrayed him by allowing any lost souls to appear.

Nathan pulled his backpack off the chair and Alyssa sat. She handed him a root beer. "I thought maybe you'd be hungry and could use some company."

Warily, Nathan took the soft drink, unscrewed the top, and took a drink. "Thanks."

Alyssa stared at him and shook her head. "What were you thinking, Nathan?"

"Hey, I admit nothing."

Alyssa rolled her eyes. "You don't have to. Arda and his goons spread the story all over school how you were downtown asking questions about John Montoya."

"No way." That surprised Nathan.

"Way. Not everybody at school lives the way you do, Nathan. Kids come here from all kinds of families, and some of them connect to the kind of people who were answering your questions. Something like this is going to attract a lot of attention. That's why Arda was so upset. He's tried to get past his father's death, and now you've started up the pain all over again." Alyssa looked at him. "Why'd you do it?"

His head was throbbing. Nathan leaned back in his chair and sipped more root beer. "Would you believe John Montoya's ghost has been telling me to do it?"

Alyssa crossed her arms and gave him a let's-be-serious look that could freeze a high school senior in his tracks.

"Okay," Nathan said, "after that, I got nothing." He drank the root beer.

"That's it?" Alyssa was incredulous. "That's your story?"

"Yes."

"You're deranged."

Nathan nodded. "Okay. We can go with that one if it makes you happy."

"You've got to admit, it sounds pretty insane. I mean, you and Arda have been at each other's throats nonstop for the past two years."

"I know. Why would I help him?"

"You know, most of the kids at school think you're stirring things up just to stick it to Arda."

It made Nathan feel sick to think people believed he'd go that far. "That wasn't it at all."

"I assumed that was too low even for you, but that's the general consensus."

Nathan took a deep breath and let it out. "I didn't even know Arda was involved until yesterday. What I did, I did to help."

Alyssa didn't answer for a while. "Look, I know you admit to nothing, but those two security guards whose pictures you didn't email to me? I checked into them. Harry Rollins and Christopher Dillon left the Wright Guard Security Company shortly after John Montoya was killed and formed Sleep Easy Security. A couple of months later, they were both killed while on their jobs. The weird thing was, the circumstances of their deaths was pretty ambiguous—like a supercharged version of wrong place, wrong time—but no one was ever charged with any wrongdoing. I know you suspected them of being involved in John Montoya's death, but if they were, it's sort of a dead end. And, we'll never know if he was working with them or against them."

"He's not the kind of guy who would have worked with them."

"Nathan, people will do anything if they're pressed hard enough." Alyssa tapped her fingers on the table. "The motive in this case that puzzles me the most is why you would get involved in this in the first place. And the whole 'I talk to dead people' won't fly."

Nathan thought about everything he'd learned. "If he wasn't killed for either being involved in the burglary ring or interfering in it, then it has to be about something else. Maybe something in the tunnel itself."

"Do you have anything to base that on?"

He shrugged. "Just that the tunnel seems to connect everything that was going on during that time. And hey—you have to start a hypothesis somewhere."

"Have you figured out why Officer Montoya was in the tunnel that night?"

"No."

"It would help if we knew."

"I know. But he told me he doesn't have a clue."

Alyssa looked at him with an expression of concern. "Who told you? Officer Montoya?"

Nathan didn't answer.

"You're talking real weird, Nathan. Are you sure you don't need to go to the doctor?"

"Yeah. I'm sure. But I think I need to get another look at that tunnel."

"Another look? You've already been in there?" Alyssa stared at him in wide-eyed astonishment.

"Yeah."

"How did you get in? It's roped off and under the supervision of the construction crew and the university archeological team."

"I haff my vays," Nathan said in a Hollywood vampire voice and waggled his eyebrows; even that hurt. "I thought you said something about buying me lunch."

"I buy you lunch, I go with you. And I'll get us into the dig site."

Nathan wondered what the trick was. Alyssa didn't make statements she couldn't back up.

"I can get in by myself."

Alyssa arched an eyebrow. "Can you?"

Actually, Nathan was wondering if his dad had gotten the permit that would allow him on site. "Why do you want to go with me?"

"Because, for whatever reason, events around this case seem to be centering on you at the moment. I want to know how and why.

If I figure it out, it could be big bonus points on my project."

Hoping he didn't regret his decision, Nathan nodded. "All right."

◻━◻━◻

There was a new crowd milling around in the street in front of Manny's. He was surprised by how everyone seemed to voluntarily get out of Alyssa's way. Maybe she exuded charm as a by-product of simply breathing. Nathan found it intensely irritating.

When she got to the front of the line, Alyssa stepped up to one of the construction guys guarding the security line and handed him a business card. "I'd like to speak to Professor Richards, please."

"Sure, miss." The construction worker took the card and looked at Nathan. "You're the professor's kid, right?"

Nathan nodded. "Yeah."

"Didn't figure you'd be back." Without another word, the worker turned and walked back to the dig.

"Wait." Nathan was irritated. "That's cheating. You can't just ask my dad for permission."

Alyssa raised an innocent eyebrow. "Why not? It's the way most of us get things done."

"You knew you could get us in."

"Of course. I don't gamble. And it's only us if he doesn't make you stay outside."

A few minutes later, dressed in a hard hat and coveralls, Professor Peter Richards appeared. He looked pleased to see Alyssa.

"Alyssa, you took me up on my invitation."

"I did."

Invitation?

His dad's gaze moved to him, and surprise caused his smile to slip. "And Nathan? You came back too? This is a surprise."

Alyssa jumped into the conversation. "I figured I could get Nathan to take pictures for the article I'm writing for the school paper about the artifacts your team is preserving."

"Okay. Well, come this way." Professor Richards handed them each a hard hat and waved at them to follow him to the pit.

Nathan fell into step beside Alyssa. "You stink."

"See this look?" She pointed at her face. "Yeah, this is the one. This is smug. This is beating Nathan at his own game. Cool, isn't it?"

37

"Frankly, I was surprised your school paper would be interested in this, Alyssa." Professor Richards led the way down the tunnel.

Lights hung from the ceiling, illuminating practically every corner. The area was so barren Nathan felt like he was walking on the surface of the moon. Nearly all of the debris he'd seen on Friday had been removed. Archeologists worked carefully among the exposed ruins, photographing and removing pieces as they found them.

"Blame it on Indiana Jones and Lara Croft," Alyssa said. "A lot of the students think archeology is cool."

"It is cool." Nathan's dad sounded excited and happy, the way he always did when he was talking about museum pieces or dig finds. "I love this stuff." He turned to look at Nathan. "I really didn't expect you to come back."

Nathan shrugged. He didn't know what to say. If he showed too much interest in his dad's work, then he heard more about it at home. Nathan inadvertently learned all sorts of things about history, but nothing at all about his dad.

"I think he's getting some extra credit for helping me," Alyssa said.

"That's good. The way William is going on about Nathan's grades, Nathan can use extra credit."

His dad stopped at a table where various artifacts were being cleaned and recorded. "These aren't staggering finds—what we're digging up won't change anybody's idea of this particular historical period, but they will give us a little more information about the Native Americans in this area during the Beaver Wars."

"What are the Beaver Wars?" Alyssa peered more closely at the pottery and tools that had been collected.

"It was a war over the fur trade," Nathan said. "The local tribes joined with either the French or the Dutch to try to seize control of the market."

His dad looked at him in surprise. So did Alyssa.

"Well," his dad said, "I have to admit that I'm surprised you knew that. It's not one of the subjects most schools cover very well."

Nathan shrugged again. "I probably heard you mention it."

His dad continued staring at him for a moment. "Perhaps." Nathan could practically see the wheels turning in his dad's head as he tried to decide what this meant.

Nathan felt himself getting angry. *I do listen to what you have to say, Dad. You just don't listen to me.* He used his phone to take a few pictures of the artifacts and then moved away from his dad and Alyssa. If there was something here, he needed to make his own opportunity to find it.

As he walked slowly through the tunnel, trying hard to be inconspicuous, he considered what tools he had to work with. *John's not here; Thomlinson didn't seem to have any insight into what might make the tunnel interesting; the urbex kids were here for a whole different reason.* One thing everyone's story had in common, however, was that it had looked like someone was digging around in the tunnel during that time.

The more he thought about that, the more he liked it as a starting point for his hypothesis that the tunnel was the link. *Maybe someone found a buried treasure.* That would be cool. He knew just how to look around, too—the same way he'd seen John Montoya's body in the tunnel. And where the body had landed was a good place to start.

He walked toward the small spur where Kukulkan had shown him John's body and looked around. This area hadn't been cleaned yet by the archeology students, and Nathan guessed it had probably been undisturbed for the past year or more. He studied the tunnel and thought about it in terms of a video game; if he was in this tunnel and was trying to find a key or a hidden exit, what kind of clues would he see?

Brick walls and floor, a single bulb back at the intersection with the main passage, dust, chips of brick, a small pile of dirt . . . *why would there be a pile of dirt in the tunnel?* Nathan backed up to the entrance to the spur and ran his hands along the wall. His palms quickly turned black, but he actually found something for his trouble—there were a couple of loose bricks at one place in the wall.

After a quick check to see if anyone was paying attention to him, Nathan pried out one brick, set it on the floor, and took a step back. He took a deep breath and listened for the frequencies, then carefully began to move away from his home frequency, one frequency at a time, keeping his eyes on the hole where the brick used to be.

The tunnel faded away, then he saw a small mass, about the size of an Xbox controller, just where he was looking. Made of something dull yellow that had an appealing luster, the object's surface was rough and oddly shaped.

Nathan reached out and touched it. The mass felt cool and dense. He tried to pull it out of the air but couldn't. *I think it might be gold—and it's still stuck there in the tunnel.*

Nathan listened for his home frequency and returned.

Sure that he was on to something, Nathan began pulling the bricks out more quickly and stacking them near his feet on the ground. Some dirt spilled out as he was working, and it was clear even to his unpracticed eye that someone had been digging around behind the bricks. He began brushing dirt out of the hole with his hands, which of course was when someone finally noticed him.

"Hey, kid! What do you think you're doing back there?"

Having had lots of practice, Nathan ignored the voice of authority and continued brushing the loose dirt out of the hole, wondering desperately how deep the gold might still be buried.

"Stop! You're destroying the integrity of the dig site!"

Nathan pulled out one last handful of dirt, then stepped away from the wall and held up his hands. "Chill, dude. I was just messing around back here when I found a couple of loose bricks, and I just wanted to know what was behind them." He could hear the dirt still sifting out of the hole behind him, and he hoped he'd gotten deep enough to expose the gold.

A large clump of earth rolled out of the wall and hit the ground, and dust partially filled the side tunnel. Dirt showered Nathan's shoes. When it cleared, Nathan saw the clump of dull yellow melted rock partially exposed in the resulting hole.

"Look!" a man said. "Is that what I think it is?"

Nathan's dad leaned into the hole, brushed away more dirt with a small brush, and picked up the yellow rock. As small as it was, he looked like he had trouble lifting it. He turned with a surprised expression.

"It's gold," he confirmed.

"How did you find the gold, Nathan?" His dad sat on one of the stools in front of the table containing the artifacts. The gold rock sat on the table. Between the construction workers assigned to guarding the nugget and the archeologists waiting to get their hands on it, Nathan figured he might be allowed to hold it—oh, approximately never.

"It wasn't like I was looking." Nathan shrugged, uncomfortable with all the attention. "I was just messing around in the tunnel, thinking about how it would be a great environment for a game, and I noticed the loose bricks. Then I was just curious what might be back there."

"You started digging without thinking to get someone trained to do excavation?" Alyssa arched an eyebrow at him, and he knew she knew he was making it up as he went along.

"Didn't occur to me. I was just curious. I didn't ruin anything, did I?" Nathan packed as much innocence into his words as he could.

One of the other university people picked up the melted rock. "There were no gold mines in this area, so this discovery doesn't fit what we were expecting."

Professor Richards turned his attention to the chunk of metal. "That's not raw gold, either. It's been refined."

"This wasn't poured into a foundry mold," the first man objected.

"No, but I'd wager it's been in one already." Professor Richards looked up and grinned. "Do you know what we're almost directly beneath?"

"The Chicago Fire Academy," Alyssa answered promptly. "Which was built on the property where they believe the Chicago Fire of 1871 started."

Nathan scowled at his cousin. *Brainiac showoff.* He considered reminding everyone that he'd found the gold, but remembered just in time that he'd already gotten into trouble over it once.

"That's right." Professor Richards said. "Source please, Alyssa."

"I researched the Chicago Fire Academy for a report last year."

"Impressive." Nathan's dad smiled at her, then studied the gold rock again. "What if there were gold in one of the original buildings on this site? It could have melted in the intense heat of the fire and trickled down through the strata."

"But where would the gold have come from?" someone asked.

There was a moment of silence as the group contemplated the possibilities, but no one offered a theory.

"You know," one of the young students finally said, "the hole Nathan found is pretty deep, and the dirt was loose—like someone else had been digging there not so long ago." He pointed at the gold. "Do you think there was more than this in the ground? That someone might have found other gold and missed this chunk?"

Someone did, Nathan. John Montoya's voice sounded like he was standing right behind Nathan. *And I think I know who it was.*

38

Nathan slipped away from the crowd.

"What are you talking about?"

There was this guy I bumped into a few times down in the tunnel. He was on the team working on the telecommunication upgrades they were putting in, and he was down here late a lot. I checked him out and then forgot about him, because I just figured he was pulling a lot of overtime. But nobody else on his team was ever with him at night.

"Was he digging?"

I never saw him doing any digging, but he was always in the same area of the tunnel—which doesn't make any sense, if he really was laying fiber optics.

"You never saw any gold?"

I'm sure I would have remembered that. But I must have seen something that night. Or maybe he just thought I did.

Nathan watched his dad, Alyssa, and the others still speculating about the gold. "This is great. We can tell Aunt Jennifer, and she can make new inquiries with this guy, figure out if he was involved."

That's not gonna work, Nathan. If this guy found gold and still has any of it—and he might, because it's pretty hard to fence gold nuggets—then he's going to get rid of it as soon as this story hits the media. And the discovery of a big gold chunk is going to be big news, at least for a day or two.

Nodding, Nathan took a deep breath and let it out. He wasn't sure he wanted to deal with a guy capable of murder, but he had to admit to himself that the adventure had been pretty cool so far. "What's our next step?"

Check this guy out, find out where he lives. Maybe you can do that thing you do with the frequencies and see if he's still got any of the gold at his place. It should show up there just like you were able to find it here. Then you can call in an anonymous tip. If they're able to match him up as the guy working in this tunnel the night I was killed, the police will have enough probable cause to do something. But only if he still has the gold.

"Fine. Where is this guy?"

His name and address will be in my field reports.

"You don't remember?"

Do you remember everybody you talked to Saturday?

"Point." Aristotle had taken him around to a lot of places and introduced him to too many people.

See? And I talked to this guy two years ago. I don't remember his name, but I know I wrote it down. I always did. You'll just have to get access to my logs.

"Yeah, I'm sure that will be perfectly simple." Nathan said sarcastically, then stopped talking because he suddenly had a brainstorm. "Hang on. What about this guy Thomlinson? He was working down in these tunnels for a communications company about the time you were killed. They interviewed him on one of the archived reports I watched about your case. A follow-up report called him a 'person of interest helping the police with their inquiries,' but they eventually stopped talking to him. Even if you don't remember his name, it makes sense this was the guy.

"I already talked to him once, and he didn't seem to like me asking questions. We can get his address from his phone number."

John looked dubious. *That seems too easy, but it's worth a try. We've got to make it fast, though—whoever found the gold, once this story breaks he's going to bury the evidence so deep we'll never find it.*

Nathan tried one more time to talk John Montoya into turning over their suspicions to the DA's office, but he didn't try too hard. Truth be told, he felt like he'd been making so much progress on the case that he was anxious to follow this new lead himself.

How would you explain this new insight you have? You going to tell them you talk to dead people? I think they'd have a psychiatrist check you out before they went knocking on Thomlinson's door. Use the gift Kukulkan gave you, Nathan. Let's find out if this is the guy first. If not, we don't need your aunt or the Chicago Police Department thinking you're a nutjob. Not if you need to give them more information later. Right now you've got cred as the kid who found the gold in the tunnel.

Nathan knew that it was no use arguing. But if Thomlinson murdered Montoya, who was to say he wouldn't murder Nathan? The game board flashed in front of his eyes once more, and he hoped that he would see himself winning. To his surprise, there were four white pieces in the center of the board and only three black pieces. The game board faded from his vision and left Nathan confused. *Why is Kukulkan winning? I've almost solved the mystery!*

Nathan felt defeated. Then he noticed his dad waving him back to the table. "Speaking of which, I guess the press has arrived. I'll get through this as fast as I can, then we can head out." He already knew he was going to hate his fifteen minutes of fame, and as it turned out, he was right.

39

The tunnel in front of Manny's was less than four miles from Marcus Thomlinson's house. Nathan flagged down the first taxi he saw and gave Thomlinson's address. He wanted to go home and burrow in his bedroom. But he knew he needed to see for himself if Thomlinson was the bad guy.

Just hold steady, kid. You're going to be okay. John Montoya sat beside Nathan in the taxi, reflected in the window glass. *You should know something about this guy in the next few minutes.*

"You want to know what I know?" Nathan was too scared to even be embarrassed about how his voice broke as he spoke.

The cab driver, a large man with a bored expression, looked up at him.

Nathan took his iPhone from his pocket and pretended he was having a conversation. "I'll tell you what I know." He tried to speak more quietly, but the tension ratcheting up in him wouldn't let go. "This could be really dangerous."

I know. It's my fault.

"Of course it's your fault. I wouldn't be going there by myself if you hadn't talked me into it."

We've both gotten really wrapped up in this. We both want to get it solved.

"'We'? I don't think you're going to potentially get hurt because of this. I don't think you're going to have to worry about dying."

Nathan, get a grip. But cut me some slack. I've been wandering around for two years, watching my family deal with hard times, and not knowing who killed me.

"We don't know that information now."

Maybe we will. No matter what, we gotta check out this lead. I swear to you, you can blow an investigation all over the place, step over lines everybody tells you not to step over. But if, in the end, you can deliver the goods, you're golden. Please, just hang in there with me a little longer.

Frustrated and angry, Nathan pretended to hang up the phone and looked away from John. Not that it really did any good, because the police officer was reflected in the opposite window as well.

Nathan's phone vibrated in his hand. He glanced down and saw that he'd gotten a text from Alyssa.

Every1 is worried sick. Where r you? Txt back ASAP!

"Oh man. This just keeps getting better." Nathan ignored the curious stare from the taxi driver. "Evidently everyone is looking for me."

You're in the soup now, kid. The best thing you can do is push through to the end.

"Yeah, well, not exactly Vin Diesel here, John. Have you ever stopped and considered that I'm so far in over my head they're going to have to pump sunlight down to me?"

Every minute since we started this thing. John talked quietly and contritely. *I wish there'd been another way, Nathan. I really do. But there wasn't. I just can't watch what this is doing to my family anymore.*

Nathan took a deep breath and thought about Arda and his mom. They *were* having a hard time, and neither of them deserved it. But he didn't deserve it either, and he had put himself in a tight spot with the school, and his family.

Nathan stared through John's reflection at the passing buildings and wondered, "Is this really part of the Game? Because if it is, I'm not sure I want to play anymore."

□─□─□

L ess than ten minutes later, the taxi delivered Nathan to Marcus Thomlinson's address. The house was located in a small, older neighborhood. Lately, Pilsen was being remodeled as more established citizens moved into the area and brought their money with them. Only a few blocks away, renovated homes had started marching through the neighborhood.

Thomlinson lived in a small two-bedroom that had seen better days. The paint was peeling, and the roof needed to be replaced.

"If he found the gold in that tunnel," Nathan said, "he sure hasn't been spending it on his home."

There are other ways to spend money. For all you know this guy has a lake house somewhere and a Lamborghini in the garage. He may be keeping this place so no one gets suspicious.

Nathan started to get out.

Don't get out here. Have the driver take you a couple blocks down the street. If Thomlinson's here, he's going to see you. And you don't want that.

Panic clutched Nathan's stomach and tightened his lungs. He looked at the driver. "My bad. This isn't the address. It's further down."

"Sure." The driver nodded and put the car in gear.

Two blocks later, Nathan paid for the cab ride with some of the money his dad had given him for his birthday. He stood for a moment on the sidewalk and took a deep breath.

Scared?

"Oh yeah. I feel like I'm going to throw up."

I felt that way a lot when I was playing football. I always felt better after I threw up.

"Great. You think I'd attract any attention blowing chunks on somebody's lawn?"

I was thinking maybe you could sneak up on the house through the alleys. If you want to throw up there, it should be fine.

"Just for the record, I don't want to throw up." Nathan's phone rang. When he checked, it was Alyssa. He switched the phone to silent and tucked it into his coat pocket.

As quickly as he could, without looking like a burglar, Nathan went between the houses and reached the alley behind Thomlinson's house. Strangely enough, once he got moving he didn't need to throw up nearly as badly as he thought he needed to.

Movement helps. Gets the blood going.

Nathan didn't say anything, just concentrated on his breathing.

What's our plan with this, Nathan?

"I'm trying to find a position where I can hide myself from view but still see the house. When I peel back the frequencies, if there's gold, I'll see it."

Right. I'm betting if Thomlinson's the one who killed me and took the gold from that tunnel, he hasn't traded it all in. Not if he's smart. Probably took enough of it to buy that lake house, maybe a boat.

"And the Lamborghini. Yeah, I got that." Nathan crept across the corner of the alley until he could see all of Thomlinson's shabby house. He didn't see a car in the driveway, but there was a garage.

Get this over with as quick as you can. If the gold is there, we call your aunt.

"And tell her what?"

We'll figure that out when we get there.

"I guess you don't know what we'll tell her either."

John chuckled. *Not yet. We're making this up as we go along, kid. Sometimes that's the way you gotta do it.*

"I really hate doing things that way."

I've seen your homework.

"Not talking about homework. Talking about important stuff. You always gotta have a plan."

We got a plan. Just don't push it.

Nathan tried to breathe and calm himself down.

Can you sense anything?

Not answering, Nathan slid through the frequencies, but he quickly lost the house and the neighborhood. The street remained, but it was no longer a street. It was more of a straight path that crossed at an intersection.

"I don't see anything," Nathan said.

Maybe you have to dig deeper. You had to peel back a dozen frequencies to see where the gold was in the tunnel.

Pulling back into his home territory, Nathan looked at the house.

Nathan, if you don't want to do this—

Taking a deep breath, Nathan waited until a noisy ice-cream truck sped by, then moved to face the house directly. His knees felt like they might go out from under him at any minute. "Do me a favor. Just keep an eye out for Thomlinson."

I will.

40

His heart beating furiously, Nathan moved through the frequencies. The house vanished quickly, but there were a few personal items, antique furniture, and several pictures, that remained for several frequencies.

When those items vanished too, Nathan felt certain he and John had been wrong. He was incredibly conscious of standing exposed, aware of how vulnerable he was.

Stay with it, kid.

"Everything's disappearing. Don't you see that?"

Yeah, but you can still see the basement.

He was right. Nathan concentrated on the rectangle of ground occupied by the basement. In one corner, under the ground, there was a collection of irregularly shaped yellow rocks, just like the one Nathan had found in the tunnel. One of them looked like a sharp tool had been used to chisel off a chunk.

Bingo! We got him. Now we call the police and—

Nathan felt a pain in his arm. He snapped back to his home frequency and discovered Marcus Thomlinson standing next to him, twisting Nathan's arm behind his back.

"What are you doing hanging around my house?" Thomlinson was a thin, muscular man with a shaved head and a goatee. His dark eyes looked like they'd been burned into his head, and his gaze was restless, constantly darting suspiciously back and forth.

His voice was soft but sounded like sandpaper on hardwood.

Nathan looked around too, desperate for someone to be around at this moment. The streets were so empty he could practically see the tumbleweeds blowing past.

I'm sorry, Nathan.

"I'm just walking my new paper route." Nathan said the first thing that came into his head. "I like to see the houses I deliver to from both sides, so that I can figure out the best way to get everyone their paper on time."

Thomlinson looked at Nathan like he could smell the lies on him. "Uh huh. And you need to carry your computer with you to do that? You must think I'm some kind of idiot."

"No."

"Here's what I think. You're the kid I just saw on the news who discovered the gold in the tunnel, and now you're here trying to involve me in something."

"That's it. You caught me. You should call the police now and turn me in."

"Oh, no. You're coming with me."

Thomlinson twisted his arm up higher, and Nathan awkwardly matched Thomlinson's stride. He led him to the garage and then pressed the code into the keypad to raise the garage door. A sleek black sports car sat inside.

"What made you connect me to the gold?" Thomlinson held Nathan against the car and reached for a roll of duct tape.

"Occam's razor."

Thomlinson slapped him. "Don't get smart with me, kid."

Nathan worked his jaw. "I meant, there were only a few people in the tunnel on a regular basis, and you were the most reasonable suspect for this kind of job. The most logical explanation is usually the right one."

"Turn around, but be careful, and don't scratch the finish on that car or I'll drop you on your head a few times before the police get here."

If only the police were on their way. Nathan turned around.

"Hold out your hands," Thomlinson growled.

Nathan held his hands out in front of him as Thomlinson tore off a strip of tape to bind his hands, blinking back tears of fear and frustration.

In the car's shiny finish, upside down, Nathan spotted John's reflection.

Just stay cool, Nathan. You're going to be fine.

Nathan squeezed his eyes shut and thought about fleeing to another frequency. But if he did, his body would still be here, at the mercy of Thomlinson.

"Tell me how you found that gold."

"I don't know. I was just messing around in the tunnel. When I found the loose bricks, I found the gold."

Thomlinson slammed Nathan's head against the car. "I don't believe you. Know why I don't believe you?"

Nathan tried to shake his head, but that hurt because of the grip Thomlinson had on his hair.

"Because I spent weeks looking for that gold after I stumbled across it. If there'd been any there to *just find*, I'd have found it. Do you understand that?"

"Yes."

"Then tell me how you found it."

"I was just messing around in the tunnel and—"

Thomlinson cursed and slammed Nathan's head against the car again. "Tell me how you found it! That's what brought you here, isn't it? You figured I found more gold than what was there, and that I might still have it."

"I have visions." Nathan swallowed hard and tried to sound believable. "Sometimes I get these dreams."

"Do you expect me to believe that?"

"I don't know what else to tell you. It's the truth."

"Someone else—"

Nathan interrupted. "If someone else knew about the gold, they'd be here too, wouldn't they?"

Easy, Nathan. Don't make this guy any angrier.

"Look, you can still take the gold and run," Nathan suggested desperately.

Thomlinson leaned in, putting his weight against Nathan. "Lemme tell you something, you nosy brat. I like my life here. I don't want to walk away from it." He stepped back. "But if I have to, then you're going to pay. And since you came alone, I'm gonna assume you're the only one who knows my secret."

"What are you going to do?"

"Well, we're gonna take a little drive."

Nathan struggled to get free, but Thomlinson was too strong, and he flattened Nathan back up against the car with his body.

"Now that—that was a stupid mistake. I wasn't going to hurt you any more than I had to. Now I may enjoy this just a little." Thomlinson held Nathan up against the car with his body and pulled a gun out of his pocket. "You keep squirming around, I'm going to shoot you."

Nathan stared at the upside down reflection of John Montoya, but the police officer didn't have any advice.

Grabbing Nathan roughly, Thomlinson shoved him into the passenger side of the sports car, slammed it shut, and locked the door.

Then he walked back around the car to get behind the wheel.

The car started immediately, and the purr of the powerful engine filled the garage.

"I'll be long gone before you can get loose and find help. Not that anyone will believe you anyway; I don't even believe you, and I'm not as critical as the cops."

Thomlinson reached for the gear shift between the seats.

"Hey!" The voice came from outside the car, muffled by the soundproofing, but it was loud enough to be heard.

Thomlinson looked up just as Arda brought a crowbar around in a tight swing that pierced the driver's side window.

41

Glass shot all over the interior of the car as the crowbar crashed through the window. Nathan turned his head at the last second, but a few stray pieces razored across his cheek, chin, and nose. Blood wept from the small wounds and ran down his face. The pain followed, like biting black flies, but by that time he was so scared he could barely think straight.

Arda! But only Nathan was able to hear John Montoya's scream.

Arda swung again, this time going for Marcus Thomlinson.

Thomlinson cursed and dodged away from the crowbar. The makeshift weapon bounced through the steering wheel and stabbed into the instrument panel. Thomlinson roared in anguish at the damage to his car and then swung up the revolver and aimed it at Arda.

"Look out, Arda!" Nathan yelled. "He's got a gun!"

Instantly, Arda dove to the floor.

Thomlinson pulled the trigger. The detonation sounded like a cannon shot.

Nathan was suddenly deaf. He opened his mouth and tried to equalize the pressure in his ears, wondering hysterically if any permanent damage had been done. He started scrabbling for the lock, trying to get out of the car.

He watched helplessly as Thomlinson pushed open the driver's side door and jumped out of the car.

Nathan! John stood at the passenger side door, reflected in the glass and the mirror. *Help Arda!*

I'm trying!

"Come out from under there, you stupid brat!" Thomlinson stood beside the car and held the pistol in both hands.

"So you can shoot me?" Arda yelled back. "No thanks!"

The lock popped up, and Nathan grabbed for the door handle awkwardly as he saw Thomlinson duck down with the pistol in both hands. "Look out, Arda!"

As soon as Thomlinson leaned over, Arda slid out from under the car on the other side. He leaped onto the car's hood and launched himself at Thomlinson just as the man stood back up.

Nathan couldn't believe Arda was there. Much less that he had attacked Thomlinson.

Nathan yanked open the car door. The gun went off again, and a bullet hole appeared in the ceiling, letting in a shaft of light. Afraid that Arda had been shot, Nathan slid across the car's hood, landing awkwardly.

Arda was hanging on to the pistol as Thomlinson beat on him with his free hand. Thomlinson tripped Arda, leaving him stumbling backward. Thomlinson raised the pistol and pointed it at Arda.

Arda tried to roll out of the way, but there was nowhere to move.

Noooo! John Montoya shouted somewhere in the garage, but Nathan had lost track of him.

"*Noooo!*" Nathan shouted as he threw himself at Thomlinson.

Thomlinson turned, and Nathan grabbed the pistol. The shot from the pistol went wild. Arda rolled to his feet and attacked Thomlinson from the back.

Wrestling for control of the gun, Nathan felt himself losing his grip. He couldn't get enough leverage with his hands still bound together. Desperately, he listened for another frequency, held tight to Thomlinson, and pulled the man through with him.

The floor beneath them opened up, and all three of them fell onto the white sand of a beach. Nathan landed hard on top of Thomlinson, who lost his hold on the pistol. The weapon skipped away over the sand.

Nathan scrambled up and ran toward the pistol, hoping to grab it and throw it into the water. Thomlinson wasted precious time gazing around in astonishment.

His hand had barely closed on the gun before Thomlinson smashed into him from behind and took him to the ground again, scraping Nathan's chin through the sand.

Arda hit Thomlinson from behind in a pile-up, and an avalanche of sand spilled over the pistol and hid it from view.

Cursing all the while, Thomlinson threw Arda off him, punched him in the face, and searched for the gun. He found it a second later, while Nathan was still getting to his feet.

Wide-eyed and frightened, Thomlinson pointed the gun first at Nathan, then at Arda, then back at Nathan.

Nathan stood up and spread his arms, trying to ignore how scared he was. "Are you going to shoot us? You want us to turn around to make it easier?"

"Shut up." Thomlinson peered around nervously. "Shut. Up."

John Montoya, given form in this frequency, rushed in from the side. He grabbed the pistol and pointed it up as Thomlinson fired. Without pausing, John hammered Thomlinson in the face, bloodying the man's nose and knocking him senseless. He flipped the man over onto his face, then took a pair of handcuffs from the back of his belt and cuffed Thomlinson.

Turning back around, John gazed at Arda and Nathan. "Are you two all right?"

"Yeah." Nathan brushed sand off his face and stood up.

"Dad?" Arda's voice cracked in surprise. "Dad?" He ran across the sand to his father, throwing his arms around him in a huge bear hug. John held his son to him so tightly, Nathan couldn't see how Arda could breathe.

As he stood there in the shade of a palm tree, Nathan saw the strength of the bond father and son had shared. *No wonder Arda has been so hard to get along with. Nathan couldn't imagine losing someone so close to him.* He searched for Kukulkan and his mother, but neither of them was in this frequency.

Nathan settled down to wait. They had plenty of time.

Epilogue

Nathan sat on the edge of his bed, nursing a headache and a massive amount of bruising. The last thing he wanted to be right now was awake. He glanced at his computer and saw that it was almost one o'clock—afternoon. Nathan covered his face with a pillow. He'd dreamt about the fight with Thomlinson all night. He kept hearing the conversation that he and Arda had had with John, about how he was at peace now and needed to move on to a permanent frequency, one that didn't interact with Nathan and Arda's home frequency. As much as he tried, he couldn't forget the way Arda had wept when they had to leave his dad. That hurt Nathan more than his own aches; there was pain in loss, and Nathan couldn't know how that felt.

"Are you awake? Are you decent?"

"No. Go away."

The door opened anyway and Alyssa walked in, looking as fresh and carefree as always. She looked at him. "You weren't even sleeping."

Nathan sighed in disgust and flopped back on the bed.

"Look, I'm here to make your day. Show you what a chick magnet you're going to be when you come back to school." Alyssa patted his knee. "You'll love this."

"No, I won't."

With a flourish, she opened the newspaper she'd brought in

with her. At the bottom of the first page were pictures of Nathan, Arda, and John Montoya. Not together, of course, because no journalists could have accessed the beach frequency where they'd collectively made up the story Nathan and Arda were going to tell about what happened.

"You're a hero. Listen while I read about you."

The news story started with Nathan's fortuitous discovery of the melted gold in the tunnel. Where it had come from remained a mystery.

Then it moved on to how Nathan had gone over to Arda's house, told him about the gold, and they'd searched John Montoya's notes until they found mention of Marcus Thomlinson showing up in the maintenance tunnel a suspicious number of times.

Arda and Nathan had gone over to Thomlinson's house to find out if he'd really found the gold, only to surprise the man in the act of moving the cache. That last part had been John's suggestion; Nathan and Arda had put a few chunks of gold in the trunk of Thomlinson's car to back up their story.

According to the two boys, Thomlinson had caught Nathan, and Arda had busted in to save him. Together they had overpowered Thomlinson, and Arda had used a pair of his dad's handcuffs to hold the man until the police arrived in response to the shots that had been fired.

In fact, Nathan had been curious about how Arda had found him at Thomlinson's house and interfered with his plan. When Nathan asked, Arda told him that since his dad died, he'd been going to Manny's at least once a week and eating a sandwich while looking out the front window onto the street—he said it made him feel closer to his dad. He'd been at his usual table when Nathan came up out of the dig site, and he had bolted out of the deli and followed him.

Anyway, their sounded mostly logical, and way better than the explanation Thomlinson was giving of being transported to some other place and getting beaten up by John Montoya.

"Look," Alyssa said with glee, "they even quoted me. 'Nathan gets misunderstood a lot—'"

Nathan groaned.

"'—but he's always been there for me whenever I needed him.'"

"That's scandalous." Nathan cracked an eye at her. "That's not the truth."

"It is the truth. I have *never* needed you." Alyssa stood and folded the newspaper. "Gotta go."

"Hey—how come you're not in school?"

"I'm adding all of this new information to my report on our now-solved cold-case murder. The professor already told me we'd get an A, but I don't like to disappoint." Alyssa smiled at him.

Nathan covered his face with the pillow again and was glad to hear the door close after her. Then he sat back up and glared at the thing that most bothered him.

The pieces sat unmoving on the game board. He'd lost.

Nathan.

Recognizing Kukulkan's voice, Nathan shifted across the frequencies until he found him. Kukulkan stood on a cliff next to a sparkling waterfall that plunged at least a hundred feet before disappearing in a misty rush into a river. He wore Mayan robes that stood out brilliantly white against the burning orange and red of the sky behind him.

Nathan flew down and landed beside him. "I've been looking at the game board. I think I lost."

"You did."

Nathan couldn't believe it. "I don't understand. I found out who killed John Montoya. The investigation is going to show that he wasn't guilty of stealing anything. He's practically cleared already."

With an unaccustomed seriousness, Kukulkan nodded. "You achieved the goal, Nathan, and for that you are to be commended. But you didn't choose the wisest path."

"What?" Nathan smiled uncertainly. "You're kidding, right? This is some kind of joke."

"No. The Game requires you to do more than simply reach a goal. This time, you were asked to reach outside yourself, to get help in order to achieve the goal."

"I was supposed to go around telling people I was talking to John Montoya's ghost and he was telling me he was a good guy? That's crazy. They would have thought *I* was crazy. I'd have been locked up."

"There are other ways to get people to help you, Nathan. You prefer to stay locked up inside your own shell, to rely only on your own resources; that strategy will not be good enough for you to win the Game." Kukulkan pierced him with his gaze. "So much depends on you being more than you are now."

Nathan was angry. "You know what? Nobody explained those rules to me. Nobody let me know that the Game was based as much on *how* I did something as it was on if I got it done. Maybe I don't want to play your Game anymore."

Kukulkan's voice was a study in controlled rage. "You don't have a choice."

Nathan wanted to disagree, but he kept his mouth shut. For the first time, Kukulkan scared him.

"When you lose," Kukulkan said sternly, "the Game demands something from you. You never play without risk. I told you that in the beginning."

"Yeah, back when you were nice."

"Silence!"

Nathan wanted badly to say something, then decided against it.

"You have been given great gifts, Nathan, but there is great responsibility that comes with them. You must learn to shoulder that responsibility."

Folding his arms, Nathan met Kukulkan's gaze with difficulty, but stubbornly held to it.

"This Game will cost you." Kukulkan gestured, and suddenly Felicima Richards stood at his side. Tears ran down her cheeks.

Shocked and confused, Nathan took a step toward her. "Mom?"

"Nathan, this isn't your fault. I didn't have time to explain everything that I learned." She tried to smile and almost pulled it off.

"What's going on?"

Suddenly, a blur of black swept down from the sky, sharply defined by a deep streak of red that seemed to flare at its passing. Nathan realized it was a soul vulture an instant before it reached his mom. Instantly, the soul vulture turned her into a feather and caught it in its beak. Then it flew high into the flame-colored sky.

Leaping into the air, Nathan flew after the monstrous bird. "Mom!"

The soul vulture tucked the feather in among its plumage. For an instant, Nathan saw his mom's screaming face trapped among hundreds of others. He tried to catch up, but the soul vulture swiftly disappeared.

Crying, unable to control himself, Nathan flew back to Kukulkan. "Bring her back! This isn't her fault! If you want to punish someone, punish me! I screwed up!"

"I *am* punishing you." Kukulkan's gaze pierced Nathan.

"I apologize," Nathan said. "Please. I just got to meet her. There's so much I don't know. Don't take her away from me. Not yet."

"It's done. Study the Game. We will play again soon. You need to be ready." Kukulkan gestured—

—and Nathan was back on his bed in his room. Nathan wiped away his tears, took a deep breath, and tried to remember the sound of the frequency to which Kukulkan had called him. He couldn't. He hadn't been paying attention.

His mom was lost.

Nathan crouched in front of the game board and rearranged the pieces, putting the colored pieces back in their reserves and the sun piece back onto the first square of its path. He closed his eyes for a moment, thinking about what his first move might be. When he opened his eyes, a white piece had moved into play.

He shivered at the thought of what the next Game might cost him. He took a slow, deep breath and tried to let go of his anger.

He stood up and focused on the good things that had happened in his first Game. He held the image of his mom clearly in his head, determined now to win at any cost. He would be the best opponent Kukulkan had ever faced.

Nathan sat down to play.

The Game of Lost Souls

According to ancient Mayan legend, a representative is chosen from the human race to play the Game of Lost Souls against the gods to guarantee that mankind passes into the new world.

The game is a battle of wits, strategy and luck. Understand your opponent's choices and make wise ones of your own. The fate of humanity rests in your hands.

The Goal

The goal of the game is to have the most pieces in the center when the Sun reaches the end of its path.

Background

The game board represents the Mayan calendar. Each of the rings on the board represents a **frequency** with its own unique symbol. The center of the board bears the face of Tonatiuh, the Mayan god of Heaven. The game pieces represent creatures on the calendar whose powers differ from each other, and whose effects often depend on which frequency they're in at the moment. The pieces can take any path, but the goal is to travel the frequencies and pass through the squares with the yellow borders, called **gateways**, and advance safely into heaven.

Set Up

- Each player rolls a die. The player with the highest result plays with the White pieces. Reroll ties.
- Move the board so that each player has the correct color Start space in front of them.
- Put your pieces into your Reserves area.
- Set the Sun on its starting space.

Playing the Game

The White player takes the first turn.

On your turn, you will;
Roll the die
Move one of your pieces
Battle (this won't happen on every turn)
If you are the **Black** player, you will advance the sun piece along its path.

Each piece has a special ability that may change the basic game rules. Special abilities are listed on the Piece Identification Chart.

1. Roll **one** die to determine how many spaces your piece can move.

2. Choose one of your pieces and move it up to that many spaces.

Movement Rules

You do not have to use all of your movement.

You can choose to move a piece already on the board or you can move a piece from your reserves onto the board.

If you select a piece from your reserves, move it through your Start space onto the first frequency. The Start space counts as one space of movement.

A space with an open side is called a **gateway**.

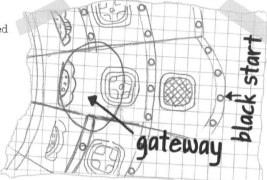

You may move through a gateway to another frequency.

You may move around a frequency in either direction.

Once a piece enters the center, its movement is ended. Pieces in the center may not be moved back onto the board.

You may move through a space occupied by one of your pieces. You may not stop on a space occupied by one of your pieces. If your movement would end on a space occupied by your own piece, your movement ends in the space before your piece.

3. If you move onto a space occupied by an opposing piece, stop your movement and start a battle.

Battle Rules (may not occur on every turn)
Running into an opposing piece ends your movement and starts a battle (Bate'il - *bata-EEL*).

To battle, each player rolls one die. Be sure to check the Piece Identification Chart for abilities that will change your die result. The player with the higher result wins.

If the result is a tie, the player whose turn it is wins.

If the battle takes place in the 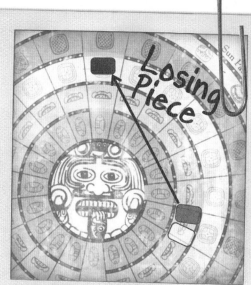 frequency, the losing piece is moved off the board back to its owner's reserves.

If the battle takes place in the , or frequency, the winning player moves the losing piece to **any** unoccupied space on the next frequency out from the center.

Losing Piece

TIP: Move the losing piece far away from a gateway that gets them closer to the center!

4. If it is the Black player's turn, advance the Sun one space along its path at the end of his or her turn. The Sun does not move at the end of the White player's turn.

5. Your turn is over and the other player begins his or her turn by rolling the die (#1 above).

The End

The game ends when the Sun has gone all the way around the board and returned to its starting space.

Each player gets one point for each of his or her pieces in the center of the board. Some pieces, such as the K'an piece, may be worth more than one point so be sure to check the Piece Identification Chart when adding up your points.

The player with the most points wins.

If both players have the same number of points (including if both players have 0 points), move the Sun to the Wayeb area of the board and continue playing. The next player to land a piece in the center of the board wins the game.

•Attached you will find a Piece Identification Chart

Piece Identification Chart

The Sun *(K'in)*
Marks the passage of time and signals the end of the game

Jaguar *(Ix)*
+2 to your battle roll when landing on opposing piece

Deer *(Manik')*
Move one extra space when in the  frequency

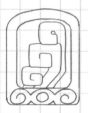

Wind *(Ik')*
Can move through spaces occupied by opposing pieces

Wisdom *(Kib')*
+2 to your battle roll when an opposing piece lands on a space occupied by this piece

Maize *(K'an)*
Worth 2 points when in the center

JORDAN WEISMAN is the creator of the successful MechWarrior line of PC games, one of the best-selling PC games of all time. As co-creator of the *Cathy's Book* series, Jordan changed the face of teen publishing with his interactive/new media approach to storytelling. He is also the owner of Smith & Tinker, whose new venture Nanovor launched Fall 2009 with a series of hand-held video games, online sites, and books published by Running Press Kids. He lives in Bellevue, Washington.

⊏—⊏—⊐

MEL ODOM has written more than 150 books for young readers. His book, *The Rover*, was selected as an Alex Award winner, and his book, *Apocalypse Dawn*, a spin-off of the popular *Left Behind* series, is a bestseller. Mel wrote a three-book *NCIS* series. He lives in Oklahoma with his wife and five children.